STRANGE COMPANY

A NOVEL OF THE AMERICAN REVOLUTION

By Pierre V. Comtois

Special thanks to Gregorio Montejo for help with Chapter One.

"Strange Company: A Novel of the American Revolution," by Pierre V. Comtois. ISBN 978-1-60264-360-4.

Manufactured in the United States of America.

"What is truth?" said jesting Pilate; and would not stay for an answer. Certainly there be those that delight in giddiness, and count it a bondage to fix a belief; affecting free will in thinking, as well as in acting. And though the sects of philosophers of that kind be gone, yet there remain certain discoursing wits, which are of the same veins, though there be not so much blood in them as was in those of the ancients.

Francis Bacon
On Truth

Cease then, nor order imperfection name: Our proper bliss depends on what we blame. Know thy own point: this kind, this due degree of blindness, weakness, Heaven bestows on thee. Submit in this, or any other sphere, Secure to be as blest as thou canst bear: Safe in the hand of one disposing Power, Or in the natal, or the mortal hour. All Nature is but art, unknown to thee; All chance, direction, which thou canst not see; All discord, harmony not understood; All partial evil, universal good: And, spite of pride, in erring reason's spite, One truth is clear: Whatever *is*, *is* right.

Alexander Pope
An Essay on Man

PROLOGUE
December 1782

The Chaumont House in Passy near Paris was swathed in a light drizzle. For the past few days, the only evidence of approaching winter had been the lowering clouds that clung over the city like balls of dirty cotton. Even in the most dazzling city in the world, the streets were nearly empty of traffic as the weather cast its pall of gloom over nobility and ordinary citizen alike. The Tuileries lay silent for once, the shouts and calls of the vendors in local markets, never losing an opportunity to be heard, seemed to be the only life in the great metropolis.

Most of the city's activity had long since moved indoors; with the new rages for gaming of all sorts and wild speculation for those with plenty of money. Of these indoor activities, none matched the frenzy that ruled on the Rue Vivienne. There, situated in the Hotel de Nevers, was the Paris Bourse. With the huge increase in the national debt, the Bourse became the ideal market for public debt bonds and it was all the *Caisse d'Escompte* could do to keep up with the traffic. But now, a new element had been added to the mix.

The United States, the former British colonies in North America, had won the war with their former masters (indeed, they were one of the main reasons why France had such a huge debt), and now rumor had it that a peace treaty had been signed. Hopeful speculators, financial sharks, and knights of industry prowled the parquet at the Bourse making deals with powerful stockbrokers for the immense opportunities they saw in the infant nation. Every hour it seemed, more news about the Americans would come, throwing the crowded exchange into a new flurry of agitation.

However, the Chaumont House stood quiet and peaceful, its beautifully manicured gardens wilting slightly this late in the season. A gravel footpath wound around the house, along rows of shrubbery, and out where the vegetable garden had been. On the far side of a former pea patch, where the house back along the path would just begin to lose its distinction in the gathering drizzle, the path picked up once more, piercing a brick wall where an arch opened onto a neatly cropped lawn on the opposite side. There, nestled in the center of a grassy clearing, sat a spacious gazebo, domed and enclosed against the weather. Inside, figures were moving.

"Damnable! Simply damnable!" said Henry Laurens as he turned in exasperation from the tiny window.

"Now, now, we can endure it for a while, can't we?" chided John Jay. "Look at Dr. Franklin now..."

Benjamin Franklin laughed from where he sat in an overstuffed chair, his feet propped on an enormous pillow. "Come John, no need to patronize an old man. I may be getting on in years, but I'm far from an invalid."

"No disrespect intended," said Laurens, who had only recently been released from captivity, "but the good doctor hasn't just spent almost a year in the Tower of London."

Franklin inclined his head and Jay grunted in agreement. Anyone, such as Laurens, who had spent time in the Tower and lost a son in the war had a perfect right to complain.

"But it's still a damnable situation that forces the diplomatic negotiators of a sovereign nation to huddle in an unheated summer house like..."

"I hope you weren't going to make an unfortunate reference to peasants," said Franklin, his earlier mood of understanding quickly dissipating. "We've fought a long and vicious war to rid ourselves of such unfair distinctions."

"I wasn't going to say any such thing," protested Laurens, "but merely make the point that we are not yet treated with the proper respect due us as representatives of a sovereign nation."

"Henry certainly has a point," said John Adams, speaking for the first time. "We've been treated with condescension since the start."

"I wouldn't say that..." Franklin began to say.

"You wouldn't," snapped Adams, conscious of the tone in his voice. "You've grown too close with our French hosts." He did not add his own doubts about Franklin's personal loyalties.

Ever since Adams had arrived in the country as an ambassador, he found his partner's camaraderie with the French too comfortable for his role as a representative of the United States. The French people loved his portly figure, lining the streets of Paris just to catch a glimpse of him as he passed by in his carriage. The country's famed *philosophes* trooped dutifully to his house every day for conversation; but most of all, Adams detested the old man's easy acquaintance with the nation's ladies. He had proposed marriage to Madame Helvetius and allowed Madame Brillon to sit on his lap, even played chess with her during her bath! Also, Adams did not like the attitude the Pennsylvanian had toward his official duties. He counted the group lucky to have persuaded Franklin to attend their meeting this morning seeing as how the old man never left bed before one o'clock in the afternoon.

Franklin was chuckling. "Now John, I..."

"Never mind that," interrupted Laurens, "what are we going to do about Lee?"

"Arthur? He's perfectly harmless," said Franklin aware of Lee's questionable involvement in an arms smuggling operation and efforts to discredit fellow diplomat Silas Dean.

"You can say that, knowing your own valet is a French spy?"

"I do nothing in private any spy isn't welcome to; besides, my valet gives good service."

Laurens was flustered in the face of Franklin's equanimity in regard to espionage.

"Nevertheless," said Jay, who never trusted the French anyway, "it's a fact that very solid information is making its way to the French Government. If it isn't Lee, then it's definitely his secretary...what's his name?"

"Thornton," Adams helped.

"Thornton's been on the British payroll for months now and the fact that Vergennes never gets upset at our dealings suggests to me that he has his own informants in London."

"And you still don't trust Lee either?" asked Laurens.

"Absolutely!" said Jay. "Why else did you think I insist we meet out here in this drafty outhouse?"

"You sound confident of your opinion, sir," said Franklin.

"You're wise enough to know, Doctor, that we're like children in a nest of vipers," said Jay. "The French and British have had centuries to refine espionage to an art. We shouldn't trust anyone."

"That didn't stop us from negotiating the preliminary treaty with England. How do you explain the well-informed Vergennes not knowing anything about that?"

Jay snorted. "Because the British wanted to keep it all confidential. If I know their foreign office is riddled with spies, they do too, and they would have taken steps to limit those who knew of the negotiations."

"Perhaps it might have been better if Vergennes had gotten some warning about our negotiations," Franklin mumbled.

"Why?" demanded Jay. "So he could whisper into the ear of the English and destroy the talks?"

"In case you've forgotten, John, the government of the United States had an agreement with France not to negotiate a separate peace but to keep Louis' government fully informed."

"I was in Spain for months before coming here," said Jay, "and I'm convinced it was France that kept that government from moving on any of my proposals. It's not in the interest of France for our nation to be free. The only thing in it for them is that our independence would be a thorn in England's side."

"I think Dr. Franklin is still smarting over your giveaway of Canada, John," suggested Laurens.

"Were we to let a few acres stand in the way of the treaty?" demanded Jay. "A treaty that gave us more than we could possibly have had a right to expect?"

"That treaty still almost wrecked our delicate position with France," said Franklin with some heat. "If not for me, we'd have had another very powerful enemy to contend with. Luckily I managed to smooth things over with Vergennes."

"And even get an additional loan in the bargain," laughed Laurens.

A light rain began to fall outside, filling the interior of the gazebo with the sound of raindrops on the roof.

"It's too early to begin congratulating ourselves on our accomplishment," cautioned Adams, ever the dour Yankee. "The international situation is yet very fragile. America's enemies in Parliament will jump at any excuse to wreck the treaty."

"And there are also forces at Versailles in whose interest it would be to see that happen," added Jay.

They all nodded, even Franklin.

"The position of King George's government is yet very weak," said Laurens who had been approached by British officials after being released from the Tower about opening negotiations with his fellow diplomats in France. "There are still British troops occupying New York, Boston, and South Carolina, and tens of thousands of Tories still armed and angry at the prospect of losing everything they own. And worst of all, the Articles of Confederation are too weak an instrument to give our nation room to maneuver. In fact, I hear that some states are not even represented in the Congress. Furthermore, our army has suffered a number of mutinies over payroll and our frontier has been continuously ravaged by savages for as long as anyone can remember. No, everything rides on this preliminary treaty holding."

"Then it's understood that we must do everything in our power to keep anything, any scandal or provocation, from occurring?" asked Adams.

The others nodded, confident at least, that no one else could possibly reveal the tenuous nature of their position while the meeting took place out of doors.

"Our outward demeanor must be one of confidence and goodwill at all times, and above all, we must pray that our countrymen at home realize the gravity of the position to control matters at their end," concluded Adams.

"I included a very definite warning about that in my last message to Congress," said Jay.

"Well, I don't think we have anything more to discuss...?" asked Adams.

"Good," said Franklin presently. "This *tete a tete* has delayed my social calendar considerably. My appointment book tells me I've been keeping a very charming young lady waiting. Very uncivil of me." He winked at Adams knowing his colleague's disapproval of his private life.

Adams adjusted his waistcoat and said nothing as he and the others made their way through the rain to the carriage house.

Over Paris, the clouds turned an angry black. Lightning filled the sky and with a boom like the crack of a cannon, the rain that had been threatening for days flung itself toward the city.

CHAPTER ONE

"A toast to our esteemed member," said Dr. Rittenhouse raising a frothing tankard in the air.

"Here, here," agreed the others in the small gathering raising their own cups in the young man's direction.

Thomas Jefferson smiled broadly and raised his own cup to his lips. There was silence a moment as the four men slaked their thirst with the warmed ale then wiped the froth from their mouths.

"It's not good Madeira, but it will do on a cold winter's day," said Dr. William Shippen from where he sat near the open hearth.

"Thank you gentlemen for this most hearty welcome to your city," said Jefferson.

"Well what else could you expect, Tom?" asked Rittenhouse, drawing a shade across the tavern's window to keep out the bright afternoon light. "I must admit, I am quite pleased with the honor bestowed upon you by the College of William and Mary."

"Certainly to be given an Honorary Degree of Doctor of Civil Laws is a good deal to be proud of," said Dr. Shippen.

"But then, who else could they have given it to?" said Bartholemew D'Estaing, speaking from the corner.

"Delegate to Congress, writer of the Declaration of Independence, the Virginia Statute for Religious Freedom, governor of Virginia, writer of his wonderful *Notes on the State of Virginia...*"

"Enough, enough!" pleaded the embarrassed Jefferson, with his hands before him as if warding off danger.

"...and now minister plenipotentiary to France," finished D'Estaing amid general chuckling.

"I think it's too soon to be awarding me that title," admonished Jefferson.

"Too true," agreed Rittenhouse. "How many times is it now you've been nominated? Ten or twelve?"

"So many that I just can't take it seriously anymore," Jefferson said. "I've stopped worrying about it and have decided to take what comes. In the meantime, I'll enjoy the present company and the many distractions to be found in such a metropolis."

"You will find Philadelphia small and quaint after arriving in the capitals of Europe," said D'Estaing.

"That may be so, but I prefer the rugged simplicity of America and her citizens than the corrupt over-crowding of the Old World," replied the Virginian. "Here a man can live as he chooses, breath free, and grow healthy and strong without the encumbrances of the twin scourges of an overbearing church and state. No, gentlemen, give me the life of the farmer that naturally breeds virtue than the corruption any concentration of mere artisans and manufactory workers inevitably engender."

"Admirable sentiments," said D'Estaing, "but somehow, I suspect you'll find more to admire in Europe than you're willing to admit."

"In any case, if you want your appointment, you might have to chase after it," said Shippen. "With British troops still in New York and restlessness among the

Continentals, the Congress might try to slip from the city."

"I hear Princeton is supposed to be safer than Philadelphia," said D'Estaing.

"Well, if the Congress wants me, they know where to find me," said Jefferson.

"You insist on displaying little interest..." Rittenhouse stopped in mid-sentence as a passing barmaid caught his attention. "Over here, young lady, and this time, let's have a real drink. Your finest wine for another toast."

"I think John must have little to keep himself busy as he can spend so much time drinking," joked D'Estaing.

"If that's the problem, I have just the solution," said Jefferson. "A project that could serve both a diplomatic purpose and to keep our friend from the evils of idleness."

"And what is that?"

"Simply that I propose that the Society engage Dr. Rittenhouse, as America's foremost genius, to build one of his wonderful orreries to present to King Louis in appreciation for all his help in the crisis just passed."

The others nodded in agreement, although Rittenhouse seemed less than enthusiastic about the idea. In truth, he was not getting any younger, and he found the painstaking exactness needed to create his astronomical invention with its myriad of moving parts illustrating the movement of all the heavenly bodies in relation to one another, almost more than his fading senses could withstand.

"Then we'll raise it in the next full meeting of the Society," said D'Estaing.

The American Philosophical Society to which those seated belonged, had been created by Dr. Franklin nearly thirty years before for the purpose of gathering and disseminating useful knowledge. Jefferson's own exhaustive, *Notes on the State of Virginia* was the most recent addition to the group's growing body of knowledge.

"Here then," said Rittenhouse, raising a slender glass again.

"Another toast, to Dr. Benjamin Franklin on the occasion of his seventy-seventh birthday; may he continue in good health and as the guiding spirit of our Society."

"Aye," they all said tilting their glasses toward the ceiling.

As the conversation veered in the direction of stories about Franklin, Jefferson found that his thoughts began to wander. He wondered with glowing affection about his young daughter, Martha, or Patsy as the family called her, and the contentment she gave him knowing she was always close by in the city; the two younger girls, Polly, and Lucy who was just an infant, whom he was forced to leave behind in the care of his sister; and finally, inevitably, to Martha, his wife. Even now, nearly five months after the terrible event, he could hardly tolerate thinking of her. When she had died, quite literally, the light had gone out of his life. He had loved her more than life itself and her passing had gouged a gaping hole in his heart that had forbidden him to leave his bedroom at Monticello for weeks following her death. Or at least that was what he was told; he hardly remembered how much time had passed while he fought his way from out of the depths of despair to which he had fallen. Finally, when the summons from Congress came, notifying him of his being chosen to augment the negotiating team in Europe, he took the opportunity for an extended trip away from the torturous environs of Monticello and its awful memories. To bury himself in the endless paperwork and diplomatic intrigue of the Old World was a Godsend. His thoughts having gone full circle, he once more found himself sitting at a table in the City Tavern.

"...and remember his 'electric dinner?'" D'Estaing was saying. "Benjamin and a number of his friends had killed a turkey by electric shock and roasted it on an electric spit using the resources of a Leyden Jar."

"And then they toasted all the famous electricians in electrified glasses to the sound of a discharging electric battery!" concluded Shippen.

"Certainly there shall never be another like Dr. Franklin," said Jefferson, trying to get back into the conversation. "But let's not forget the marvelous gift to the world of natural philosophy he gave us with his *own* experiments with electricity."

"Yes, until Franklin drew electricity from the clouds with a common kite, the phenomenon had been discounted by those in Europe as nothing more than an interesting toy," said Rittenhouse.

"Collecting it in a glass bottle covered in tin foil was enough for them," said D'Estaing. "And wasn't the king entertained by watching a row of monks holding hands all jump at the same time due to receiving an electric shock?"

"But now as I understand it, there are hundreds of lightning rods all over Europe," said Rittenhouse.

"I've actually heard of experiments being conducted with living organisms, wherein it is hoped to prove that living tissue can not only conduct but store electricity."

"I think they go too far," chuckled Shippen.

D'Estaing shook his head. "Electricity has already been stored in batteries and the artificial currents have been observed to turn water into steam. This could once have been considered magic but today, we need to define it in more precise terms; in the rational language of science."

"The phenomenon you describe," said Jefferson, "suggests a breakdown in the physical properties of liquid into what Democritus called atoms, the fundamental particle by which all matter is composed." He paused, struggling with a new thought. "I wonder, would it be possible to actually measure the strength of a particular jolt of electricity by the amount of material, in this case a liquid, it can dissolve?"

"Electricity and chemistry related?" mused Rittenhouse, rubbing his chin.

"The mere thought makes my head swim," said Shippen, by profession a physician. "Such an unknown country would need to be mapped for simple accuracy!"

"I don't think that would be a problem," said D'Estaing, "one only needs to decide which map is the better."

Jefferson smiled, "My old tutor, William Small, always said that mathematics is the hub from which all other sciences branched out."

"But which method would be most appropriate?"

"That's the question I'm afraid we will have to leave to the mathematicians of the future," said Jefferson. "Whether present geometric models will prove more advantageous than the older methods..."

"Fluxionary versus differential calculus, for example?" said Rittenhouse.

"Exactly," agreed Jefferson.

"Mathematics *is* the language of rationalism," said Shippen

"The ultimate logic of mathematics as the basis of modern science and the definition of God?" asked Rittenhouse, seeking clarification.

"Descartes used mathematics, however unknowingly, to challenge the old aristotelianism in searching for a rational proof of God; it was only later that Spinoza took his methods and used them to remove all personality from the act of creation and with it, purpose and design."

"There can be no God," concluded D'Estaing.

"Or at least the existence of Newton's God, clockmaker and timekeeper."

"The difference between the two schools of thought in Europe," said Jefferson. "One that believes man is an instinctive creature endowed with unconscious knowledge and the other that holds he is a tabula rasa, a blank slate on which all the knowledge he can garner for himself will be used for his own continuing perfection."

"What monumental hubris all that is," said Shippen. "To think that man is infinitely perfectable. And where does this leave his feeling and emotions? Are we merely empty shells to be filled with knowledge without any consequences to follow? How are we to interpret this new knowledge; to use it for good or ill?"

"This is all true," agreed Jefferson, thoughtfully. "Of all the creatures on the earth, man is the only one possessing not only reason, but the ability to decide in which direction that reason shall lead him. He is different, not merely another beast. Even Locke in his *Essay Concerning Human Understanding*, reaches the conclusion that our very awareness of ourselves is one of the simplest and surest elements in experience. From that, he concludes that God exists calling it 'the most obvious truth that reason discovers.'"

"'Its evidence is equal to mathematical certainty,'" quoted Rittenhouse.

"But let's not confuse Locke's belief in a God to supernaturalism. Though he believed in a revelatory Christianity, he yet used reason and logic to strip it of its supernatural trappings to reveal the simple truths imparted by the historical Jesus. Locke was not a supernaturalist but a realist." Jefferson leaned back in his chair and stretched. "Someday I'd like to take the New Testament, and strip it of all supernaturalism; what I'd have left is what I believe Jesus actually taught."

"Don't expect cheers from the ordinary citizen," warned Shippen.

"In any case," said Jefferson, "I think we have Newton to thank for the spirit of the times. Our age of rationalism has already gone far in banishing priestcraft and superstition from the world of nature, relegating it to the world of conjecture where it belongs. And now, with the hoped for conclusion of our own political struggle, we also banish it from the realm of government."

"Then you condemn nations to lawmaking without regard for morality," said Shippen.

"By no means," said Jefferson. "All government, led by men of enlightened minds, cannot but conform to nature. Natural law is supreme, ruling over every area the mind of man can penetrate. Nature must be their ultimate standard; all laws must be judged by their conformity to what natural laws Voltaire has said, reveal themselves at all times to all men. We must believe that men are endowed with reason, so that they can live well in this world. Natural law must reign supreme even in the realm of morality where independence and autonomy can be substituted for the divine will."

"That's fine in a perfect world ruled by logic," said Shippen, "but everything must be filtered through man's emotions. Jean-Jacques Rousseau has said that logic alone cannot satisfy the heart of man, that emotion too claims a piece of his soul. In the name of sensibility, he advocates a simple life of reverence to God and love toward one's fellow man. He admitted nature to be fundamentally good; that it was a man-created environment that fostered evil. And even though I do not see the attraction of his bucolic views, I can understand his assertion that there can be no ignoring of the duality of man: that logic and emotion are forever at war in his soul."

"And don't forget Hume's warning about pure logic," added D'Estaing without conviction. "That it is an uncertain instrument at best. Although ideas are born of sense impressions, our senses are very fallible organs of judgment. Ideas which the senses convey may often turn out to be false phantoms created from error, bias borne directly out of the way we've lived our own particular lives or even our imagination. We can never know more than the appearance of things because that's all our finite minds are capable of grasping."

"Like the Platonic idea of mimesis, that the real perfect object can exist only in a perfect world; since man lives in an imperfect world, by his own life experiences, he's foiled right from the start in his attempts to comprehend the true state of things. He's hopelessly biased," said Rittenhouse

. "Exactly; the idea that man can arrive at truth by a process of elimination, running a series of causes down to the First Cause or vice versa is preposterous. We'll only find what we want to find, not what's actually there. Causality is far from fact."

"But how can we live in a world where all is in doubt?" said Jefferson rhetorically. "If Hume is to be believed, we can trust no one."

"That is the fundamental paradox of our age," said Shippen. "We have come to the point where doubt now lies side by side with confidence; where our logic wars continually with our emotions and we find ourselves trapped halfway between the angels and the brutes of the fields."

"Nevertheless," persisted Jefferson, "I think you've dismissed causality too swiftly. There is much to be said for the tracing of logical progressions, from one event to another. How easy is it to see that the invention of the telescope and its use by Galileo confirmed the existence of the heliocentric system; with the discovery of Jupiter and its moons, a new aid to oceanic navigation was developed; with easier access to the high seas, commerce was able to expand a hundredfold; with the expansion of trade, comes the riches a young nation such as ours will need to grow strong; and who knows? with that strength may come the conquest of a continent."

"Your explanation is simple and quite easy with hindsight," said Shippen, "but I daresay, would be a bit more difficult to trace in the opposite direction. In which direction, suppose, would you go if you were to trace causes backward from the discovery of the telescope?"

Jefferson smiled. "Now you have me there, William. Any tracing of prior causes from the telescope would necessarily involve a myriad of paths; any one of which could lead to the First Cause. But which one? I don't want to bore the present company with a thorough search now, but I don't doubt it's possible."

"I don't see why it can't be done either," added D'Estaing. "Logically, there's nothing to stand in its way. After all, the point is not that it can be proved with a real example, but that in theory it's possible. Just as in theory, it's possible to count the grains of sand on a beach..."

"But don't you see that way lies madness? Just as Hume warned. The logic of infinite possibilities is a trap from which there is no exit," said Rittenhouse.

"In any case, you admit the logic is sound," said Jefferson.

"I admit logic has become an end in itself. An end that can never be realized as long as man is a being of sense impressions; as long as his very brain is fashioned and formed by the variety of experience each individual is the victim of in just being alive."

"Then in the electrical experiments we discussed earlier, the results cannot be trusted," said D'Estaing.

"Oh, they can be trusted, but how far? Are the results being interpreted objectively? Or are they colored by the unconscious desires of the experimenter? Did the experimenter miss vital information because it wasn't what he was looking for?"

"Then, if you'll pardon the expression Dr. Shippen," said Jefferson, "logic dictates that the ultimate truth can never be found by the observer; that all conclusions are subjective."

"Exactly; man must ever be a subjective being. Theoretically, it is quite possible for two observers, because of their different backgrounds, to interpret the results of any experiment in two different ways. What might occur to one, might never be noticed by the other."

"This is a novel way of looking at the world," admitted Jefferson, never one to assume a dogmatic position. To him, the natural world was in flux, until irrefutable proof could be established. "I'll have to think it through...And reread my Hume!"

The others laughed and would have continued the conversation if they had not been interrupted by a small commotion at the door

The City Tavern was a popular meeting place for members of Congress and the city's political and scholarly communities and so was almost always a bustling enterprise. This particular afternoon was no exception; the winter weather always reduced the city's outdoor activities and moved them indoors. The central floor was crowded with occupied tables and patrons weaving from them to the door. A thick haze of tobacco smoke lingered near the low ceiling that made the room seem smaller than it really was and over all was the hubbub of conversation, the calls of the bartender to the barmaids and the scrub boys and the incessant tinkling of the little bell over the main door as people came and went.

With all this activity, it was surprising that the small drama near the entrance caught the group's attention at all. A young boy, snowflakes melting on his shoulders and his tricorn in his hands, was trying to make himself understood to one of the barmaids. It was his voice, which kept cracking into high pitched notes, that cut through the noise of the room.

At last, the bartender wormed his way over to the scene and, relieving the exasperated barmaid, managed to calm the boy down enough to make sense of his speech. Catching Jefferson's eye, the bartender dragged the boy over to his table.

"Looks like another nomination, Thomas," laughed Rittenhouse.

Before Jefferson could reply, the boy was standing before him, nervously fingering his hat.

"Mr. Jefferson, sir?" he asked.

"Yes, my boy."

"I come from the Congress sir. Mr. Thomson begs you come to the State House as quick as you can sir."

CHAPTER TWO

"Thomson?" said Rittenhouse. "Perhaps Charles desires another look at your *Notes*."

"Quite a dramatic way to ask for them, I'll say," said Shippen, smiling.

"I'm afraid I can't say, sirs," replied the boy seriously.

"Well, it must be important for Mr. Thomson to send you over in this cold, young man," said Jefferson, slipping into his coat and luxuriating in the residual warmth from where it had hung toward the open hearth.

"I'm sure it must be sir; as he told me to be quick about it."

"You'll come by tonight for dinner as planned won't you, Thomas?" asked Rittenhouse as Jefferson began to follow the boy through the crowded room.

"If I'm not delayed," he called over a receding shoulder.

In another moment, the tinkling of the doorbell announced his exit and the others left at the table resumed their seats. "Thomas is such a gentleman," said Shippen.

"How do you mean?" asked Rittenhouse sipping the rest of his wine.

"Why, he's left us with the cost of our drinks, and we don't resent it in the slightest!"

Outside, Jefferson pulled up the collar of his coat and brought the brim of his hat down closer over his eyes against the cold winter wind. The warmth collected by his coat rapidly dissipated as he tried to reconcile himself to the weather in Philadelphia.

Not that he hadn't experienced cold winters at his mountaintop home at Monticello, but they were not as severe as those in a city situated so perilously close to the sea.

He looked up for the sun but couldn't find it amid the featureless whiteness of the sky. Scattered snowflakes pecked at his face.

"Hurry sir," urged the boy, beckoning with his hand

Together, they began toward the city center and although Jefferson was able to reconcile himself to the weather, he found it more difficult getting used to the citizens' habit of disposing of their household slop by tossing it out any window. Where occasional smells would waft over the city on still days, on windy ones like this, the stench was almost constant. Prisoners, heads shaved and sometimes in fetters, worked along the streets cleaning up the mess. Jefferson sidestepped and narrowly avoided a half decomposed animal of some sort. Even *his* trained eye could not make out what exactly it was.

In the distance, the raucous sounds of the market could be heard and beyond that, the busy noises of the dockyards with their rows of warehouses and forest of masts. A church bell was ringing somewhere and Jefferson reached instinctively for his pocket watch. It was early.

He bumped into someone. "Excuse me, sir," said a voice in almost unintelligible English. A foreign sailor from a visiting ship no doubt. Though Jefferson disliked many things about the city, any city, both practically and philosophically, he had to admit there was plenty to like about it too. Besides its many bookshops and good libraries; its balls and fetes and museums; its centers of learning; there was too, the sense of cosmopolitanism about it. Particularly here, in Philadelphia, where one was just as likely to run into a German sailor as a buckskinned frontiersman or proper Quaker. And just at the moment, Philadelphia played continuous host to a stream of visiting French officers who charmed and dazzled the city with their refined continental ways.

But the city was still considered to be a place of loose morals with its continuous demand for entertainments and novelties, its excessive drinking and lately, its cries for a new theater! On the other hand, he had heard visiting French officers claim the city was alarmingly virtuous, with its maidens prim and proper and hardly a wife of liberal attitudes about!

Which made Jefferson all the more worried about the city's, and the nation's, youth. He looked at the boy with him and wondered if he would ever be able to take advantage of the opportunities that had most recently been won for him and his fellows. Would that every boy could avail himself of a proper education and not be allowed to abandon himself to nature! If only Virginia had accepted his pyramidal plan for educating the people! Perhaps it would have been followed by the other states and boys of promise would have been educated and groomed to assume the leadership of their new nation in their proper time. Then, he and his contemporaries could retire in old age with confidence in the rising generation. He shook his head. But now, education must remain a haphazard affair, available mostly for those who could afford it and, he was sure, the country was the poorer for it.

They were just passing the old Carpenter's Hall where the first Continental Congress had met. Jefferson well remembered those days of drama, except at the time they did not seem so dramatic with their interminable meetings and long, dull speeches; but great things had been accomplished within its red brick walls. He remembered with pride the day the Declaration of Independence had first been read to the people from the balcony. It was hard to believe that words he had penned could assume a life of their own; and even now, when he saw them, it seemed as if they must have always existed, that he had just snatched them from the air and captured them on paper.

"I remember the first Fourth of July," the boy was saying. "My father held me on his shoulders when the Congress read the Declaration."

"You were there?"

"Yes. Mr. Adams said the day should be celebrated with whistles and bells and firecrackers and ever since, the city has done it. I remember that day because I thought every bell in the world was ringing."

"And did your father explain the words to you?"

"He tried, but I was still too young you see," said the boy seriously. "The next day, my father joined the army. He fought at Yorktown. Someday I'm going to join the army too." He paused, then stopped and faced Jefferson. "Mr. Jefferson, sir; may I shake the hand of the man who wrote the Declaration?"

Jefferson did not know what to say, so he simply held out his hand and the other grasped it; not with a boy's weakness but with a man's firmness.

"Well done Mr. Jefferson," the boy said. "I couldn't have said it better myself. Your words expressed exactly what I felt in my heart but that I could never have explained to anyone."

Then, as if nothing had happened, the boy turned and started off toward the State House again leaving Jefferson to wonder at his own hubris. Why did he think he had to worry about the rising generation? It was clear it could take care of itself! The values of the new nation it seemed, transferred themselves naturally to its young.

At last the State House came into view, its elegant, yet simple lines marred by the scaffolding that surrounded the aging steeple. As they entered Walnut Street, Jefferson steeled himself for the ordeal of passing by the old stone prison that faced directly across the street from the State House. In seconds, he and the boy were being assaulted by begging prisoners who held out long poles with little baskets on their ends from between the bars of their cells. If offerings were not made, the most vile epithets and calls would follow. Jefferson looked around, hoping there were no ladies within earshot.

Quickly, the two entered the State House grounds where the building itself rested far back from the street. Together with its twin wings and dividing piazzas, the property presented a very dignified and elegant air. A snaking gravel walk led along rows of young saplings, denuded by winter, and up to the main entrance of the building.

The building was not only host to the Congress, but also the governor of Pennsylvania and the state judiciary and legislature, so its halls were far from quiet. The boy knocked on a door just to the rear of the stairway that led to the second floor and in a moment it was opened and they were beckoned inside. Jefferson knew the four men in the room: Charles Thomson, Secretary of Congress and a member of the American Philosophical Society; Alexander Hamilton, recently arrived delegate from New York and protege of General Washington; James Madison, delegate from Virginia and a close friend and finally, John Pembridge, delegate from South Carolina.

"Thomas! I'm glad you were able to get here so quickly," said Thomson, giving the boy a coin and ushering him from the room.

Jefferson held out an arm, preventing Thomson from closing the door and said, "Tell me boy, just what *is* your name?"

"Todd, sir; James Todd," the boy said.

"Well James, good luck with the army."

"Thank you sir!"

Jefferson just had time before Thomson closed the leaf of the door and blocking view of the corridor to note that the boy headed to a chair near the entrance where he was accustomed to sit and wait his next errand.

Turning toward the room, Jefferson shrugged out of his heavy coat and draped it across a chair. His hat he hung on a peg by the door. Thomson was already moving behind a desk cluttered with papers while the others took chairs that had been grouped in a semi-circle around the desk. A fire burned brightly in a nearby grate.

"Thomas, please have a seat," said Thomson, waving him in.

Jefferson took a chair as the others turned to face Thomson.

"Thomas, we have a very grave matter to discuss with you," Thomson began. "It requires the utmost discretion..."

"Now Charles, if this is about another nomination..."

"No, no, nothing like that," said Thomson impatiently. "Look," he continued, moving back around the desk to face Jefferson, "I must ask your word that anything said in this room between the five of us and our colleague William Few who is not here at present, must remain completely confidential."

When he did not continue, Jefferson assumed a reply was expected and gave one. "Of course, you know you can rely on my discretion."

"We were counting on that," said Thomson, visibly relaxing. "Now then, since you have been nominated as a member of the negotiating group in Europe, you've been fully informed of the status of the situation?"

"Of course." Why was Charles bothering to tell him of something he already knew?

"Then you know the extreme delicacy of our position? That nothing is definite. There are certain demands we must make on the King that are non-negotiable and others we may suggest and just hope the Foreign Office will go along with. Also, the French government must be a partner in any talks we have on settling the war." Jefferson nodded, still not hearing anything he had not been aware of before. "Though the United States is not officially recognized by England, this city is still host to its representatives..."

"Not to mention ten thousand of its troops in South Carolina," said Pembridge.

"Of course, John. In any case, what I'm trying to impress on you Thomas, is the extreme precariousness of our whole situation. We're at our wits end in this war. At the moment, we enjoy a fragile peace, but if hostilities break out again, our treasury is empty and the troops are near mutiny for lack of pay. The country has been bled white and if we ask for more French aid, we'll have more of their troops on our soil than British. It's imperative that the enemy do not suspect our weakness and in turn force us from the bargaining table. I have been informed that they have already made clandestine, tentative contact with our men in Europe and so am hopeful; but all rests on nothing disturbing the enemy. There are still those in Parliament, on the defense at the moment, but ready to seize any opportunity to scuttle a peace treaty. England is as tired of the war as we are, but unlike us, still retains the resources to fight."

"I understand all that, Charles," said Jefferson, crossing his legs. "But just what are you trying to say?"

Thomson moved in closer, instinctively lowering his voice, "Thomas, the very thing we have feared has come to pass."

"Something has happened that threatens the negotiations?"

"Yes..."

"What is it?" asked Jefferson leaning forward.

"Nothing less than murder; murder right here, in the halls of Congress."

"Murder you say!"

"The body was found not four hours ago by Mr. Madison," said Hamilton. "Papers on the body have identified the man to be a Mr. Jonas Singer, a wealthy businessman from New York."

"And worse than that," said Thomson, "a Loyalist of very high regard in the British army with connections to the royal family. His death would not go unnoticed by Parliament. A scandal of this magnitude would surely wreck the negotiations and plunge our nation again into war; a war we are in no condition to continue."

"You're aware of the King's concern for our Tories," said Madison. "Even now, we're informed that no treaty will be signed that does not make allowances for the restitution of Tory property and safe passage to a destination of their choosing; either Canada or England. The questionable death of a man of Singer's prominence will surely give the war party in Parliament their excuse for continued hostilities."

"I see the gravity of your position, gentlemen," said Jefferson. "The problem would seem to be twofold: to conceal nothing and let events take their course or to cover up the affair and risk later discovery, making matters appear even worse."

The four congressmen exchanged nervous glances before Thomson continued.

"Realizing the implications of the situation immediately, Mr. Madison locked the room and came directly to me. After informing Mr. Boudinot, the President of Congress, I was instructed to form a committee of the most trusted men in Congress to decide what to do. We made our decision and informed the

President of our recommendations. He approved of them, and so, we've summoned you."

"What exactly did the President agree to?"

"To a combination of both your scenarios," replied Thomson. "That an immediate investigation into the affair be made, and at its conclusion, report the findings and the guilty party to the proper British representatives."

"But we must impress on you the little time we have," said Pembridge.

"We expect a boat from Europe any week now with news of the negotiations, perhaps even a preliminary treaty. If word of this affair were to get out, it would scandalize Congress and provide the British envoy with an excuse to refuse us the treaty." Hamilton was in earnest now.

Jefferson had heard that Hamilton wanted a treaty with England badly; was the war interfering with his new father-in-law's business? He forced the unkind thought from his mind and said, "This is all very alarming gentlemen, but what exactly do you want of me? Shall I be engaged to speak to the envoy when he arrives?"

Thomson straightened and returned to his chair. Young Hamilton leaned back and glanced at Madison, who of all in the room, was closest to the red headed Virginian.

"Thomas, it was the decision of the committee that the murder must be investigated and that the guilty party be brought to justice," explained Madison. "But we couldn't just call in the local constabulary. The affair must remain within the family so to speak. Nothing must get out about it, you understand? Nothing."

"I won't say a word."

"That's good Thomas, because we want you to be the one to investigate the murder," said Thomson.

"What!" Jefferson was genuinely surprised. What did he know of murder? Of course, he'd had his contact with the unsavory business when he practiced as a lawyer in Virginia, but direct investigation? Whoever heard of such a thing? How would one go about investigating a murder? It did present an intriguing problem. "But why?" was all he could say.

"For a number of reasons," said Thomson. "You are available of course. We've not received word from London of guarantee of safe passage for you to Europe, and so you're marooned here in the city for the time being. You're not a member of Congress or of any other political body at the moment so you'll not be missed by anyone. You're discretion is above reproach and, finally, I know you have a fine and inquisitive mind filled with all sorts of useful knowledge that you can bring to bear in your investigations. You are the perfect vehicle to look into the affair."

Jefferson sat back and breathed out, his mind already awhirl with possible angles to approach the puzzle; and though he was not aware of any regular methods of crime detection, he was certain he could apply the rules of logic to the mystery as he could with any other intellectual problem. He grinned. Perhaps he could prove the effectiveness of causality in his investigations. Wouldn't William be surprised!

Thomson must have noticed the smile that creased his face, because he said, "Then you'll take on the assignment?"

"What else can I do gentlemen? As you've so aptly put it, the fate of the nation is in the balance. Although I don't think it's a good idea to cover up the crime in the long run, I'll do my best not to disappoint you."

"Excellent!" said Thomson, delighted at the prospect of reporting his success to the President. "But you must realize that you cannot tell anyone else of the business? If you must seek help, you have to come to me first for permission, understand?"

"Absolutely."

"Good..."

"Where's the body now?" asked Jefferson suddenly.

The abrupt question took Thomson by surprise. His mind had not had the time to reconcile itself to the reality of a man's death. Up until this moment, he had treated it as an intellectual exercise rather than a bloody reality. Jefferson's habit of wasting little time was going to be hard to get used to, but it was the more sanguine Hamilton who spoke first.

"We moved the body as quickly as we could to keep it from being discovered. Mr. Madison and I have it hidden in the basement. Luckily the cold weather will prevent putrefaction from setting in long enough for us to dispose of it when no one is likely to see us."

"How do you intend to dispose of the body?"

Hamilton seemed nonplussed. "Why by burial in pauper's field for now. Later, when we're able to reveal the whole business to the British, we can have it exhumed and moved for proper burial if necessary. No need to concern yourself on that account, Mr. Jefferson."

"You don't understand, Mr. Hamilton," said Jefferson, steepling his fingers. "I may wish to examine the body before you dispose of it."

Hamilton's brow furrowed. "Why on earth for? If it's the cause of death you need to know, I'll tell you: he was shot twice in the back. As for his identity, we were able to retrieve some papers we found on his person."

Thomson extended some envelopes, obviously opened, to Jefferson.

"Be that as it may," said Jefferson, taking the envelopes, "I yet may wish to see the body."

"Now Thomas," said Thomson, "there's no need to be morbid..."

"I'm nothing of the sort. I have certain ideas that information may be gleaned from the unlikeliest places.

Gentlemen, if you want me to take on this assignment, I must insist that I have complete autonomy." He looked around at the others, seeking eye contact.

"Of course, Thomas, we never expected to give you anything less."

"Good. Now then; I'd like permission to bring Dr. Shippen into our confidences."

"But why?" demanded Pembridge.

"Because I'll need him when I decide to examine the body. And besides, we can't keep it in the basement forever now can we?"

"That's true," admitted Thomson, already nervous about being able to keep the whole affair a secret.

"The body must be transported to Dr. Shippen's hospital as soon as possible. I'm expected for dinner at his home tonight, so I'll inform him then. Afterwards, he and I can take his cart over here and collect the body when everyone has gone. All I'll need is the key."

By this time, Thomson was definitely feeling a bit uneasy. Now that the secret was out, he felt that he had lost control of events. Perhaps it would have been easier to forget the whole thing? He reached into his pocket and handed Jefferson a key.

Jefferson took the key and pocketed it. "Now I'd like to see the room."

By this time, Hamilton was losing patience. "Mr. Jefferson, I'm willing to give you every doubt, but why do you want to waste time there for? We gave you Singer's papers and you will have the body to examine, what more do you need?"

"Mr. Hamilton..." Jefferson began patiently.

"Never mind, Mr. Hamilton," said Thomson. "This way Thomas."

CHAPTER THREE

Jefferson rose with the others and followed Thomson from the office and back out to the hall. The Secretary of Congress did not wait, but ducked immediately behind the staircase to a passage that ran along the rear of the building.

A row of windows let in the light from out of doors casting the shadows of their panes in strange patterns across a row of closed doors on the opposite side. A man sat in the alcove of a window facing one of the doors.

"Has anyone tried to enter the room since this morning, William?" asked Thomson.

"No, sir."

"Good," Thomson said, turning to the door.

"Mr. Secretary," said Few. "If my presence is not needed here, I have some other business to attend."

"Of course," replied Thomson. "We can brief you later on our meeting."

Nodding, Few hopped down from the alcove, and left them.

"I had William stay here to keep an eye on things just in case," Thomson explained as he inserted a key in the door. "We've cleaned up as much as we could, but still didn't want the room available so that there might have been someone here if we brought you over."

"I still don't understand why we're even bothering," said Hamilton. "There's nothing to be seen here. The killer, whoever he was, has long since gone."

"That's most certainly the case, " said Jefferson patiently, "and though I don't claim to have any experience in this sort of work, I can't help feeling that we mustn't leave any stone unturned."

"So what do you expect to find when you turn this stone over?"

"I haven't the vaguest idea," said Jefferson truthfully.

Hamilton put his hands on his hips and opened his mouth to say something else, but Thomson interrupted him.

"This way gentlemen," Thomson said, swinging the door open wide and ushering them all in, his hand still resting on the knob.

As the Secretary quickly closed and relocked the door behind them, Jefferson moved into the center of the room. It was not very big, but large enough to hold a circular table with six high backed chairs; a comfortable fireplace; a number of stuffed wing-backs and two waist high coffee servers. The tables faced each other from opposite sides of the room and held complete arrangements of silver tea sets. Over the fireplace hung a painting of a scene depicting William Penn speaking before a gathering of Indians (Jefferson identified them as Delaware), and on the mantelpiece, locally crafted vases containing flowers (*Orchidaceae*) sat at either end, their contents wilting and browned. Seeing the flowers, he became conscious of the room's odors; among them, the last residues of the orchids, old tobacco fumes, and another that he assumed belonged to some agent employed by Thomson in cleaning up the room.

Because obviously, the room *had* been cleaned. If a man had been shot here, Jefferson mused, blood would have been all over the floor.

Thomson must have noticed the Virginian's searching look when he said, "As you can see, we've...tidied up a bit since this morning."

Jefferson nodded and moved further into the room, hands at his back. "The room's used for committee meetings isn't it?"

"Yes."

Jefferson stood silent a moment, then said, "Since the room hasn't been used for the last two days and you say Mr. Madison only discovered the body some hours ago..."

"This morning around eight o'clock to be exact," said Madison.

"But you couldn't say just how long the body had lain there before you discovered it?"

"Well...no."

"So, theoretically, it could have been here for almost a full day before you found it?"

"Now how the devil can you make such an assumption?" demanded Hamilton.

Jefferson pointed at the flowers over the fireplace. "It's well known that once pruned, orchids have a short life. They're beauty is very fragile. What's more, in our country, most orchids must be cultivated in controlled environments such as greenhouses; furthermore, it being winter, I'm certain that these particular flowers came from a local grower. My conclusion is that judging by the state these specimens are in, they haven't been changed since at least yesterday morning. If any meeting were to be held in this room since then, then certainly the housekeeper would have replaced them. Consequently, barring any commotion prior to James' discovery, I must assume that the room has been unused for at least thirty hours."

At these deductions, Madison and Thomson felt encouraged to believe that they had made the right choice in getting Jefferson to look into the affair; but Hamilton's demeanor had not changed. He was dubious about Jefferson's reasoning at best. Not one to ruminate over the niceties of philosophy, he was not impressed with the Virginian's application of causality. Instead, he was disturbed by the needless complication of simple common sense. What possible connection could rotting flowers have to the murder?

"Had the corpse begun to stiffen when you and Hamilton brought it to the basement?" was Jefferson's next question.

"Not quite." Madison gave Hamilton a questioning look as if seeking confirmation for his reply.

"It still held most of its resiliency," agreed Hamilton.

"Hmmm; now, just where was the body found?"

"Well," Madison moved over to an open space on the far side of the room from the fireplace. "When I came in, I found it lying right here." He circled around the spot as if the body was still there, bent slightly, and stretched out his arms to indicate its position.

"The rug has been cleaned?"

"Replaced," said Thomson.

"The soiled one is in the basement as well," said Pembridge, lingering near the door.

"And in what condition was the blood?" The surprised looks of the others forced Jefferson to explain. "I mean, had it coagulated? Was it pooled or splashed? Was the body soaked in it or merely lying in it? How far from the body did it extend; I mean were there residues cast about the furniture and such and how far from the body? Was it smeared?"

"Oh come now, Mr. Jefferson!" cried Hamilton.

"Surely, Mr. Hamilton," said Jefferson, "as a soldier, you're no stranger to violence."

"Of course, sir; but what need is there to dwell on such unpleasant subjects? They belong to the battlefield, not the halls of Congress."

"I'm afraid that such explicit language is necessary for the accurate collection of facts, sir. In applying the language of science to the investigation, we allow for the most objective conclusions. If the sanguine nature of this affair is too much for you, I suggest you concern yourself with less disturbing duties."

"I don't find the affair too sanguine, sir!" retorted Hamilton angrily. "I merely find your approach..."

He was interrupted by a noise at the door.

"Damn the secrecy in this place!" a voice said from the other side of the door. "Is there to be no honesty even in the halls of Congress?"

"That's Samuel Adams, if it's anybody," hissed Pembridge.

"Adams!" said Hamilton. "I thought he was back in Massachusetts; running for governor or something."

"No, I'd heard he was back in the city," said Thomson. "And how could you expect a natural conspirator like him to stay away from Congress?"

"He's a rabble rouser," said Madison. "If he should suspect anything, the secret is as good as revealed."

"We have to get rid of him," said Pembridge, unconsciously leaning against the door.

Thomson went to the door and stepped quickly from the room. Adams' impatient, self-righteous voice was heard easily over the more level tones of the Secretary. Gradually, however, the savage breast was soothed and Thomson reentered the room.

"He said he'd wanted to use the room to meet with the Massachusetts delegates and what the devil do we have it locked for? But I promised him he could have it within the hour."

"Well then, we'd better get going," said Hamilton, starting for the door.

"About the blood?" said Jefferson to Madison, who was still standing over the imaginary corpse.

"The blood was pooled with the body lying on top of it."

"None on the body?"

"Not much; it was mostly beneath him."

"No splashing."

"Not really...no. I mean, we cleaned the furniture regardless, but we never saw any blood but what was pooled beneath the body."

"This pool had regular edges; there was no sign of dragging, or movement?"

"Nothing of the kind."

"Coagulation?"

"Definitely, but the part beneath the body and a few inches out from it might have still retained a fluid aspect."

"And I recall you saying there were two bullet holes in its back?"

"That's correct."

"They weren't knife wounds were they?"

"Most definitely not."

"Now then, the position of the body."

This time, Hamilton merely snorted.

"It was a bit crumpled, not full length..."

"Show me."

Madison stood back, his sense of dignity offended.

"Then I'll do it," said Jefferson, moving to the area of the floor indicated by Madison. "Just describe to me in what manner you found the body."

Madison collected himself. He could not allow the older man, and his mentor to boot, to so treat himself. "Never mind, Thomas, I'll show you." He went to the floor and lay on his left side with his knees bent partially to his waist, his right arm lay near his face and his left lay back, palm upward.

Jefferson said nothing, but carefully circled him and compared him to certain objects and places in the room. "Where exactly were the two holes?" Hamilton pointed a finger once at the spine just below the shoulder blades and once just to the right of the spine in the lower back. "Very well James, you can get up now." Madison wasted no time getting back to his feet.

"There were no signs of a struggle?"

"Nothing..." began Madison, then stopped. "Except for this chair here. I found it overturned alongside the body. But I'm sure it wasn't used to down him."

"Perhaps he merely used it to support his weight as he fell," mused Jefferson.

"You don't suppose the murder had anything to do with Congress do you?" asked Thomson, at last voicing his greatest fear. If the killing did involve politics, it would make explaining it all infinitely more difficult and might even present him with a dilemma involving political expediency.

"No way to tell," said Jefferson, examining the chair. "Shooting a man in the back is a coward's doing. Anyone with such low self-esteem strikes me as being nothing more than a common criminal. But the world is filled with all kinds of men and cravenness knows no station. Even a crime of passion cannot be ruled out."

"That would make things so much simpler," said Thomson hopefully.

Jefferson straightened. "Now then, what do we know of the man's identity? You say his name was Jonas Singer, a prominent Loyalist and wealthy businessman."

"From New York," said Pembridge.

"Since Mr. Hamilton is from the state of New York, perhaps he knows something about Mr. Singer," said Jefferson.

"I don't know him personally, but I know *of* him, and that merely what everyone else knows," Hamilton said. "He inherited his wealth from his father and put it to use in the China trade. He had very close ties to the East India Company, Britain's state supported monopoly. It was through the East India Company that he made contacts with the royal family some of whom may have had investments in his company. I suppose it was those attachments, the source of his continuing financial success, that proved stronger than his fidelity to his country. In fact, he was seen regularly here in Philadelphia in the days when it was occupied by the enemy. Anyway, it came as no surprise to many that in the end, he opted to ally himself with the crown. His wealth allowed him to move easily in New York's social circles and he was regarded as quite a catch for any young lady of ambition."

"You seem well informed Mr. Hamilton," said Jefferson.

"As a delegate from New York, I found it expedient to acquaint myself with those who had the resources to place me here," Hamilton said smoothly. "Mr. Singer was not a stranger to these circles before the war."

"Hmmm, yes. Well, there doesn't seem to be any lack of possible motivation for the crime; after all, Tories have not been well liked during the course of the war," said Jefferson.

"To say the least," said Madison. "There have been many instances of abuse that have gotten out of hand among the citizenry."

"The papers I gave you were found on his body," said Thomson, changing the subject.

Taking them from his pocket, Jefferson looked the papers over as carefully as he could under the circumstances then grunted in mild surprise.

"He was in Philadelphia under letter of mark from General Washington himself to see about those Tories wishing to leave the country."

"Mr. Hamilton who, as you know, served as Washington's aide de camp throughout the war, has verified that the signature is genuine," said Thomson. "You see how much more embarrassing that makes the affair; Mr. Jonas was under official protection, his safety the responsibility of Congress."

"It seems he also intended to take care of some private business," said Jefferson. "These are local letter heads."

"I suppose he intended to leave the country himself after his assignment was completed," observed Thomson. "Perhaps planning to have others watch over his business affairs after he left."

"That's natural. Unfortunately, some of these assets have already been seized by patriots," observed Hamilton.

"You disapprove?" demanded Pembridge.

"I do. Half the business community of our country is controlled by Tories. If that half disappears, where's the badly needed revenue we'll need to rebuild to come from? This country will be cash poor for years to come and we cannot continue to allow the pilfering of valuable, taxable property..."

"Enough, Alexander!" said Thomson. "You don't have the floor in Congress at the moment."

"And here's his name and address in the city," said Jefferson, studying the outside of an envelope. "I think I'll pay a visit to his rooms next."

"What!" exclaimed Thomson, alarmed. "If you do that, you're sure to be seen and questioned."

"Charles, how else am I to discover any reason for this murder? Mr. Hamilton himself said there's nothing here to see," he waved his arm about the room. "What do you suggest I do next?"

"I just think going to his rooms is a very risky thing to do."

"I gave you my word to be discrete and I intend to keep it; if anything should arise that would threaten that discretion, I'll back away."

"Then I suppose I can live with that."

"Good. I'll hold onto these."

Jefferson had already stuffed the papers into his waistcoat before Thomson could say, "By all means."

"I'll be going now," said Jefferson moving to the door.

"Are you sure there's nothing else?" asked Thomson, "I'm going to open the room up to Adams."

"There's one thing," said Jefferson, "don't forget to have the flowers freshened."

CHAPTER FOUR

Jefferson hardly noticed the late afternoon bustle of the city as he wound his way to the address indicated in Singer's papers. His mind was preoccupied with the myriad disparate facts of the man's murder. When exactly was he killed and for what purpose? Why in the very halls of Congress? Was it indeed a political killing designed to upset the young country or simply a crime of passion? Certainly there was no evidence to support the former except the location where the body was found. As a matter of fact, there was more evidence to the contrary: there had been a scent in the room that he began to associate more and more with a woman and his difficulty in believing anybody so stupid as to kill a man in such a public place where anyone could have heard the shots fired. But it had been done, and presumably, no one saw or heard a thing. The murder must have occurred either late at night or so early in the morning that no one had yet been about.

It was a loud curse that finally brought him back to his senses as he was nearly run over by a coach and four and abruptly realized that he had reached Fourth Street. The papers discovered on Singer's body indicated that he had found lodgings in an establishment at this address and despite the lateness of the hour, Jefferson was determined to view his rooms as soon as possible before the cleaning lady decided to tidy things up and perhaps erase vital information. It was strange the way he had begun thinking in such a manner; first at the State House and now here, yet he could not shake the apprehension that evidence might be destroyed in the process. After all, if he had had to rely on the testimony of others regarding the murder room instead of viewing it himself, how different a picture it would have created when instead of facts, he would have had only the narrow minded assumptions of his colleagues (as well meaning as they might have been) to go on.

Fourth Street was not quite a residential area and not quite commercial, but rather a concentration of boarding houses and hostels, very fashionable for visitors to the city. And, as he soon learned, lodging was not so difficult to find if one had the money to pay for it. It was well known that at most lodgings in the city, it was not uncommon to find two boarders per bed, but in the case of Mr. Singer, a private room was somehow found. Jefferson knew how difficult *that* was, he was just lucky to have a standing invitation from his own landlady, Mrs. House, for a private room at her home.

He decided to approach the property quietly first. After ascertaining the address, he walked over to the side entrance where a narrow driveway led to the rear of the building. Crunching along the path, he came to the carriage house whose doors stood open, revealing a shiny new gig of the latest British fashion and a stable area where a group of well bred horses stamped nervously, sensing the approach of a stranger. Indeed, Mr. Singer had done well for himself. He noticed also the receptacles for storing waste until the servants could cart it away, far enough from the house to free it of unwanted odors. He nodded in approval. Sanitation was still little understood, but the owners of this establishment were at least aware of the advantages of premises free from foul stenches.

Walking back around to the front of the building, he knocked at the door. His eyes roamed about the windows and potted plants and admired the overall neatness of the establishment and made a note to remember the place when next he needed rooms of his own. But then his eyes stopped. Ranged along the side of the door were a number of mail boxes, mostly empty as mail was usually delivered by hand so the deliverer could collect his fee, but the one with the name "Singer" on the front contained a number of pieces easily visible through the slot. Something tugged briefly at his conscience, but was soon overruled by his common sense. The man was not only dead, but his death could have serious repercussions for the nation. The three envelopes were snug in his waistcoat before someone had opened the door.

"Yes?" a slightly rotund woman asked hopefully.

"Is this the residence of Mr. Jonas Singer?"

"It is."

"I wonder if you might tell him a Mr. Pass, is here to see him...on business." He had not really thought of lying.

The woman's demeanor changed as she realized that he was not another potential boarder. "Mr. Singer has been gone these past few days, and I'm not sure when he'll be back."

Gone a few days! "Exactly how long has he been gone, Mrs....?"

"Simms, and he left Tuesday morning, but I don't see as it's any business of yours."

That was three days before. Where had he gone all that time before showing up dead in the State House? And more importantly, *whom* did he see?

"Perhaps, Mrs. Simms," he said, rolling a shiny gold piece between his fingers, "you might have noticed if Mr.

Singer had any visitors in the time he's been in the city? Or if he left with anyone?"

It was clear Mrs. Simms was warring with her responsibility to her patron's privacy and her natural greed; but Mr. Singer had been absent for three days and the gold piece was here. "No, he's had no visitors. Unless you count a boy who was here earlier in the week to give him a message..."

"The mail?"

"No, it was private...and a woman who called yesterday while he was out," she finished.

"A lady? Can you tell me anything about her?"

Mrs. Simms shrugged. "Not really. She wasn't young, but still well preserved, if you know what I mean, soft spoken and nervous. She had on a new dress and," she hesitated and finally whispered, "a line of lighter skin around her finger as if she were accustomed to wearing a ring there but removed it recently; not that I took particular notice mind you." She reached out for the coin.

Jefferson pulled it back and said, "One more thing, Mrs. Simms. Can you tell me where the messenger boy came from?"

Mrs. Simms straightened proudly. "Mind you, I'm no eavesdropper, but I did hear him mention the Cobblers'."

The Virginian smiled and handed the woman the coin. If only all witnesses could be as observant as she had been!

Mrs. Simms was about to retreat indoors when the movement of her visitor's hand caught her attention again. "Is there anything else...Mr. Pass?"

"Why good of you to ask, Mrs. Simms. I was wondering if I might be allowed to leave a note for Mr. Singer in his room?"

Mrs. Simms took the second coin. "Mind you, it's generally not allowed, but in your case I'll make an exception. But make absolutely sure you disturb nothing! I run a respectable house here."

"By all means, Mrs. Simms," said Jefferson as they mounted the stairs.

The house was indeed well kept with many furnishings of surprising value about the place. "The Captain, God rest his soul, brought back many fine things from his voyages," said Mrs. Simms, noticing his looks.

"He had marvelous good taste."

Apparently it was the right thing to say, as Mrs. Simms became more loquacious if not more informative as they came to a door on the third floor landing. Jefferson noticed it was set to the back of the house.

After a moment's fumbling, the landlady pushed open the door and Jefferson stepped into a good sized room, well lit from the two windows facing the yard. A hearth and accompanying wingbacks stood to one side and a small desk and chair on the other. Numerous books and papers lay in obviously ruffled but neat piles on the floor along one of the walls and a Persian rug protected one's feet from the cold floor. A doorway directly facing the hall entrance led into a small bedroom hardly bigger than a closet.

Jefferson walked into the room and over to the piles of paper on the floor. Hunkering down, he began to riffle through them, quickly scanning their contents and finding nothing more than business notes. Just the same, he realized they would be invaluable to the Congress as a source of Tory activity and identity, but this time, he could see the material had no bearing on the present affair. Mindful of unlawful searches and seizures, one of the very objections the former colonies had with their late monarch, he left them alone. It was enough to know the general outline of the man's Loyalist activities. Jefferson could not understand them, but was willing to allow the man his freedom of conscience. Next, he moved to the desk in the corner. He made a pretext of searching its drawers for writing material for Mrs. Simms' benefit, but knew he wasn't fooling her. He found some blank paper, quill and ink and also a small notebook written in what looked like Anglo Saxon. Certainly, the regular notations made at the beginning of each entry at least indicated that it was probably a diary. As he looked closer, Mrs. Simms cleared her throat. He made as if to replace it but managed to slip it into the cuff of his coat. He scribbled something inconsequential on the paper while scanning the pockets on the desk's headboard and then began to replace the material, wondering at the disorder of the desk. One would think that a man able to keep his other papers, and his room so neat, could do the same for his desk, which Jefferson regarded as the center of an educated life.

Finally, to Mrs. Simms' embarrassment, he stepped into the bedroom, giving it a quick scan. There appeared to be nothing of interest except for the neatly made bed and window in the back wall.

He was being impatiently herded into the hall by Mrs. Simms when he stopped suddenly and asked, "Mrs. Simms, did your guest bring any bags with him?"

"Of course sir! An important man like Mr. Singer traveling without a change of clothes! Why the very idea..."

"Yet there were no bags in either of his rooms."

"But that's..." she stopped as she realized the same thing.

But the missing bags meant different things to Mrs. Simms and her visitor. To the landlady, it meant a client who had managed to slip away without paying his board; and to the Virginian, it meant something more sinister. He remembered the disorder of the desk and the ruffled piles of papers on the floor; had the room been searched? By whom? Who was the mysterious female caller who had asked to see Singer and from whom did the messenger come? He could see it had been well worth his coming to visit Singer's lodgings although he was not at all sure what he had gotten out of it.

In the street again, he pulled a timepiece from his waistcoat and checked the hour. He would have to hurry if he was going to have dinner with Dr. Shippen!

A half an hour later, astride one of his favorite mounts, he reigned up in a small spray of gravel before the doctor's home. A servant appeared from somewhere to take his horse and another beckoned from an open door from which bright light spilled out onto the veranda.

"May I take your coat sir?" asked the man.

Jefferson let it slip from his shoulders and had just stepped out before the narrow stairs that led to the upper floor when he heard Shippen's voice call from the dining room.

"It's about time, Thomas; we were going to start without you!"

Jefferson entered the dining room and exchanged greetings with the other members of the household. "Sorry I'm late William, but I had some business to attend to." He slipped to the empty chair alongside his host.

"The nomination?" asked the doctor, seriously this time.

"Not really."

Doctor Shippen was accustomed to such reticence and knew when to drop a particular subject. It could be raised in more private circumstances. Conversation wound about a number of inconsequential things as the meal progressed until it was almost time for dessert.

As usual, any conversation between the two old friends eventually devolved into reminiscences of old times.

"And do you recall the day we first met?" asked Shippen.

"Do I? I spent days in your hospital sick as a dog from your smallpox inoculation!"

"I remember that; hardly a complaint out of you, I was surprised at that. You see, at the time, inoculation was still a very dangerous procedure and we had lost a patient or two in the past. And those who came to us, though convinced of the operation's worthiness, still had their doubts. Consequently, we had beds filled with patients who thought their mild symptoms meant certain death. Why, we almost had to keep a minister on permanent duty just to keep them calm!"

"Well, I didn't approach the whole thing with complete confidence. As you said, the process did still carry some risks."

"Nevertheless, some years later, you did have your entire family inoculated."

"Certainly. As you know, my family has not been without its tragedies and I wasn't about to stand idly by and watch my surviving little ones taken from me when there was anything I could do about it."

Shippen nodded and sobered. "I really was quite shaken when I heard of Martha's death. I'm truly terribly sorry about the whole thing." He placed a reassuring hand on his friend's arm.

"Your sentiments are appreciated, William; and though I can never have my Martha back, I'm determined to apply all my energies to my daughters."

"Patsy is a charming girl."

"But what of inoculation these days," said Jefferson suddenly, changing the subject. "Any news?"

"The whole process is becoming safer by the day; unfortunately, the wall of fear and doubt we experienced twenty years ago still persists. I don't know what it'll take to overcome that, but if it ever is, I know we can wipe the curse of small pox from the country."

"I've heard that a Dr. Waterhouse in Boston is interested in applying certain research done in Europe to America."

"You've heard of him then? Yes, I spoke to John Adams once about the state of medicine in Massachusetts...did you know he had his entire family inoculated as well some years ago?"

"He mentioned something of the sort to me during the First Continental Congress," said Jefferson.

"In any case, Dr. Waterhouse's work has been stalled because of the war, but he's optimistic about renewing his contacts in England when a treaty is signed. One of the great barriers to inoculation as you know, is the problem of its transportation. Because of the vagaries of temperature and the open air, the media loses its potency."

"I've given some thought to the problem."

"I know what that means! Have you come up with anything?"

"What would you say to putting the media into a phial of the smallest size, corking it well, and immersing it into a larger container filled with water and that sealed as well? The water in the larger container would act as an insulation, absorbing heat and keeping the smaller phial relatively cool. In addition, the whole thing would be kept in the shade as much as possible to further reduce warming."

Shippen rubbed his jaw. "It sounds as though it might work. But I still think it would be easier to pay a carrier of the disease to be handy at various locations to be used as a ready source of the matter. But enough of this," he said, pushing his chair back from the table. "Let's retire to the parlor for a bit of wine."

A few minutes later, the two men were comfortably seated before a warm fire, savoring their drinks. Jefferson spoke.

"William, a few minutes ago you mentioned the certainty of the treaty with England being signed."

Shippen lowered his glass, aware that something serious was about to be discussed.

"Yes..."

"What if I said that the treaty may be in the greatest jeopardy?"

"You mean of not being signed at all? That the war may be continued?"

"Exactly."

Shippen leaned back and said, "From all I've heard, it would be a disaster, to say nothing of the men called on to continue to fight and die. I've seen too much of the price of war in my own hospital not to be concerned about the possibility of diplomatic disaster."

"Disaster is exactly what I'm talking about," said his friend. "William, I know I can count on you to do whatever you can in our nation's best interests."

"Of course."

"Then I must have your word of honor that what I'm about to tell you will remain strictly between the two of us."

"You have it," said the doctor seriously.

Shippen listened incredulously, then with mounting seriousness as the Virginian recounted the events of the day, his special role requested by Congress and finally his findings up until his arrival for dinner that night. "Will you help me, William?" he concluded finally.

"Why, it goes without saying Thomas."

"I was hoping you'd say that, because I want to leave now to fetch Singer's remains."

"Now? But the hour..." said Shippen, glancing at the clock on the mantel.

"The hour is perfect for what we have to do," said Jefferson. "The State House will be long since empty at this hour and it's late enough so that we can transport the body from there to your hospital without anyone suspecting anything."

"The hospital? Don't you mean the graveyard?"

"No, I wish you to examine the body..."

"Examine it! But you already know it had been shot..."

"That's so, William, but there's more to be learned from a dead man than that."

"Well then, what are you expecting to find?"

"I don't know, but I'll know it when I find it. They say dead men tell no tales; but I have a feeling this one might."

Shippen scowled as he stood. "In any case, we'd better be off then. Though it's not readily visible, a body begins to decompose as soon as the spark of life is extinguished."

"Its been kept in the basement of the State House, exposed to the winter cold..."

"That will help, but not enough. It's been unseasonably warm this past week and though it won't be visible just yet, the rate of decomposition will only increase as time goes by."

"Do you have a place at the hospital where we can examine it without fear of discovery?"

"The morgue room in the basement will serve," said Shippen, "that is, if you don't mind being in the company of madmen."

"I'm beginning to get used to a great many strange things after today."

A little later, Shippen had sent the remaining servants to bed so there were no witnesses as the two men harnessed a horse to a wagon and walked it quietly to the street. They waited until the night watch passed before they felt it safe to emerge from the driveway and head out toward the town center.

It was approaching midnight as, circling to the rear of the State House, they disembarked and gently urged the horse to back the cart up to the steps leading to the rear entrance. Shippen tethered the horse to a convenient hitching post while Jefferson used the key given him by Thomson to gain access to the darkened corridors inside.

Immediately to the right of the entrance stood another he knew to be the door to the basement. Cautiously, the two men stepped into the cold blackness, using their feet to find the way down the narrow stone steps. Presently, they stopped and the doctor lit the candles they had brought with them. Suddenly the basement, really nothing more than a crawl space beneath the first floor of the building, leaped into view. At first all they saw was the sloping earthen floor and the rubbish of years scattered about it. A rat squeaked somewhere in the unlit corners and dusty cobwebs draped down from the great beams overhead.

"Well, where is it?" whispered Shippen.

Jefferson shrugged his shoulders and held up his candle for a better view. "I don't know." Fear that it had been discovered suddenly filled his mind and he moved farther out along the foundation kicking loose boards and broken tools as he went. Behind him, the doctor followed, brushing cobwebs from his head. Jefferson was moving out to the center of the basement, and getting ready to go on his hands and knees when a hiss stopped him.

"Over here," said Shippen, beckoning with his hand. "I found it."

As Jefferson made his way over to where the doctor was crouching, he saw that the reason they had missed the corpse was because it had been hidden directly behind the stairs. It lay wrapped in a rug that was dirty from the floor of the basement.

"Well, let's get it out of here."

Shippen set his candle in the dirt well away from the body while Jefferson set his on the edge of the stairs. When he turned back, the doctor had already pulled the body out from behind the stairs and was removing the rug.

"No, leave the rug," said Jefferson. "I may want to examine it."

"A rug?"

Together, the men manhandled the stiffening bundle over the floor to the stairs and, not without difficulty, managed to haul it outside and into the wagon. While Jefferson retrieved the candles and relocked the doors, Shippen arranged the body in the back of the cart and covered it with a soiled sheet.

"Ready." he said.

"Let's go," said Jefferson as he clambered aboard.

The ride back to the hospital, which was just next door to the doctor's home, was slow as they took many detours to avoid the night watchmen on their rounds and the more closely populated neighborhoods of the city.

At last they wheeled into the yard again and replaced the wagon and horse. Shippen disappeared for a few minutes then returned saying, "All's clear. Everyone has gone to bed and the lunatics are quiet. But don't count on it to last, as soon as we have some candles going they'll be up and about."

"Will they be heard?"

"No. It's the reason why we keep them in the basement floor in the first place."

Together, they carried their strange burden across the yard to the hospital.

CHAPTER FIVE

Though the hospital's size was not very large, its reputation overshadowed the small American medical community as though it were. Established some years before by Shippen and Dr. Phillip Physick, it incorporated all the most advanced methods of medical practice. Because of the unstinting efforts of the two doctors, the study and practice of medicine in Philadelphia flourished as it did in no other colony, even Massachusetts where the first inoculations on the continent had taken place.

The very latest innovations were always eagerly adopted by the hospital staff including the use of extended rooms or wards where beds were arranged to either side. The increased wall space in these rooms allowed for more windows, and more windows meant plenty of light and ventilation for the sick and the lame. In addition, spacing between the beds permitted ample room to change the linen as frequently as possible. The light, airy atmosphere created by this arrangement was believed crucial to the patients' sense of well being and was in contrast to the more usual practice of enclosing sick rooms with shut doors and drawn shades. More specifically, the new focus was to alleviate anything that might cause the patient distress over his infirmity. This condition in the patient's humor was seen and verified as being important in any eventual recovery, and everywhere, the rooms were kept spotlessly clean.

Shippen and Physick were justifiably proud of their hospital, but they took the most pride in the radical method in which they treated the mentally disturbed. Beneath the main floors of the hospital, in the rooms belowground, small, individual cells held the lunatics. These blighted individuals, through no fault of their own, were considered a menace not only to society, but to themselves; and so, they were placed here. Each cell was rather small with only a single tiny, barred window near the ceiling, a cot against the wall, and a chamber pot on the floor (that inmates sometimes even used). The patients were as well cared for as time and effort allowed but the important thing was that they were not abused but treated with kindness and understanding. They too were treated with the same habits of cleanliness as the patients above (or as much as the hospital staff could supply and keep up with their charges), although efforts to reason or study them had mostly failed. Up until the time when the medical community had recognized lunacy as a legitimate malfunction of the body and not of the soul, lunatics were considered mere criminals and treated as such. Only those lucky enough to have wealthy and compassionate families received better care by being placed in private homes for safekeeping or the rare home of a broadminded doctor.

Now, somewhere in the hospital, a door squeaked, and Jefferson froze.

"What's the matter?" asked Shippen, struggling to regain his grip on the rolled up rug.

"That door made enough noise to wake the dead...if you'll pardon the expression!"

"Nonsense; I hardly heard it myself. And besides, the wards are separated from the corridors with their own doors and they're all firmly shut. No one heard a thing."

"You're right of course," admitted Jefferson a bit sheepishly. "I'm not used to this creeping around."

"A man who's had a price on his head for the last eight years and who's been chased by that savage, Banastre Tarleton, is not used to 'creeping around?'"

Jefferson chuckled. "At the time, I was hardly aware of any jeopardy I may have been in."

"It's all right, I understand your nervousness. But we should have the body out of sight in good time. Here, let me get this door." The doctor rested the body precariously on a knee while reaching over to open a door that led downward to a dimly lit room. "Careful now, these stairs are quite steep."

Slowly, they negotiated the stairs to the bottom and placed their burden on the floor. Shippen climbed the stairs again to shut the door and then disappeared through the blackness of another doorway at the bottom of the steps. Presently, Jefferson saw a glow come through the low arch revealing a long corridor leading to another wooden door at the far end. The door was ajar and it was from the other side that the light issued.

Shippen came back saying, "Everything's all ready," and helped lift the body again. "But remember, absolute silence is necessary here as we'll be passing along the cells of the lunatics. I'm sure they're all asleep now, but some are light sleepers."

Jefferson nodded, aware that his lower back was beginning to ache; he would be glad to see this part of the night's work finished.

Except for the soft scuff of a foot now and then, their passage along the corridor was completed successfully. The only sounds Jefferson heard were those of the snoring patients. The doors to each cell, he noticed, were as stout as those for any prison and each held a small barred window in its upper portion. The foul stench of human waste wafted from some of the rooms and from one came the low mumbling of one of the blighted creatures. The Virginian marveled again at the mysteries of the human mind; that some could learn and appreciate the finest achievements in art, science, and law and others be condemned to lives of ignorance and illusion. How was such a dichotomy possible? If there was a God, how could He arbitrarily decide which of His children were to be gifted and which to be condemned to a life of mental darkness? Or was it that men had too little knowledge of lunacy to make such judgments? Did not the native Indians hold lunatics in awe as specially touched by the Creator? It was hard for Jefferson to understand that way of thinking, but he did not fool himself into thinking that he had all the answers. Better to be ignorant than to proceed on false assumptions.

At the end of the corridor, Shippen bumped a door open and steered them past the frame and into a small room that terminated the corridor. A wooden table stood in the center of the room with shelving all around the walls. Lowering their burden onto the floor, the two men unfolded the rug and lifted its contents onto the waist high table. The rug was folded and placed in an empty corner.

As the doctor moved about the room lighting candles, Jefferson took the opportunity to study its features. He had never been to this part of the hospital, but readily guessed its purpose. Shelves lining the walls held an array of jars, some obviously labeled as chemicals, both natural and man-made, and others seemed to hold anatomical remains, both animal and human. A counter that ran along two of the walls was clear of any clutter except certain tools used in the medical profession; strangely fashioned utensils whose purpose even he was forced to guess at. Not one, but two microscopes sat side by side, each covered with a protective cloth to keep dust from their delicate instrumentation. A series of medical charts hung on the wall behind the door.

Shippen was just coming into the room again, weighed down by a bucket full of water that he set on the ground. The earthen floor had already absorbed the water he had used to clean the table just after they had come in with the body.

"Do you know what it is exactly that you're looking for?" asked Shippen.

"Not really," said Jefferson, joining his friend by the table. "Mostly I'd like to recover the two balls that killed him; but I'd hoped that something else unforeseen might be found as well."

"Well," Shippen sighed, "we should be able to determine the exact time of death which might help you somehow. This sort of thing is quite new to me you know."

"Surely you don't mean vivisection itself?"

"I've done my share of cutting with criminals, but that was always for the sake of science, to study the ways of the human body. I've never done it for any other reason. Certainly, I've never thought of doing it to help in a criminal investigation."

"Is it done so rarely then?"

"Not at all. In fact one of the earliest post mortems was done on Pope Alexander V in 1410. Mostly it's done to determine if the deceased had been poisoned or not. Before that of course, some truly garish things were done in the name of vivisection."

"Anatomy has progressed far beyond any of that blind groping."

"Definitely. In any case, this room is where Dr. Physick and I conduct our research when we do have a cadaver to study. It's conveniently situated well away from more sensitive natures."

"Hmmm. Vivisection I take it, is still not quite accepted medical practice among the general populace?"

"Maybe in jaded Europe, but certainly not in Philadelphia!"

"So how do we begin?" asked Jefferson, moving over to the anatomy charts.

Shippen cleared his throat. "Thomas," he said, going over beside his friend, "I feel I should warn you, vivisection is not a pretty sight and that if you had any idea of remaining in the room during the operation..."

"William," said Jefferson, "I'm not unfamiliar with the sight of blood. As a farmer, I've had my share of injured workmen and have had to treat them myself, and quite successfully at times if I do say so. I'm not faint of heart and I feel that I should remain in the room with you throughout the post mortem. I'm not exactly sure what it is I'm looking for, but I'll know it when I see it. I promise to keep back and not interfere." He smiled and clapped a hand lightly on Shippen's shoulder. "Besides, if I feel sick, there's another empty bucket here I can use."

"Very well," Shippen laughed, "you can stay."

"Now then, doctor," said Jefferson, waving a hand at the charts before them, "how do you intend to proceed?"

"Well, you understand there's no accepted procedure for a criminal post mortem except some very sketchy material when poisoning is suspected, so we're going to be on our own. I think the best way to proceed is by deciding just what it is we're looking for. In this case, two lead balls that have apparently entered the victim's back, killing him. But I think there are certain steps we should follow regardless of what we're looking for simply because they're good medical practice."

"A scientific method..."

"Exactly. We examine the body step by step, carefully gathering information, and when we're finished, our conclusions can only be drawn from our chains of established facts. I know this'll make you feel a bit better."

"You know my position on the medical profession as practiced by our local doctors..." Shippen raised an eyebrow. "Present company excluded of course! But seriously, I've never met a more stubborn and ignorant set of people anywhere. When bleeding is considered the best cure for every ill, well, my credulity stops there. You know as well as I do, the typical American doctor's reliance on procedures that bear absolutely no relation to proven fact."

"That's quite true, but America isn't Europe and we have some methods garnered from our studies of nature that work perfectly well. Also, another fact we have over our more doctrinaire brethren in Europe is the ability to merge the different branches of medicine into single individuals. I think that alone will one day lift American medicine from the stable boy apprentices we're stuck with now."

"That day cannot come too soon for me," said Jefferson. "Until then, I prefer the advice of my library as often as possible to that of my local physician."

Shippen decided to change the subject. "In any case," he said, pointing at a chart depicting the internal organs of the human body, "from what I've seen, the two balls have entered the body here and here." Jefferson nodded. "But first, we have to strip the body," said Shippen, turning back to the table.

"Not so quickly," warned Jefferson.

"What's the matter?"

"I'd like a chance to examine the clothing before we take them off."

"Why on earth for?"

"I'll know it when I find it."

The doctor shrugged and leaned over the corpse.

Jefferson moved over to the opposite side of the table and began fingering the clothing. The body lay on its stomach, exposing the two holes in its back.

"Ah, now you see what I mean?" said Jefferson, pointing to one of the holes.

"About what?"

"This hole here, the upper one has slight powder burns around the edges, while this one," he pointed at the other hole, "is clean."

"So?"

"So it follows that one shot was taken almost directly in contact with the victim and the second from farther away."

Shippen shook his head. "I still don't see how that could be important."

"It may not be, but it's interesting, don't you think?"

The doctor shrugged as he watched his friend continue his examination of the clothing, working his way down to the feet. There he bent a bit closer, then straightened. "Do you have a small container I might use?" Shippen took an empty jar from a shelf and handed it to the Virginian, who produced a pocketknife from his coat and began to scrape around the soles of the man's boots.

"What have you there?"

"Probably nothing," said Jefferson, holding the jar up to his face. "But there's nothing like a man's dirty boots to tell you where he's been." He placed the jar on one of the counters.

"Can we remove the clothing now?"

"I suppose so, yes." It took only a few minutes to strip the corpse, but considerably longer to clean it up with water and sponge. When that was finished, the doctor had donned a leather apron that covered his body from head to foot.

"His hands don't have any calouses; he didn't do much heavy labor," he said unnecessarily. "Hmmm, here are some scars. Dueling scars I'd say."

"Now there's something interesting; he has enemies."

"You don't say?"

"Just get on with your examination!" said Jefferson in mock anger.

"He broke his finger once; it must have been set wrong, because it healed improperly. No bruises or contusions..." The doctor continued to examine the skin for some minutes then spoke again.

"Judging by the skin color, I'd say right off that this man's been dead for at least fifteen hours, but it's still hard to tell because of the time the body spent in that cold basement." He moved his scrutinies to the head. "No cranial damage or contusions. At least he wasn't hit on the head before being shot." Next came the bullet holes. "They're quite clean and regular," he said, "except for the grains of powder embedded in the skin around the upper one. I can say right now that this upper shot would have killed him instantly."

"How so?"

"It shattered the spine. Help me roll it over." When the body was on its back, both men expressed surprise. There were two holes on that side too. "Well, you're not going to find your balls here, Thomas, they passed right through."

"But for that, the charge in the gun must have been enormous!"

"That's for sure. Either the killer was unused to firearms or he wanted to make absolutely sure his shot killed and not merely wounded his victim." Shippen began to poke the skin, testing its resiliency then bending the various limbs. "From what I can see, I'd say this man has been dead between..." he looked at his watch, "twelve and fifteen hours."

"You've deduced that from the pigment of the skin and the resiliency of the limbs?"

"That and the condition of the blood. You're familiar of course with William Harvey's studies on the nature of blood?"

"That the heart is a pump that pushes the blood in a circular motion throughout the body from arteries to veins and back to the heart again at least several times a day."

"Actually you forgot the capillaries, but they were only discovered by Marcello Marphighi when he pioneered microscopic anatomy. In any case, the important thing here is, that when alive, the body must constantly circulate its supply of blood and when life is gone, the blood merely sits idle in its tracks. But not for long, by defining gravity, Newton not only explained the forces that keep the universe in motion, but also the smaller universe of all living things. Without the action of the heart, gravity takes control of the blood and draws it toward the earth. It's by the rate at which the blood gathers at the lowest point in the body that is the simplest measure of how long it's been since life left it."

"The mathematically proven gravitational constant of Newton, governs all things equally, regardless of size or importance; from the vastness of the universe to man himself. Who would've thought that an equation used to define the very fabric of the universe, could be used to solve the time since a man's death as well?"

There was silence as the doctor stood in thought a moment, staring at the body.

"He has a venereal disease," observed Jefferson, suddenly.

Shippen shifted his attention to the infected area. "Quite true. Our man wasn't very careful with the company he kept." He looked up suddenly. "Was he married?"

"No, but he had a lady friend," replied Jefferson, making a hasty note on the back of one of the letters he had in his waistcoat.

"Then I suggest you warn her about the possibility of infection."

"Me? Such an intimate subject ought to be the province of a doctor."

Shippen laughed. "Just joking! Let me know when it's safe to say so, and I'll have her warned."

Jefferson relaxed making another note.

"May we continue?" asked the doctor.

"Of course," said Jefferson, replacing the envelope.

Shippen then began to probe forcefully with his fingers about the abdomen of the body, verifying the positions of its various internal organs. Finally he handed Jefferson a number of vicious looking tools, keeping a long knife for himself. "I'm going to make my incision now," he warned. His friend nodded wordlessly as he watched the doctor begin to cut. "Luckily, most of the body's blood supply has been lost and what remains has settled toward the left rear of the body, so we shouldn't have too much of a mess."

Jefferson watched fascinated as the doctor deftly made his first incisions. In a few minutes, he had the skin pulled aside, revealing the internal scheme of the body. He had been right, there was very little blood. He handed Jefferson the knife he had been using in exchange for a long wooden probe, which he began to use with a bit of vigor, poking about and investigating the path of the two balls that had torn their way through the delicate machinery of the body. The Virginian wondered at the mysterious fleetingness of life. How such a gift could be transmitted from mother to child and even survive with only the most delicate balance of little understood organs and arteries to depend upon. The experience of nature seemed too arduous for any such finely tuned machine to survive for long; but it did. And then that mysterious spark left the body, sometimes for no apparent reason. He had seen people die, every part of their bodies still in perfect condition, but the animating force was gone. What was it that imparted vigor to bodies that without it, no body could be animated; even with all its parts in perfect order?

"Now you see here?" Shippen was saying. He had lit a few candles along the edge of the table for better lighting.

"What?"

"Right here," he said, his reddened hands holding aside a path into the body. Multi colored organs glistened wetly in the flickering light. "The first ball shattered the spine as I guessed, just below the shoulder blades, punctured the heart just here," he bent the organ to show his friend where it had been shredded, "was deflected by this rib; here feel that," he said, making room for Jefferson's hand.

The Virginian ran his fingers along the rib indicated and felt the slight nick in its smooth surface.

"You see?"

"Yes."

"It was deflected from the rib across the right lung, deflating it," Jefferson saw that damage plainly, "and exited the body here, just below the thorax."

"The second ball entered the lower back, passed through here, destroyed the pancreas and the spleen and exited here, between these two ribs." He straightened. "No balls though."

Jefferson rubbed his chin. "Maybe they're in the rug there." He moved over to where they had tossed the rug and opened it across the floor. It was caked with dried blood and it took quite a bit of searching to find a pair of small holes verifying that the two balls had not embedded themselves in the rug but had passed through it. "They must still be in the State House then."

"Here's something interesting," said Shippen from his place by the body.

When Jefferson approached, he saw that his friend had the mouth open and was poking around inside with a flat stick.

"What's interesting?"

"Come over here and smell this."

Jefferson wrinkled his nose at the suggestion, but did as he was told. He shrugged.

"So?"

"So nothing. I just thought I smelled something peculiar. Did you?"

"I don't think so," said Jefferson, sniffing again to be sure. "No, nothing. Except the usual bad breath. Nothing a little snuff wouldn't have taken care of."

"Hmmm," said the doctor, passing a finger around the inside of the gums. When he pulled it out, there was some half-decomposed residue on the tip of his finger. He smeared it on a microscope slide and slid it beneath the instrument.

"Anything?"

"Not really. I hate to admit it, but I've not had much time to use this microscope so I'm not sure what I'm looking at. But I'll go through some of my books and see if I can match up what I'm seeing with any of the illustrations."

"Are you sure it's not just food? I mean, what else do you expect to find in a man's mouth?"

"Of course you're right, Thomas, but it's that smell really..."

"Well show me how to put some of this material from his boots on a slide." In a minute, Jefferson had entered the strange world first pioneered by Anton van Leeuwenhoek. He had almost forgotten what it was he wanted to check, so fascinated was he by this intriguing new universe.

"And what are you looking for?" asked the doctor.

"Now I'm not sure. Perhaps I don't really need this instrument to get my answer, but its power is so seductive! I think what I've got here is horse manure."

"Well of course, what else did you expect?"

"I was hoping it may have been mixed with other sediments that might be peculiar to certain areas. If I could identify something of that nature, I might be able to recreate Mr. Singer's movements in the hours just before his death."

"Makes perfect sense when you put it that way, but if you're having trouble identifying anything, why don't you try comparing your sample to the items in Peale's museum?"

"Good idea," said Jefferson, "but first I have one more thing to do..."

"Not before you get a good night's sleep!" said Shippen. "As your doctor, I prescribe plenty of rest for now." He looked at his watch again. "Good heavens! It's after three o'clock in the morning! Do me the honor of staying what's left of the night in my home?"

"That's the best offer I've heard all day!"

CHAPTER SIX

Earlier in the day, another meeting had been held, this one in a private, windowless room over the Black Horse Tavern in Philadelphia. A small group of men sat around a table littered with the remains of a recently consumed meal. Drinks had been served as they settled back for conversation.

"Well, John, what are they up to?" asked Samuel Adams from the head of the table.

John Pembridge sipped his wine before replying. "You were right of course, Sam. Not only have they called in Jefferson, but he's started his investigation already. The President of Congress deems this whole matter of the highest importance; he and the committee have agreed that the murder must be kept secret until it can be solved because the international ramifications of its exposure will surely sink the peace negotiations."

"So they've gone ahead and recruited that popinjay, Jefferson have they?" said Whitmer Stiles of Georgia. "What do they expect him to do?"

Pembridge shrugged. "Solve the murder of course; but what *exactly* do they expect from him? I don't know." He scratched his head. "He wanted to look at the murder room; he even had Mr. Madison pose as the dead man on the floor! If you ask me, the man hasn't a clue to what he's doing."

"Let's not write Jefferson off too quickly gentlemen," said Adams. "I don't know the man personally, but my cousin did, and from he and others, I'm not inclined to place any doubt in Mr. Jefferson's ability to do something with the case. No, gentlemen, I think we should not underestimate the man. He's single minded, tenacious and, yes, brilliant, with a first class mind. In short, he's a dangerous man to have against you."

"I've known him professionally for many years," added Increase Stevenson of Massachusetts, "and Sam's right. The man can make a dangerous opponent."

"The man's a coward!" sneered Henry Bolton, a Virginian and close friend of Patrick Henry who bore little love for Jefferson. "When he was governor of Virginia, he ran like a scared rabbit from that turncoat, Arnold and his British masters when they invaded the state."

"I understand Henry was also one of those rabbits," mumbled Pembridge.

The clatter of shattering glass marked Bolton's anger as he surged to his feet, "I'll take such talk from no man...!"

Adams was on his feet as well and, laying a hand on Bolton's shoulder, said, "Henry, we're not here tonight because we all love one another, but because in this one instance, we all agree that the destruction of any peace treaty with England would be in the best interests of our country. I suggest you two leave your differences outside, or on the floor of Congress, where they belong."

Bolton's ardor had cooled by the time Adams had finished speaking and sat back in his chair. Stevenson poured him another glass of wine.

"Now then," continued Adams, "I think we're all agreed that Jefferson does pose a threat to our plans?" The others nodded. "All right, now, thanks to Mr. Pembridge, we've been able to head off Mr. Jefferson at a crucial juncture in his investigations."

"Then my warning came in time?" asked Pembridge.

"Just barely, John," said Adams. "It was all I could do after you slipped me Singer's address, to get to his rooms and search them in the short time we had before Jefferson appeared. As it was, I was still clinging to the roof when he arrived with the landlady. I heard him rummaging about inside through the window; and believe me, I'm not a young man anymore!"

The others laughed, taking some of the tension out of the air. Everyone but Pembridge, who was visibly disturbed by Adams' boasts, although he managed to hide his displeasure.

"So you found what you were looking for?" asked Stevenson.

"I'll tell you, there was a gold mine of evidence there that every state in the Union could use to seize millions of pounds of Tory property, but that I had to leave behind. Not only couldn't I have hauled it all out with me, but I felt I had to leave something for Jefferson. In any event, I did manage to take a satchel fill with enough inconsequential papers to confuse any investigation."

"Good, that ought to stop Jefferson," said Jenks Howell of Vermont.

"Don't count on it," said Pembridge. "He also wants to look at the body."

"The body? What on earth for?"

"I don't know, but if what Sam says is true, he may deduce something from it."

"Gentlemen," said Howell, "I can't express enough how strongly I feel about any treaty with England. I was with George Clark at Vincennes and saw firsthand the suffering of those people on the frontier at the hands of those red savages; savages who were goaded on by the

British! Too much American blood has been spilled in the conquest of the west to allow it to remain in British hands."

"And besides that," said Stiles, "the Mississippi is the life's blood of any commerce to be done west of the mountains. With the region becoming increasingly important to our western counties, we cannot allow it to be controlled at the whim of a monarch across the ocean."

"And don't forget," added Stevenson, "Canada too, must be made part of the equation if at all possible, otherwise, we'll have British mischief making on our frontier for years to come."

"Well, isn't that why we're here?" said Pembridge. "Imagine the shock in some quarters to see northerners and southerners sitting together and agreeing on something!"

"Whatever treaty there is, must be wrecked!" cried Stevenson, slamming his fist impatiently on the table. "The British will never allow this country to claim the lands west of the Proclamation Line; at least not until they've been bled a bit more."

"Well, we've taken our first step in that direction," said Howell.

"I can't see why we just don't leak the information of Singer's death to one of the friendly newspapers..." said Bolton.

"You know we've agreed not to do that," said Stevenson. "If the source of the leak is ever traced to us, it would destroy our states' interests in Congress. Perhaps even endanger the Confederation itself."

"Not to mention putting an end to our public careers and disgrace," added Howell.

"Well, everyone knows you're running for governor, Whitmer!" said Adams to general laughter all around. When it had died down, he continued, "Stevenson is right. We've already agreed to let events run their course in

74

public, but to do everything we can short of discovery, to force those events our way. The easiest way to do that right now, is to get Jefferson off the case; he's just too competent."

"I've already moved in Congress to renominate Jefferson as minister plenipotentiary to France," said Pembridge.

"Again?" grumped Bolton.

"Could we help it if the man was completely disinterested until only recently? It would help if he did some campaigning of his own. In any case, I'm moving to expedite his nomination and get him out of the country as quickly as possible, hopefully before the arrival of the next diplomatic ship from England."

"Good," said Adams. "So if there's nothing else to discuss, we'll call it a night."

At about the same time, and just outside the city at Fairhill, the estate of John Dickinson, sometime member of Congress, anonymous author of the influential *Letters From a Farmer in Pennsylvania,* and full time patriot, a second group of men was meeting.

The big house was well lit with a small knot of carriages before it throwing long, strange shadows across the perfectly trimmed lawn. Liveried servants moved noiselessly about the property and kitchen maids busied themselves cleaning up after the master's meal.

In the study, with its walls of bookcases filled with texts on law, philosophy, and government, a bright fire was crackling in the grate, warming the room and giving it its only source of light. Three men sat in overstuffed chairs around the fireplace fingering glass cups of the finest craftsmanship. Dickinson, the President of Pennsylvania, stood leaning on the mantelpiece. "So, Mr.

Hamilton," he said, "what is so important that you had to call this meeting under so short notice?"

Hamilton rose to his feet and walked over to the corner of the hearth opposite Dickinson. He appeared to be gathering his thoughts. "Gentlemen," he said at last, "I'm worried about the pending treaty with England."

"So are we all," said Agamemnon Jones, a representative from Connecticut and a very rich man. He risked everything when he decided to join the patriot cause. The others agreed.

"Bear with me, gentlemen, as I perhaps state the obvious," said Hamilton, the youngest man in the room at the age of only twenty-six, but with a rising reputation for brilliance. Some even whispered he was Jefferson's intellectual equal; but in a curiously opposite way. Where Jefferson was more philosophical and democratic, Hamilton was realistic and aristocratic. Where the Virginian was a dreamer, the New Yorker was practical. Above all, where Jefferson had difficulty balancing his budget, in monetary circles, Hamilton was an inspired visionary. To the others in the room, the two men appeared to be on an inevitable collision course.

"The pending peace treaty with England may or may not have a clause relating to the western lands, but because of the nature of communications, we may never know its make-up until too late, when Congress will be called upon to vote on it. We all know the unlikeliness of Britain's giving up title to the western lands, no matter in whose hands they presently lie. We also know that sentiment in Congress leans strongly toward an end to the war at almost any cost. To many there, the western lands appear to be nothing more than a liability with their tribes of savages and sparse but troublesome white population. There's every reason to believe that they would give away the west at the first opportunity for peace."

"Hmmm. But there are many in Congress with real estate interests in the west..." mused Jones.

"Of course, but they are few, not enough to overturn the will of the majority," countered Hamilton smoothly. "And unlike that majority, we here know the vast potential value of the western lands. The fur trade alone is worth countless millions of pounds; taxes from which will be sorely needed to repay this new nation's crushing foreign debt. We know there are mineral deposits of every kind there also: gold and silver. And millions of acres of arable land.

"There is the matter of Spain to contend with as well," Hamilton continued. "The United States will require a buffer zone between it and the empire of New Spain whose interests in the southwest are well known. Even France may still have designs on the west with its islands of French populated towns along the Mississippi and Missouri Rivers. And finally, there's the matter of the chain of forts all along the Lake Champlain region and the Ohio Valley still manned by British troops and their Indian allies. All, gentlemen, obstacles to the expansion and enrichment of the United States."

"So what's your point?" asked Desmond Tench, a wealthy furrier from New York.

Hamilton set down his empty glass, "My point is that the treaty must be wrecked until our position in the west is so strong, the British will be forced to cede it to us."

"I think we can all agree to that," said Dickinson.

"Yes, except there's been a little wrinkle added to our problems, which may or may not serve our purposes."

"And what's that?"

Hamilton told them of the discovery of the murdered Loyalist in the halls of Congress. Their reactions were predictable and it took some time for them to sort out all the facts.

"We can't just leak this out," concluded Hamilton. "If we're discovered as the source, it would ruin our effectiveness in government and hand our opponents a weapon with which they could cast suspicion on our motives."

"Yes," agreed Tench, "it would look as if it was again, commercial interests versus agricultural interests."

"I think the best thing to do is to get rid of Jefferson," said Dickinson. "He's intelligent with a scientific mind that is well suited to the sifting through of facts."

"John Pembridge of South Carolina has already moved to nominate Jefferson as minister plenipotentiary to France in Congress," said Hamilton, "even to getting the whole process moving as quickly as possible."

"Things couldn't go better for us!" said Jones. "Our sometime rivals are doing the work for us."

"That may be so," said Tench, "but I've heard stories that Samuel Adams is back in the city and that he's been seen with Pembridge."

Dickinson straightened from his place by the fireside, losing his equanimity for the first time that night, even after hearing of the murder. "Samuel Adams! That firebrand! What the hell's he doing back here?"

"I thought he was back in Massachusetts running for governor or something," offered Jones, nervously.

The elder Adams' reputation had preceded him even before the first Continental Congress in 1774. A key figure in the Boston revolutionary movement from the earliest rumblings when James Otis was the only voice speaking out against royal injustice, Adams had been involved in nearly every phase of the coming storm. He helped organize his state's committee of correspondence, fought the legal battles in its assembly, gave rabble-rousing speeches at patriot events, and recruited his cousin, John Adams, into the movement. It was even rumored that it was he who bent the nearly lawless Guy

Fawkes' Day celebrants to the patriot cause by having them burn down the governor's mansion and chase the Crown's representatives to the safety of an island in Boston Harbor. More tenuous, but yet believed by a good many radicals, was the rumor that it was he who had shouted "Fire, fire!" when the mob pressed too closely to British soldiers, resulting in a misunderstanding that led to the Boston Massacre. And this was all before his behind the scenes maneuvering when Massachusetts finally sent him to Congress. Small wonder that his name made certain people nervous.

Hamilton shrugged. He was one of the few people whom the name of Sam Adams meant nothing; after all, in some circles, his own name was just as formidable. "He lost that contest to his erstwhile student, John Hancock as you'll recall. Yes, he came to the door of the murder room when the committee was there with Jefferson, demanding to be let in. He was his usual bombastic self."

"At the scene of the murder?" said Dickinson, still trying to recover himself. "How the devil does that man do it? He always seems to be at the place where he can do the most damage. Why, I heard from Increase Stevenson of Massachusetts that it was he who'd fired that first shot at Lexington Green! That he was present, saw reason prevailing and feared the perfect opportunity for the start of war would be missed and took a shot at the British officer in charge from an upper story window overlooking the Green."

"An apocryphal story at best," said Hamilton, unimpressed, who was no stranger to violence himself, having led an assault team into hand to hand fighting at the siege of Yorktown.

"Then how do you explain his coincidental appearance at the scene of the murder just as it was being shown to Jefferson?" said Dickinson. "How do we know it wasn't Adams himself who killed the man?"

Hamilton shrugged. "It's possible of course, but I just don't feel the man is capable of cold blooded murder."

"Well, I still don't like it," said Dickinson. "Adams makes me nervous."

"Me too," said Tench; Jones agreed.

"Well if you feel that strongly about it, gentlemen, I'll look into Mr. Adams' doings about town myself," Hamilton reassured. "If he *is* up to anything, I'll report back to you. In the meantime, we must rid ourselves of Jefferson."

He didn't say it aloud, but he still thought the man a trusting incompetent.

It was a dark, moonless night and luckily for the Chevalier de la Luzerne, French minister to the United States, the waters of the Delaware River had been relatively calm. That, however, still left the late autumn cold to be dealt with and unfortunately, little could be done about that save for holding his great coat more tightly about his body.

Looking over his shoulder, Luzern could make out a few twinkling lights along the Delaware shore and in his mind's eye, he could still picture the largest city of the new republic which, at 30,000 souls, still made Philadelphia hardly more than a provincial town by European standards. But it was the capital city of the United States for all that, the city he had just vacated by dead of night, and his own diplomatic station. Luzerne could appreciate that, as well as the importance of representing His Most Catholic Majesty Louis the XVI in cultivating the friendship of the Americans in what had grown from a colonial rebellion to a worldwide conflict of empires, but it was still small comfort for having given up the pleasures of Paris.

Sighing heavily, Luzerne turned back in the direction of the river. From his position in the stern of the boat, he could look out over the heads of the men pulling at a double bank of oars to the massive man-of-war that loomed just a few hundred yards ahead. Flagship of Admiral Comte de Grasse, the *Ville-de-Paris* still bore faint scars of the battle fought the year before at the mouth of Chesapeake Bay that ended in British defeat at Yorktown. At the moment however, the ship's 104 guns were silent, its sails furled. Furtively, other ships belonging to the admiral's fleet stood off at a discreet distance with the balance waiting down river for the return to the West Indies.

Luzern was jarred from his thoughts when his boat bumped against the curving side of the flagship soon followed by hoarse whispers and the lowering of ropes. A few minutes later, the French minister had come over the side and was met by the admiral himself. He knew that by the shadowy shape's height, a good six feet and some inches, very tall for a Frenchman, or anyone else for that matter.

"*Bienvennu*," said de Grasse in welcome.

"*Bon soir, mon admiral*," replied Luzerne, who was happy to hear the welcome cadences of his native language spoken without a bothersome provincial accent.

The admiral waved a hand in the direction of his cabin and soon the evening chill was ameliorated somewhat by the close confines of de Grasse' quarters.

Rubbing his hands together for warmth, Luzerne wasted little time in getting to the point.

"Do you have my instructions from Paris?"

"*Oui*," was all de Grasse said, handing over an envelope.

Luzerne broke the seal and opened the letter.

"It seems Vergennes suspects that the British and American envoys are close to signing a treaty of peace," grunted the minister.

"That must come as no surprise to you," said de Grasse. "The war has come to a standstill since Yorktown and everyone knows that the British have been exhausted in the effort."

"If only that were so," replied Luzerne. "But the fact is, only in America have their efforts proved useless. Everywhere else, they either hold their own or emerge victorious. All one needs is to look to India for that."

"Even so," said the admiral, "shorn of their American empire, they have been sorely weakened."

"Hmmm. Nevertheless, my instructions are the same as they ever have been: continue to encourage the Americans in their efforts toward independence from Britain while at the same time, strengthening their ties to France. With the money they owe us and their sense of gratitude for our help and support in this war, we shall tie them ever more closely with our interests and against those of the English."

"I have been instructed to ask you if your efforts in this regard have proven successful?"

"I have managed to convince Congress to rein in the headstrong John Adams, instructing him to heed the advice of Vergennes in all things," said Luzerne. "With the certainty of being able to guarantee the cooperation of the American envoys, the foreign minister can proceed with arranging his own...understanding, with the British."

de Grasse nodded, handing the minister a small glass of brandy.

"*Merci*," said Luzerne, taking the drink.

"*A votre sante*," de Grasse said, downing his own drink. "So all goes according to plan then?"

Luzerne grunted. "So it would seem, but lately, I have been getting the feeling that something is amiss with the Congress."

"Oh?"

"There have been private, unscheduled meetings between certain members and Msr. Jefferson, recently the Governor of Virginia," said Luzerne.

"Your...informants, have not been able to appraise you of the meaning of these meetings?"

"*Non*, apparently, whatever is being discussed is being kept to an extremely limited number of people."

"I understand it is unusual for the unsophisticated Americans to keep secrets," mused the admiral.

"So it has been in the past," replied Luzerne. "And for that very reason my instincts tell me that there is something of a highly sensitive nature going on."

"And what do you wish me to report on this subject?"

Luzerne thought a moment. "Simply inform the foreign minister of my suspicions and that I will take it upon my own authority, keeping in mind his previous instructions to make sure the Americans remain under his influence, to do what I can to turn the situation to the advantage of France."

de Grasse nodded, aware that the meeting had reached its conclusion. In another moment, Luzerne was once again on the open deck of the warship and was soon lowered to his waiting boat. The admiral gave him a final salute from the railing and turned to an officer who had been waiting discreetly a few feet away.

"Prepare to weigh anchor, we sail for the Indies," said de Grasse. It had been a short meeting and he expected the time remaining until dawn to be more than enough for his ships to slip from the river without being noticed from shore. Once on the open sea, he would detach one of his ships to make the run to France with his report on the night's meeting.

Meanwhile, Luzerne kept his thoughts to himself as the crew of sailors hove his boat toward a lonely landing where a carriage waited to whisk him back to the city. *What* were *the Americans up to?* he wondered. The former colonials, naive about the intricacies of international diplomacy, were terrible at keeping secrets. For that reason, he paid good money to native informants to keep him abreast of everything that went on in the halls of Congress, the legislatures of key states, and the Continental Army. He had no doubt that he would eventually get to the bottom of this affair, the question was, how soon would it happen? Information was only as good as it was fresh and he meant to know exactly what was going on as soon as possible and to exploit it for the further glory of France.

CHAPTER SEVEN

Jefferson rose early the next morning. Outside, the sun still had not risen, but when it did, there would not be any clouds to obstruct it. He had slept comfortably of course, but he wanted an early start in order to get to the State House before the legislators began to arrive for the day's sessions.

He swung his feet over the side of the bed and found a bowl of icy water sitting on the floor. He slipped his bare feet into it and soaked them for a few seconds. He had asked the servants to leave it the night before, but fully expected his wishes to be forgotten because of the lateness of the hour. He resolved to commend them to their master for remembering.

Each morning without fail for as long as he could remember, he had started every day with a bowl of cold water for his feet and he firmly believed it to be the reason for his singularly good health.

Next, he dressed and walked to the window, throwing it open. Immediately, the cold blast of winter air struck him, destroying the last traces of sleepiness he might have had. He was in one of the rooms to the side of the house overlooking a small grove of apple trees and beyond the line of shrubbery on the far side, he could make out the shape of the city beyond. At the moment, the trees were bare and the grass brown; in the summer, he was certain, the city would not have been visible.

He intended to check the temperature outdoors to record in his notebook, another duty he had conducted daily for years, but remembered that there would be no thermometer outside the window. He shrugged to himself and settled on a most unscientific method, but one that would probably be close enough to the mark to pass until he discovered the real temperature: he made a guess and decided that little had changed since the day before and noted it.

Then he remembered the murder.

He reviewed what he knew of the affair while he fixed his hair. A man named Jonas Singer, a wealthy Tory businessman, was murdered in the State House, probably early enough in the morning to avoid detection by the legislators who generally began to arrive around nine o'clock. Singer was killed with two shots in the back and his body was discovered by Mr. Madison. At Singer's local residence, nothing of interest was found with the exception of some sort of diary written in Anglo Saxon of all things. Jefferson picked up the notebook from where he had left it on the night table. Singer also had two visitors in the time he had spent at the address. A messenger boy from the Cobbler's who delivered a note, and a woman, apparently married, who had come by after he was gone. Most disturbing of all, was the fact that Singer's bag or bags had been taken from the room without the knowledge of the landlady. Since no bags were found with Singer's body, he had to assume they were either taken by his killer at the time of the murder, or from his rooms after his death. It seemed too much to expect Singer to have taken his bags with him to the State House, so Jefferson was forced to conclude that someone had searched the rooms before him. The killer, obviously;

but why? What was Singer up to that he not only had to be killed, but that certain of his possessions had to be taken as well? So far, evidence seemed to indicate that the crime was less that of passion and more of a premeditated one. But before he went to the committee with something that would destroy any hopes of a simple explanation, he had to make sure; after all, the mysterious woman (or, perhaps, a jealous lover, cuckolded by Singer?) could have had a reason for both killing her suiter and snatching some evidence of her indiscretion from his rooms.

He sat at the night table where a single candle was burning and took up the items of mail he had purloined from Singer's mailbox. It was too easy to guess where the first one came from. It was addressed in a female's handwriting and slightly scented. He brought it to his nose. He could not identify it, but it smelled good. Brushing aside the twinge of guilt that nibbled at his conscience, he tore open the envelope and unfolded the note. Once again, the handwriting was in a distinctively female hand with the body of the message of a routine nature as far as he could tell: the professions of undying love, a report on the satisfactions of their last tryst, how much she misses him, and a suggestion for their next meeting...Jefferson picked up the envelope again and checked the date of issue. According to that, it had been placed at the local post office for delivery...three days before. It would have been delivered that same day, and if Singer were at home, it would not have still been in his mailbox when the Virginian arrived. That would confirm Mrs. Simms' claim that Singer had been gone for at least three days.

Jefferson leaned back in his chair. The man disappears only to reappear dead three days later at the State House. Where had he gone for those three days? Was there any way to check if he had left the city? He decided there wasn't.

Turning back to the letter, he noticed that although it was unsigned, there was an address at the bottom of the page. The woman would not be fool enough to leave that if she were married would she? He shook his head, pocketing the letter; he doubted it, but he would have the opportunity to find out when he paid the lady a visit later in the day.

Next, he slit open another envelope which proved to be business correspondence with a Mr. John Sparhawk, bookseller. Jefferson had heard of him of course, having visited every bookseller in the city at least once, but he was not sure if he had ever met the man personally. It would be a good idea to visit the dealer to find out if his client had any other business contacts in Philadelphia and particularly, any who felt strongly enough about him to kill him.

The final piece of mail was beat up, crumpled, and soiled as if it had come a long way by various hands before being deposited at a post office. The return address stated it as being sent by a Mr. Isaac Invernol, esq. Jefferson tore that open too and found a diagram showing latitude and longitude, elevation, and figures for determining area over uneven terrain. He himself had plenty of experience in the surveyor's art to recognize their work here, but there was no information about where this particular plot of land was located. He lay the diagram down and continued with the body of the letter, which gave little more information about the land except to say that it was exactly where Mr. Singer had said it would be: at the confluence of two good rivers that gave easy portage to the Ohio and thence to the Mississippi and St. Louis and New Orleans. The perfect site for a fort and trading post and most importantly of all, the Indians thereabouts were amenable to bribery.

Jefferson did not like the tone of the letter. It boded ill for his country's interests in the west. If the United

States did manage to claim it from England, it would require the greatest of diplomacy to assuage the natives who lived there to keep from continuing to make war on the homesteaders in the region. Any exploitation of the western lands though good for the country in the long run, must yet be done under governmental law. If private enterprise were to be allowed into the region before it could be sufficiently organized, anarchy could follow. Already, the frontier people felt alienated and ignored by their fellow countrymen to the east of the mountains and Jefferson was fully aware of separatist feelings on the border. The only real thing that kept that from happening, was that the frontier was divided over which sponsor to turn to: Spain or Britain. In fact, with Spain, Britain, the United States and even France added to the continuing Indian threat, frontier divisions and even conflicting land claims by individual states, the whole region was like a powder keg ready to explode; and whoever could control that explosion, would control the region. Here Jefferson's mind began to wander wildly: and whoever controlled the heartland of the continent, all the major waterways connecting the trade of British Canada, transmountain United States, and the Spanish west, controlled everything.

He shook his head. This was all daydreaming! All he had was a surveyor's map of land Singer probably wanted to invest in. It was no crime to make contingency plans. After all, land speculation to the west had been sound business for generations in America, nothing wrong with that. Why even General Washington himself had land agents prowling beyond the Proclamation Line long before it was legal to buy land there.

He gathered his things and found his way downstairs where the servants were expecting him for the early breakfast he had requested. He surely would tell Shippen of the quality of his servants! Breakfast was completely prepared and over it, without the distraction of the rest of the household, he studied the diary he had taken from Singer's rooms.

He noticed again what he had noted the day before: that it had been written in Anglo Saxon, which was a strange thing to do in itself. Up until that moment, Jefferson had every right to believe that he was the only man in America able to read the ancient language of the English. He had learned it in the zeal of youthful bliss when he imagined it might be useful to know in his search for the origins of British law.

The first thing he noticed about the notebook, as he had when he first opened it back at Singer's rooms, was that it was obviously broken down by dates with separate entries for each. He did not have the time to go through it with the precision he wanted, so he did the next best thing: he skipped ahead to the final entry. It came as no surprise that it had been recorded four days previously, which would make it the day before Mrs. Simms noticed his absence. If nothing else, at least it now gave Jefferson a firm date on which Singer had disappeared. But why would he bother to write his diary in Anglo Saxon? Obviously for security reasons beyond the normal wish to keep his private thoughts private. But this ancient language was quite extreme. Was he aware of a threat to his life? That perhaps his diary, falling into the wrong hands, would be read? Was he, in the end, aware of whoever it was that searched his rooms before Jefferson arrived there? If so, he guessed right about using such an archaic language for his private thoughts; but Jefferson was sure it was only luck the thief did not take it. After all, would an item written in such a strange fashion not be the first thing to suspect of containing information?

The Virginian temporarily forgot his cooling eggs as he read: "January, 1783: Why am I suddenly plagued by doubt? For years I have felt sure of where I stood in all things. Sound judgment had allowed me to build my fortune and loyalty to my king has ever kept me on the right path. For the past eight years, I have suffered the scorn and barbs of my fellow countrymen in the name of that loyalty and in all that time I never doubted whether what I did or stood for was the right thing to do. I even sold off my London venture to sponsor Benedict Arnold's Legion. But now, I suddenly find myself lost and unable to decide where to turn. I still think the rebels who control the colonies and play up to the mob are wrong and that the only thing my country need do to prosper is to remain loyal to England and her traditions. What am I to do? I am at a complete loss as to my next move. Should I sit idly by and let events take their course, or become an active member in the drama? I will think on it." Jefferson closed the book and put it down.

When he tasted his breakfast again, it was cold. Instead, he settled for his tea before leaving the house for the stables.

It did not seem that the entry told him very much. Singer had been wracked by self-doubt the very night before he disappeared, before he received a mysterious message as a matter of fact. Did the contents of that message strengthen his resolve…to force a decision on him? The fact remained that he left his rooms soon after and was not seen again for three days until his lifeless body was found in the State House. As Jefferson pondered the question, he found that the tenor of his thoughts had begun to swing away from the idea that Singer's woman caller had anything to do with the murder. Innocence of the actual deed however, did not mean that she could not provide him with some idea of Singer's habits, which could prove valuable in tracing the man's movements over the three days in question.

Outside, he saddled his horse himself and rode away from the property, the cold winter air sharpening all his senses as he moved along the still darkened streets. Turning over different approaches to the mystery of Singer's murder, Jefferson realized that he had never really given much thought to the possible importance of the lead balls that should have been found in the dead man's back. Indeed, it was their very absence that intrigued him. Was it possible, he wondered, to suppose that certain information could be gleaned from a spent ball? Certainly he had never had occasion to consider the question in regard to a murder, but after reviewing in his mind the results of the post mortem and the strange position of the entry wounds in the body and the even more curious fact of having only one hole with powder burns, he had determined to have a closer look at the place where the murder was committed. But first, he had one more place to go.

———————

Dr. Rittenhouse did not like the idea of being rousted out of bed at so early an hour, but when Jefferson explained the importance of his visit, he got over it. Although the Virginian made it understood that he could not reveal exactly *why* it was so important, the nature of the two men's relationship was such that little more was needed. Trusting his friend implicitly, Rittenhouse knew that he had little to fear when his word was given.

Presently, Jefferson was in possession of the things he needed and bid his friend goodbye. A few minutes later, as dawn was just brightening the eastern sky, he reined in behind the State House at the same door he had used to recover Singer's body the night before. Looking around, he led his horse over to a nearby inn and tethered it there. He wanted to avoid any possibility of being associated with the State House during his sensitive mission and a man's horse was the easiest way for anyone to guess its owner's presence. He let himself in using the key he had been given and locked the door behind him. He listened for a moment and satisfying himself that the building was yet empty, he found his way to the murder room. He slipped inside and locked that door in turn, setting his things down on the table. The flowers, he saw, had been changed. Once again, he made sure the door behind him was locked before he unwrapped the theodolite and drafting instruments he had borrowed from Dr. Rittenhouse.

Next, he dragged the heavy table away from where Madison had indicated the body had lain and positioned it between that and the door. Approaching the edge of the new rug, he lifted and tossed it aside with a good heave, and there, in the shiny planking of the floor, he saw the two holes. He pulled a pocketknife from his waistcoat and selected the proper blade.

Kneeling on the floor, he began to probe carefully in the holes, trying to dig out the contents without enlarging the holes any more than he needed to. At last, he had the two balls in the palm of his hand. They were both mashed and wildly distorted, one more than the other indicating they had been fired at different distances from the body. Of the opinion that something more could be learned from them, he rose, pocketing them and the knife.

Now he took the theodolite, a sophisticated and delicate scientific instrument used mostly by surveyors to measure vertical and horizontal angles or altitude and azimuth, and hefted it to the edge of the table. The base of the instrument consisted of a vise-like grip that allowed it to be clamped to any surface. Generally it would be a stand designed specifically for the theodolite to be used for field work, but sometimes it was attached to the rail of a widow's walk or porch. After tightening the screws and looking through the instrument's lens tube, Jefferson shoved the table over a few inches more and checked again.

Finally, he took a roll of string and tacked one end as close to the center of one of the holes as he could, let out a good length and snapped it, then did the same for the other. Judging by the use of his eye alone, he stretched out one length of string to a height he guessed would still leave the string centered on the angle of the hole in the floor. He followed the rest of the string to the nearest object and tacked its opposite end there; in this case, the ceiling almost directly over the position of where the body would have been. No surprise. He took the second string and did the same thing; this time, he tacked the opposite end to the ceiling a few feet before the door. When he jumped from the chair he was using to reach the ceiling and looked at the second string, he grunted. He must have made a mistake. But that was why he brought along the theodolite; all he needed was a rough starting point, and eventually, with the use of the theodolite, he would be able to narrow down the trajectories of the balls to their actual paths.

Looking through the instrument, he began a series of measurements that took the better part of three hours. The process took longer than expected, but then he was not used to using a theodolite for so novel a purpose. At Monticello, he would have used his own instrument for more mundane tasks such as laying out new gardens or marking woodland for future development. It took a few false starts just to get an idea of what he needed to do, and having to climb up and down chairs retacking the strings as his measurements continued to refine the trajectories did not help. By the time he was finishing his second set of measurements, double checking the first, he began to hear the sounds of movement elsewhere in the building. He forced himself not to rush while using the delicate drafting tools he needed to complete his findings.

When he had finished, he looked again at the position of the strings and frowned. He was leaning against the edge of the table with his arms crossed over his chest and staring hard at the string that stretched from one of the holes to a spot about waist high in the center of the door. It was strange, but not completely unexpected. The powder burns found around only one of the bullet holes in the body should have told him as much.

Jefferson rebuilt the crime in his imagination. One shot was fired into Singer's back from almost directly over him as he lay face down on the floor. A string stretched almost vertically from the floor to the ceiling. A second shot was fired from the door or perhaps even farther into the corridor. But which was the first shot? He remembered the damage one of the balls had done to Singer's body as it plowed an almost horizontal path of destruction through his torso, from the lower organs to the upper, as well as the fact that one of the recovered balls suffered more disfiguration than the other. There was only a single conclusion he could deduce from the evidence: that Singer was shot from the doorway and then shot again at close range to make sure he was dead hence the powder burns. Because the least damage had been done to the ball that had entered the body at the more acute angle, that shot could only have been fired if Singer were already in a prone position. Furthermore, the angle of the other shot, whose ball suffered the most damage, indicated that it had not only been fired at close range, but from almost directly above the body. In both instances, Singer's body would have needed to be on the floor before the shots were fired. He could imagine the scene quite clearly; finding the body on the floor, the killer approached and took his first shot from close range. Then, concerned that the noise might have attracted an early visitor to the building, he retreated immediately to the door, reloading his weapon as he went. From there, it could have been anything, most likely a groan or movement from the still living victim that prompted the killer to turn and risk a second shot from the doorway.

There was definitely more activity outside the room as the members of the legislature came in for the day's deliberations. But one thing still puzzled the Virginian: if Singer had already been on the floor when the first shot was fired, what put him there? Did his attacker strike from behind before shooting him? It did not seem likely; if he could get that close, why not just shoot him and not risk a mistake and possible struggle? And if Singer had been felled, why were there not any marks on his body to prove it? Shippen had said just the night before that there were no bruises, marks, or contusions anywhere on the body, including the head. On the other hand, his measurements were as precise as science could make them, they were not wrong. Singer had already been on the floor before the killer arrived on the scene. In that case, someone or something else had already downed him and Jefferson had an idea of that might be.

CHAPTER EIGHT

Slipping unnoticed from the State House was a good deal more difficult than it was going in when it was empty, but Jefferson managed to do it without being overly conspicuous. His horse was where he left it, and after returning Rittenhouse' instruments, he made his way through the rapidly filling streets to the dock area of the city.

On the way, he occupied his mind by going over the facts he had learned until he knew them backward and forward; and though he had some definite ideas on some, others left him completely baffled. Who, for instance, had managed to get to Singer's rooms before him? This, more than anything disturbed him because it intimated that what was supposed to be a secret affair, apparently was not. Of course, if the intruder had also been Singer's murderer, then confidentiality was still preserved. Be that as it may, that still left Singer's overnight bag missing with obvious signs that the loyalist's desk had at least been gone through leaving the possibility that papers may have been taken as well. Although there was no evidence for it, was it possible that Singer was killed because of certain knowledge he possessed?

Jefferson shrugged and felt for the lead balls in his pocket. They were still there.

As he approached the dockyards, Jefferson was reminded at just how much more crowded it was here than anywhere else in the city. The atmosphere was a miasma of foreign scents, mostly foul. Over all hung the smell of the sea, but this close to shore, it was definitely tinged with that of the city's refuse: swill, garbage, and human waste. At the head of the mile or so of docks and wharves and the hundreds of masted ships they served, there stood rows of giant warehouses crammed with the treasure of the seven seas from cotton to tea to opium to textiles and alongside them, the fish market that he could also smell long before he laid eyes on it.

Jefferson ignored the strident calls of the auctioneer at the slave block as he tried to make himself heard over the hawking of the fishwives and made his way through the surging tide of humanity crowding the roadway. Finally, he broke free and kneed his mount into an alley that led from between two warehouses to the promenade along the water that serviced the great sea vessels from England, China, or Africa. Here too there was furious activity as cranes and hooks and chains swung heavy loads about the air and stacked them aside while sweating, cursing men ran about in organized chaos. Huge coils of hempen rope snaked about everywhere, forcing him to dismount and lead his horse the rest of the way on foot.

At last, he reached the place he wanted, one of the largest and longest wharves in the harbor that jutted far out into the Delaware River. Along its length, ships rode at anchor, waiting their turn to off load, and down the middle stood the dozens of shops that thrived in selling the wares of international trade; most owned by sea captains and captains of commerce but a few happily independent and it was to one of these Jefferson was aiming.

There was barely enough room for the Virginian to tether his horse in front of the weather beaten shop, but he managed to leave it on a very short leash before stepping through the front door. The tinkle of a bell announced his arrival although it was hardly necessary; the interior was so tiny and cramped, the proprietor was unlikely to miss the entrance of a patron.

An old man with a face that spoke of long years of experience looked up from behind a counter that consisted of a simple plank laid over two hogsheads and smiled. "Well, howdy Mr. Jefferson, we haven't seen you about these parts for some time."

"I try to avoid this part of the city as much as possible," said the younger man with a smile.

"Aye, it's a sight isn't it? Why if I were only a few years younger, I'd throw it all away and head back to the mountains. I shouldn'a ever left 'em. If I'd a known it was gonna be like this, I would'a died content in the wilderness. It was a good deal easier facing a screaming savage than some of the fishwives about these parts..."

Jefferson laughed at the man's hyperbole, but not because he failed to understand his feelings. The city more often than not stifled the Virginian as well, who much preferred the tranquility of his mountaintop home to the bustle of Philadelphia, which he considered like other urban centers, a magnet for the corruption of the human soul. After all, had not Europe long since concentrated a greater portion of its population into cities with the consequent rise in vice and corruption? Jefferson was convinced that only the bucolic rewards of an agricultural society were healthy for the human spirit. "I'm sorry, Necessity, what was that you said?"

Jefferson saw the fringe on the old man's buckskin shirt and leggings jiggle with his chuckling. "Youth is wasted on the young," he said, "too much in a hurry and not knowin' where they're goin'. I said, what brings you way out here?"

"Oh," said Jefferson, digging the lead balls from his pocket. "These," he said, holding out his open palm.

Necessity squinted and took them in his hand. If anyone could tell him something about the balls, it was Necessity McOntry. A backwoodsman all his life, he had spent nearly sixty years on the frontier gathering a huge store of practical knowledge that Jefferson wished could be written down but had long since resigned himself to the fact that his nation was yet too young for that sort of indulgence. As usual under such conditions, that sort of thing would be left to their descendents long after they were all dead.

"So, what do you want to know about 'em?"

"Well, I'm not sure what I'm looking for," said Jefferson. "That's why I came to see you. Anything you can tell me will be appreciated."

Necessity scratched his head.

"Well, I'll give a look, but I can't promise anything."

"That's all I ask."

"Come back tomorrow, we'll talk then."

Outside, if anything, things had gotten even more hectic and it was almost noontime before Jefferson was able to reach the well to do neighborhood of the address on the envelope of Singer's woman caller.

Summit Street was empty and the only sound was that of his horse's hoofs as they clattered against the cobblestones. It only took a few discrete questions of the occasional passerby to determine the proper house and in a little while, with his horse chewing contentedly on the lower branches of a tree, he climbed some steps and knocked at a door. He could not believe that "Adele" would be so indiscrete as to give her own address to a lover if she really were married as Mrs. Simms suspected, so what he expected was that the door would be answered by a neighbor or good friend instead. He was not disappointed.

When the tall, rather spare woman came to the door, he began by asking: "Is Miss Adele in?"

The woman's mouth opened slightly in disbelief before it shut again and her eyes narrowed in immediate suspicion. "I'm sure I don't know who you're talking about Mr..."

"Pardon me, Madam; Mr. Thomas Jefferson." He bent almost imperceptibly at the waist.

"Well I'm sorry Mr. Jefferson," there was some recognition in her voice, "but there is no one answering to the name Adele here." She made as if to close the door.

"Then perhaps you might tell me where I can find her as I have a message for her from Mr. Jonas Singer."

The woman stopped, unsure of what to do. Jefferson decided to help her. "Madam, if you'd be so kind as to allow me inside, you might have all the time you need to fetch Miss Adele from wherever she resides. I assume she lives somewhere along the street here?"

The woman knew she had no choice. "Won't you step into the parlor for some tea, Mr. Jefferson?"

"Thank you," he said, allowing himself to be led to a rather well appointed parlor and settling in an overstuffed wing chair. A moment later, a maid appeared with a tea service as the woman of the house excused herself for a moment. Jefferson passed the time by studying the Paul Revere silver work of the tea service until she returned a short time later. So short in fact, that he felt his guess correct in that Adele lived somewhere on the same street.

He rose, cup and saucer in hand, and bowed slightly to Adele as she entered the room and hesitated near the door. She glanced nervously about until the click of the closing doors almost made her jump. Her discrete friend had left them alone in the parlor. "Miss Adele, I presume?" said Jefferson. She nodded uncertainly and he waved a hand to the chair opposite his.

She took one step, then came to the chair in a rush. There was a rustle of cloth as her dress filled the chair. She looked everywhere but at him. As for Jefferson, now that he faced her, he was not at all sure how to proceed. "Tea?" he began neutrally. She shook her head quickly, hiding her mouth behind a handkerchief. Jefferson could not help noticing that she was a rather attractive woman just shy of entering middle age, but it hardly showed and he guessed that she had been spared the ravages of childbirth. The new thought added worlds of meaning to her actions. Barren, she probably blamed herself for the resulting ill will between she and her husband. Perhaps he shunned the marriage bed as a result, driving her to certain...indiscretions. If so, Jefferson felt sorry for her, but not enough to condone her faithless actions.

"Adele...is that your real name?"

"Yes, " she finally said, eyeing him hopefully.

"Adele, I'm not here to expose you or..."

"Oh thank you! Thank you, Mr. Jefferson!" she blurted, leaning forward with her relief. Jefferson could not help noticing that she had freckles along the swell of her breasts.

He held up a hand, "As I said, I'm not interested in your private affairs, but only want to ask you a few questions about Mr. Singer."

She leaned back again, much to his relief. "He was a wonderful man," she said, not surprisingly. "He loved me; my husband..."

Jefferson raised his hand again. "I told you I'm not interested in your private affairs. All I want is to ask you a few questions about Mr. Singer's business practices." Was it his imagination, or did she seem vaguely disappointed?

"What exactly is it you wish to know?" The switch from the terror of discovery to the relief of safety confused her emotionally; she seemed not to know what to feel.

"How long have you known Mr. Singer?"

"Well, before...? I...I mean...I first met him when the city was occupied...But only by sight, it wasn't until last year that we...saw more of each other." She was unconsciously rubbing her hands and Jefferson noticed that a marriage band had reappeared on the finger that Mrs. Simms had claimed had been naked of any ring.

"You only saw him when he came to the city?"

"Yes..."

"And how many times has he been to Philadelphia in that time?"

"About three or four times; it was hard getting permission from the Congress for him to move about. He was a loyalist you know..."

"He was a Tory, that's true," Jefferson corrected unconsciously. "But did you ever know what sort of business he had in the city? With what people he may have met with?"

She appeared to concentrate before replying. "He said that he had product being brought into the city by ship which he had to be present to receive; and I know he tried to help other loyalists who were in trouble with local patriots." She leaned forward again and Jefferson leaned back. "But his only concern was justice, Mr. Jefferson! He believed a man should be able to think what he wanted to without fear of consequences. Isn't that what the patriots want too?"

"Of course...Adele. But that's beside the point. Do you know any of the people Mr. Singer met with while he was in town?"

"No, he never spoke too much of business when he was with me. He said if I knew too much, I'd get into trouble. I'm not in trouble am I, Mr. Jefferson?"

"No, not with me," he assured her, hoping she would lean back again.

"Sparhawk!" she said suddenly. "That was one. I think he knew someone named Sparhawk."

"The book dealer?"

"I don't know, but that's the name of a man he said he did business with."

"Now, Adele, I'm afraid I must ask you something of a more personal nature." He cleared his throat. "Did you ever visit Mr. Singer in his rooms at Fourth Street?"

Adele nodded hesitantly.

"I know you called on him personally a few days ago..." Even he was startled at the rapidity with which her face reddened. "And he wasn't home; and that you'd also sent him a letter post marked a few days before that. How long had he been in the city before you wrote your letter?"

"Three weeks exactly," she said.

"And how often had you been with Mr. Singer in that time?"

"I ...I saw him only twice."

"And you were supposed to see him again, until he missed you at the appointed time?" She nodded. "And that was when you sent the note to his rooms?" She nodded. "And when he failed to reply to that, you risked an unannounced visit?" She nodded to that too. "How long had it been since you last saw him?"

"About a week before I sent the message."

"Was it possible on your last visit, that Mr. Singer could have been home, but merely told Mrs. Simms to refuse any callers?"

Adele shook her head. "No, because Mrs. Simms had shown me to his rooms where I was allowed to wait for about an hour on the chance that he might be back soon."

This was news to Jefferson! He made a mental note to offer more when bribing future informants.

"And when you were in his rooms, did you notice anything amiss? Anything out of the ordinary?"

"No."

"What about traveling bags, Adele? Did you notice any traveling bags or a trunk or anything else in his rooms that he may have stored his things in?"

She lowered her eyes and buried her face in her hands. "There...there was a large traveling bag he kept beneath the bed." He could barely hear her voice from behind her hands, but he was not about to shame her more by having her repeat her words.

"Is there anything at all you can tell about where he might have gone in the last few days?"

She looked up quickly, tears on her cheeks. "Is there something wrong? Has something happened to him? Why are you asking all these questions?"

He could not very well tell her the truth, even though if anyone was entitled to it, she was. "Just routine curiosity by the Congress, Madam; we like to keep track of notorious Tories." He felt there was nothing more he could learn from her and prepared to take his leave.

"You're leaving?" she asked.

"Thank you, Adele, you've been most helpful."

"You won't expose me?"

"Didn't I tell you I wouldn't?"

"Oh thank you, Mr. Jefferson..." She rose and rushed to him, taking his hand in hers and pressing it to her bosom. "You're a man of honor for certain."

Now it was his turn to blush, but her loveliness and pathetic fearfulness compelled him to speak further. "Adele, there's something more I should tell you." Damn! He had never been in a situation like this before! He had spoken thoughtlessly, and now felt obligated to forge ahead, despite his preference for having Shippen speak to her himself. "Adele...I have information of an extremely personal nature regarding Mr. Singer, don't ask me how I came about it, that I feel it is my duty to tell you..." He gulped as she looked at him expectantly. "I mean I have it on reliable medical authority, that Mr. Singer has a certain disease...Adele, there's no proper way for a gentleman to raise such a subject with a lady, but...Mr. Singer had a venereal disease and..." It was only knowing that he might have to move quickly that allowed him to support Adele before she fell to the floor. He guided her to a divan and set her down on it. "Adele, you must listen to me. Such a disease is quite contagious and it is your responsibility to have it treated as quickly as possible for your own and your husband's sake. I refer you to the services of Dr. William Shippen whose discretion I can guarantee."

Distressed at the whole scene, he did not like the way that she just lay unmoving on the divan.

She nodded at last, and began to sob lightly. Jefferson judged now was the best time for him to make his retreat and when he bumped into the woman of the house in the hall, he directed her to her friend. He could not get outside and away from such an awkward situation fast enough.

Samuel Adams was in a good mood. For the first time since losing the contest for governor of Massachusetts to his own creation, John Hancock, he felt like he was back in his element. Ever since the waning days of the Continental Congress before the reading of the Declaration of Independence, his own political career had begun to be eclipsed by the very events he had fought so hard to have come about.

His plan for manipulating Congress through his informal working group was progressing nicely. With Pembridge keeping them informed on the progress of the investigation into Jonas Singer's murder and Stiles' and

Bolton's impeccable southern connections coupled with his own and Stevenson's New England ties, he felt sure that they would be able to knit together a loose coalition in Congress that would be strong enough to not only renominate that pesky Jefferson, but to order him on his way to Europe with all possible speed, despite the lack of a guaranteed safe passage from England. He rubbed his hands in unconscious glee; after they had gotten rid of their most formidable obstacle, it would be a simple matter to strengthen the coalition and block any further attempt to work on solving the murder.

Of course any murder was a sorry affair and an act to be abhored and avenged by the state as soon as possible; but Sam Adams was not a man to look a gift horse in the mouth and he was not above using such a happy accident to further his own political ends.

Other than Jefferson, what troubled him most was that young Hamilton fellow. From everything Pembridge had been telling him, he seemed to be moving very quickly up the ladder of power. From one of the youngest officers in the Continental Army as aide de camp to General Washington (and managing to have himself treated as almost an adopted son to boot!) to a very lucrative marriage to one of New York's most beautiful and eligible young ladies whose father, General Philip Schuyler, was not only rich but politically powerful. And now, appointed to Congress. And all with the public knowledge of his illegitimate birth! It simply boggled the imagination, even one as fertile as his own! Certainly, this Hamilton will be a man to watch. He rubbed his chin; maybe he could see about one of the other representatives of New York...no, too risky. He had not been so successful in Massachusetts by playing into the hands of his enemies. Better to stay in the background; after all, who would believe a man of his reputation when he cried wolf?

Then there was the problem of Singer's bag. Well, it was not a problem actually, it was just that with all the congressional activity of the past twenty-four hours, he had not even had a chance to search it yet. He chuckled to himself at the thought; imagine a man his age scampering over roofs and through windows breaking into houses! He breathed a mental sigh of relief at the close call he had when he just managed to get outside before that meddling Jefferson came into the room! Why, he had almost fallen and broken his neck because of the bag he had in one hand! Now it was sitting beneath his own bed in his own room.

He had not had much time to search the rooms as thoroughly as he had wanted but when he heard someone at the front door and saw that it was the Virginian, he had to make do with what he could carry, only being able to sift quickly through the papers stacked on the floor and rummaging through the empty desk. Not for the first time, he wondered why Singer had been killed in the first place; and unless there was some revelatory information in his bag, there was no evidence at all to suggest a reason. His eyes narrowed as he approached City Tavern for his next round of meetings; then what was it that had been keeping Jefferson on the move since his meeting with the Secretary to Congress?

Just at that moment, Jefferson was moving along Lombard Street to the home of the noted portraitist and patriot Charles Willson Peale. It was a good deal past noon time and in the shortened winter day, the westering sun had already passed its zenith. That, however, made no difference to the Philadelphians who continued to throng the streets. Although the Virginian much preferred the slower pace of life in Richmond and the bucolic atmosphere of Monticello, he had to admit to a certain thrill at being at the center of things that business in the big city invariably visited upon him. The feeling, he knew, would pass soon enough, and so it behooved him to enjoy it while it lasted; thus, if local residents recognized him, they could often see him browsing through bookstores, the shops of furniture craftsmen, or importers of fine goods from London or Paris. Visits to points of cultural or political interest were also on his list of things to do as were congenial visits to friends and colleagues in the American Philosophical Society. One such acquaintance was Peale, whom Jefferson had met only briefly before at a Society meeting and whose famous studio he had long intended to visit but never seemed to have found the time. Well, that time was now, as he drew up before the impressive building that the eminent artist called home.

Dismounting, Jefferson walked up the short set of stairs to the door and used the brass knocker. A moment later, a servant girl opened the door.

"Mr. Thomas Jefferson to see Mr. Peale," said Jefferson, inclining his head slightly.

The girl sketched a curtsy and stood aside, opening the door more fully as she did so.

Jefferson entered, removing his hat.

"Please wait here, sir," said the girl, closing the door against the outside chill and sweeping down the corridor and into a back room somewhere.

Looking about, Jefferson was mildly surprised to see that there were no paintings on the walls of the corridor. Somehow, he had expected a man like Peale to have collected enough bric a brac in his travels to fill up any house he lived in.

His musings were interrupted by the master of the house himself as Peale swept into the corridor through a side entrance and walked up to him, hand extended.

"Mr. Jefferson!" Peale said with genuine pleasure in his voice. "So good of you to finally come to visit."

"Thank you Mr. Peale, but please call me Thomas," said Jefferson.

"Very well, Thomas, but I insist you call me Charles!"

"Done!"

"I know you've only been in the city for a few weeks," continued Peale, "but I thought sure that a man of your interests would have come by sooner than this."

"My apologies...Charles," said Jefferson. "I have many friends in Philadelphia as well as official duties to perform that have kept me from doing everything I've wanted to do, including visiting your famous studio."

"Then let's not waste another minute," said Peale, eager as any man to indulge in the object of his enthusiasm.

Engaging Jefferson in small talk, the artist led the way into the rear of the house where the back rooms had been completely given over to his studio. Upon entering the main room, the Virginian's sense of smell was immediately assaulted by the scent of paints and oils. Here, the walls were certainly not left naked as Jefferson saw many of the paintings that he had only heard and read about and others he had no idea the artist was working on. Although noted as the young nation's most famous portraitist (when not serving as a captain of volunteers in the revolutionary army or sitting in the state's legislature, Peale had studied under John Singleton Copley in Boston and had many of the heroes of the war as his subjects including Gen. Washington), there were a few nature scenes in the collection as well.

Jefferson, like many other admirers, marveled at the ability of the artist to capture the essence of his subjects through what appeared to be a few deft strokes of his brush: the firm jawline, the glistening eyes, the soft halo of silvering hair. Even the scattering of the objects representative of the subject's achievements in life seemed to suggest more significance than the hollow hubris such conventional elements had lately come to acquire.

"Excellent..." Jefferson murmured admiringly.

"Would you care to see my current project?"

"By all means."

Peale stepped across the room, careful to avoid piles of framing struts and bits of canvas, until he arrived before a heavy easel upon which rested a canvas draped lightly by a cloth. The artist carefully removed the concealing shroud to reveal the subject beneath.

Still unfinished, the painting, which Jefferson judged to be in the middle stages with only base coats showing in the background, was of an elderly gentleman in the severe habilaments of the ruling clan of Quakers that still wielded great power in the political life of Pennsylvania. The work however, was of a sufficiently advanced form that the obvious skill that had gone into it so far could be readily appreciated.

"Marvelous work, Charles," was all Jefferson could muster, woefully inadequate though he knew the words to be. "You must paint me some day soon."

"Nothing would give me greater pleasure, Thomas," said the artist graciously, replacing the cloth over the painting. "This one is a private commission of course. Ah, but here, as a man of science, I have something that I think will really capture your interest."

Peale led his guest to a corner of the room behind the work in progress where a number of paper boards lay against the wall. Picking them up, he handed one to Jefferson.

It showed a simple, though anatomically correct, drawing of a common gray squirrel.

"You did this?" asked Jefferson.

"Yes."

Jefferson thought the likeness was very lifelike, but could not help wondering why the great portraitist was spending his time making simple charcoal drawings of woodland animals.

"There is a reason for my interest in drawing such creatures," said Peale, as if sensing Jefferson's thoughts. "I believe that man can learn a great deal from the harmony that exists in nature. If that harmony could be grasped by men, how beneficial would it be in soothing the discordant emotions of the mind that prevent a fuller appreciation of the wonders of the universe?"

"There is no better teacher than the natural world," agreed Jefferson, the farmer.

"It is my belief," said Peale, handing Jefferson another drawing, "that if the full variety of nature could be gathered in a single place, making it a simple thing to see how each disparate part actually relates to and complements the other, and then presented to the public, not reserved only for the privileged classes, it could become a powerful tool for the edification of our citizens."

"I agree. It is in the interest of a Republic such as our new nation, if it is to grow strong, to have an informed and literate citizenry."

"Then you will be happy to know that I have taken the first steps to help that dream come true," said Peale, putting down the drawings and beckoning Jefferson into an adjoining room.

"You no doubt have heard of the cabinets kept by private citizens in Europe in which collections of curiosities of nature are kept?"

Jefferson nodded. "Sometimes referred to as museums, yes, but as you say, they are more in the nature of private collections, very infrequently seen by anyone outside the owners' circle of acquaintances."

"Just so. My cabinet, or museum, however, will be different. I intend to keep it open to the public, for the enlightenment of all our nation's citizens."

"A noble idea," said Jefferson, excited at the novel prospect. He had heard of Peale's cabinet of course, but before now, he had only considered it a bit of a half joke by fellow members of the Philosophical Society. Now however, as he was led into another room, this one lined with many large windows which let in plenty of light, showing off to their best advantage, the many artifacts that had been collected there by the artist, the notion seemed less droll.

"Like yourself, Thomas, I have many interests beyond my painting but for the most part, I find myself fascinated by the endless variety of flora and fauna offered by the natural world," Peale was saying as they stopped before a table holding a neatly arranged set of skeletal remains. "These, for instance..."

"Mammoth bones are they not?" asked Jefferson excitedly, leaning close to examine the relics in detail.

"Quite so. As you are aware, the Comte de Buffon has taken the position that animals native to our continent are on a whole inferior in size and number to those found in the Old World. It has been my goal to disprove his ridiculous assertion."

The theories of Georges Louis Leclerc, the Comte de Buffon, the most eminent naturalist in Europe were familiar to Jefferson. An ardent nationalist who was proud of the land of his birth, the Virginian had gone to great pains in his *Notes on the State of Virginia* to prove Buffon, and his colleague Louis Jean Marie Daubenton, wrong, by not only citing the dizzying variety of animal and plant life in America, but to research stories told by Indians of a pachyderm-like beast once hunted by their grandfathers. It was his belief in fact, that such beasts, or mammoths, still wandered somewhere in the interior of the continent.

"Collection of such fossil remains will go far in confirming our contention that the representation of natural phenomena in America is virtually endless and at least the equal in any manner Buffon would care to measure of that portion of the kingdom found in Europe," said Jefferson, straightening.

"Some day, I think I would like to recreate an antedeluvian animal from his fossil remains," suggested Peale.

"A wonderful idea!" encouraged Jefferson.

"For now, that notion will have to remain a dream, but here," Peale said, moving over to a windowless wall hung with the accoutrements of the continent's native cultures, "I have begun a collection of artifacts from native tribes." Ritual masks and headgear, weapons of war, and items of rude clothing displayed on the wall bespoke not only of the Indian's skill in craftsmanship, but of their savage nature.

"It is a worthwhile endeavor to preserve the cultural artifacts of America's native peoples," said Jefferson, who believed that the way of life of the continent's natives was doomed to extinction. To survive against an ever advancing white civilization, Indians would have to adapt to a sedentary life of farming or become extinct. Already, many tribes once known in the thirteen states had vanished with only the preservation of their ancient tongues by Jefferson himself to mark the fact that they had once existed at all.

Next, Peale showed his guest what he obviously felt was his pride and joy: a number of dioramas depicting stuffed animals and birds set in scenes that attempted to depict their natural environments.

"Your skill at taxidermy is as amazing as I have heard," said Jefferson, admiring the handful of birds and small woodland creatures whose glass eyes seemed to twinkle with the spark of life itself. "You've parted with convention it seems in placing your subjects amid the wood and rushes they have been accustomed to in life, I see."

"It is my belief as I said earlier, that all parts of nature must be seen in context," said Peale. "As all parts of the natural world exist in harmony with each other, so I feel that the observer must be made to realize the phenomena and seek to apply this unvarying principle to the conduct of his own affairs in the world."

"It strikes me as an eminently more logical premise than placing such creatures of nature against blank backgrounds as is the practice in Europe," said Jefferson, admiring the taxidermist's skill in preserving the likenesses of the squirrel and beaver displayed in what appeared to be a wooden box tipped on its side so that the open top faced the viewer.

"When I have enough specimens, I intend to arrange them in an orderly manner, perhaps in the Linnaean system, and open my cabinet, or museum, to the public for a nominal sum," said Peale.

"We are of one mind, then" said Jefferson. "It has always been my own contention that the Linnaean system of botanical classification, with its emphasis on the characteristics of a given specimen, offers the clearest and simplest method of categorization." Would he have the room at Monticello, he wondered, to create his own cabinet of natural history? Such musings, however, needed to be set aside until a more proper time as he recalled the reason for his visit to Peale.

"Charles," said the Virginian, "please forgive me, my interest in your paintings and artifacts has completely distracted me from my true purpose in coming to visit you."

"Oh?"

"Yes, you see, I have a specimen here," said Jefferson, pulling from his coat pocket the small glass container that held the residue from Singer's shoes, "that I wondered if we might identify by comparing it with some of the samples in your cabinet?"

Peale took the vial in hand and held it up to his eyes. Carefully unstoppering the top, he sniffed lightly at the opening. "Hmmm. Horse manure makes up the majority of its composition I'm sure...but there does seem to be something else..."

Moving toward a gardrobe that stood in the corner of his cabinet, Peale opened it and revealed a rank of shelving that held scores of glass containers of different sizes. Some held leaves and grasses of varying hues and thicknesses while others clearly were filled with soils of some kind. Holding the vial he had taken from Jefferson up to those on the shelves, the artist compared its contents with that of the coloring of the others. At last, he took one container down and removed its cork with an audible pop. Sniffing its contents briefly, he held it out to his guest.

"Try this, Thomas."

Jefferson sniffed delicately at the opening then did the same to the sample he had brought with him. He shook his head. "Not quite."

"Hmmm. All right then." Peale took another sample down, shook the brown soil inside thoroughly, then smelled the contents. "Ah!"

Jefferson took his turn and smiled. "That's it exactly! There's a bit of pine smell I think, as well."

"My thoughts exactly," said Peale, stoppering the vial and picking up a handwritten card that had rested before it when it was on the shelf. "Yes, it contains seven parts horse manure to two parts white pine mulch."

"And the remaining part?"

"Vegetable matter I think. The mixture makes for a fine compost found mostly in flower potting as the vegetable matter is usually taken from kitchen refuse. Most often, that means a well to do household, but as I understand, the mixture is not often used. The white pine you know."

"Which means my sample could have come from almost anywhere," mused Jefferson. "There's no shortage of well to do homes in Philadelphia after all."

"Why is its identification important to you, Thomas?"

He must remember not to think aloud, Jefferson chided himself. "I'm thinking ahead to the start of the planting season at Monticello and was told about the unique properties in this fertilizer for delicate flowers and herbs."

"Hmmm," was all Peale said and Jefferson, aware that his reply did not answer the question of why he needed to find where the sample he had brought came from, was thankful for the painter's discretion.

Suddenly eager to take his leave, Jefferson thanked his host for his hospitality and wished him every success with his plans for a museum. Peale, ever gracious, bowed slightly and asked no further questions.

Out on the street, dusk had nearly fallen and Jefferson realized that he would need to hurry if he was to make his next appointment.

CHAPTER NINE

The Cobbler's, as everyone in Philadelphia knew, was merely an abbreviation of the city's most popular method of personal message delivery. John Percy ran a profitable shoe repair establishment in the shop district of town and not coincidentally, a messenger service as well. An enterprising fellow, Percy struck on the idea of a speedy messenger service using young boys to better illustrate the hardiness of his footwear some years before. So successful had the campaign proved, that he began actually showing a profit that did his Puritan heart good. Eventually, the Cobbler's messenger service became so well known, that it was even used regularly by most members of Congress.

After a light mid-day meal served by Mrs. House in his rooms, Jefferson remounted his horse and once more entered the city's bustling streets, which seemed never to empty. Although large by the standards of America, Philadelphia was still a rather small place compared with the metropolises of the Old World and it was in no little time that he found himself again near the heart of the city. Passing through it, he slipped into the narrow street where the tradesmen kept their shops, keeping a sharp eye out for the distinctive boot shaped sign that swung heavily from over Percy's door.

After a bit of jostling and delay by the press of the crowd, he spotted the sign and urged his horse carefully to the side of the road and dismounted. After securing it to a nearby post, he pushed open the door to the darkened interior of the store.

Immediately, his nose was assaulted by the mingled scents of leather and sweat. In the late afternoon light, with the sun completely hidden behind the buildings in the crowded street, the shop was already in the clutch of creeping shadows that hid objects and obscured details. He could plainly see samples of the cobbler's art from where they hung from pegs on the upper portions of the walls, but below that, only the suggestion of shapes hinted that there was anything there at all.

A low worktable of planking met him almost the instant he stepped into the room and the wall behind it was decorated with the tools of the cobbler's art; although at the moment, most of those seemed to be scattered about the room. A short, thin man stood precariously on the sagging planking trying to hang a newly lit lantern to a hook set in the ceiling. Jefferson decided not to disturb him at such a delicate task and contented himself in waiting until the operation was completed. At last, the lantern in place, the man eased himself to the floor. He looked up and it was only then that he noticed his visitor.

"You gave me a start there stranger; didn't hear you come in."

"Sorry, I didn't want to startle you while you were up on the table."

The man rubbed his chin. "Well, thanks for that; I probably would've ended up in the nail keg if you did." He began moving about, picking up stray tools. "Is there anything I can do for you?" He spared a moment to look at Jefferson's shoes. "Those buckles need some buffing for sure, and I can tell from here, you'll be needing a new heel soon."

Jefferson, never giving too much attention to the way he dressed, smiled and said, "Actually, it's the messenger end of your business I'm interested in."

Percy's eyes widened. "Ah, of course. We deliver personal messages faster than anyone, including the post office and we never read any of the messages entrusted to us..."

"Exactly," soothed Jefferson, "It's your professionalism I seek to address in a search for certain information."

Percy's eyes narrowed. "What sort of information? I run a confidential business..."

"Of course you do, Mr. Percy," said Jefferson, fingering a coin in his pocket. He would have to speak to Charles about expenses. "But I assure you, I have no interest in the contents of any message you may have had delivered."

Percy's eyes went back to their normal saucer shapes; truly, thought the Virginian, the man's soul was expressed through his eyes! "Just what do you need to know, sir?"

Jefferson placed the coin on the counter where it was covered by Percy's hand as his eyes darted to the windows. "A message was delivered by one of your boys to an address on Fourth Street, a boarding house run by a Mrs. Simms in fact, not five days ago. The message went to a Mr. Jonas Singer."

"So what exactly is it you want to know?" the cobbler asked again.

"Who had the message sent and who exactly delivered it?"

Before Percy could answer the question, the shop door burst open suddenly, letting in among the dust and noise of the street, a boy that Jefferson guessed to be no more than ten years old. The door was unceremoniously slammed as the boy came up to the counter and slapped a paper on its surface. "All signed and delivered sir," he said, removing his cap and striking it against his arm. Dust rose in the still atmosphere of the room and Percy coughed twice.

"Damn you, boy! Do that outside, before you come in!" The boy seemed to ignore him and settled on a wooden box to eat an apple he had undoubtedly stolen.

"What was it you wanted to know again?" asked Percy to his visitor. "Oh, that's right. Who had the message sent. Well I can't rightly say. To Mrs. Simms' place you said? Hmmm, five days ago...ours is a busy service you know, plenty of customers." After another moment's thought, he finally answered. "It was a big fellow, very well dressed," he eyed Jefferson's own attire with a meaningful look, "spoke with an accent; New York I think, as it sounded like he'd just come off the boat from England. Come to think of it, I remember at the time wondering if he was a damn Tory..."

"Is there nothing else about him you can remember?" To Jefferson, the description he had just heard could have fit almost anyone.

Percy slowly shook his head. "No, nothing."

"His name?"

"He didn't leave his name. Just gave me the message he wanted sent, told me where to deliver it and paid handsomely for the service. If a man wants to keep his name out of it, I'm not one to question him."

Of course, Jefferson was keenly disappointed. No name! If there had been, he would have had the whole mess cleared up before the dinner hour. He sighed and said, "Who delivered the message?"

"Why, Homer there," said the cobbler, inclining his chin to the boy who still sat on the box looking for a place to throw his apple core. "Homer," continued Percy, "you remember that note you brought over to Mrs. Simms' place on Fourth Street a few days ago?"

The boy appeared to ponder on the question a moment before replying; "Yes."

Percy had his mouth open to say something again, but was beaten to it by his visitor's own question. "I understand you delivered the message personally, Homer," said Jefferson.

"I'm paid to do that sir; if the party isn't there, I'm to leave my own message and return immediately to the store."

"Of course. But in this case, the party to whom the message was addressed was present?"

"Yes, sir."

"You delivered the message to Mr. Jonas Singer at Mrs. Simms'..."

"Yes sir, and he tipped me handsomely "

"Tell me, Homer, did Mr. Singer open the message in your presence?"

"Yes he did; he looked as if it was quite urgent and I remember how he tore it open so fast he ripped the message."

"Can you tell me what sort of reaction he had while reading it and what exactly he said in your presence?"

Homer was not quite sure what his interrogator wanted, but tried to remember what was said. "He didn't look surprised or anything and he didn't say anything either, although I saw his lips move while he read. Afterward, he just stood a bit like he was doing some hard thinking. Well, I got tired of waiting and kind of cleared my throat. We have to wait to see if there are any return messages you know." Percy smiled at that. "After that, he gave me that handsome tip and said no, there was nothing else."

"How did his rooms look? Did you notice anything out of the ordinary about them?"

The boy shook his head.

"Thank you, Homer," said Jefferson, disappointed at the whole enterprise. Finally, he said, "Mr. Percy, I'd like to avail myself of your services and send a message of my own." Percy's eyes lit up at that as he assembled his writing utensils and record book. "I'd like a message sent to Simon Bolling in New York City to be delivered personally."

"Very good, sir, and the message?" Percy stood ready to copy down the note himself.

"If you don't mind, I already have it prepared." Jefferson produced a sealed envelope containing a message he had written during lunch asking his friend, Simon Bolling, to look into Jonas Singer's background in New York and especially to drawing up a list of his immediate family.

Percy looked disappointed as he took the envelope but promised to have the message in Mr. Bolling's hands in two days.

Jefferson deemed that a reasonable time, and quickly calculated an optimistic schedule that had a reply in his hands within a week. Now came the disagreeable part. He had to visit Dr. Shippen again, and this time ask him to take part in a midnight exhumation!

Alexander Hamilton stood just inside the shadows of an alley directly across the street from the Black Horse Tavern. Already a tall, lean man, the addition of a night black tricorn hat pulled low over his face and a flowing black cloak draping his shoulders created the illusion that some sinister figure from a popular romance had come to life. His dark hair had been pulled back into his accustomed short queue and held together with a black ribbon. At the moment, his only noticeable feature was the profile of his sharp nose whenever he decided to glance in the direction of the Tavern. The shadows of midnight almost completely engulfed him.

Across the street, he had watched as the lights slowly winked out after the tavern closed for the night and its occupants found their beds. The rest of the street had long since quieted as well and except for the night watchman, whose schedule Hamilton knew as well as his own, was as silent as the grave.

He settled back into the alley, vaguely annoyed by the scuffing his new boots were taking in the unaccustomed environment. It had been too long since he served with Washington in the Continental Army, he reminded himself, when hardship and discomfort were a matter of course. The folds of his cloak rippled slowly like the rolling breakers of the sea at night as he raised a pinch of snuff to his nostrils.

He had begun the day by fulfilling a promise he had made to the others by tracking down Samuel Adams and trying to find out why he was in the city. There was no real reason for his presence after all, he held no political position and Hamilton's contacts in Massachusetts had long since brushed Adams off as politically impotent. But everything Hamilton had learned during the day, indicated that Adams, although in the city without any official patronage, was up to something. He had learned that the old patriot had been keeping interesting company in the past few days and every indication pointed to him as the driving force behind the efforts in Congress to speedily send Jefferson on his way to Europe. Nothing could please Hamilton more of course, but the mere fact that someone else was as anxious as he was to do it, excited his suspicions.

After learning all he could about Adams' doings through normal channels, it had been time to try less orthodox ones. Ascertaining Adams' absence from his rooms at the Black Horse Tavern earlier in the day, and keeping him under surveillance by trusted agents, Hamilton had spoken to the Tavern's proprietor about a personal message for Mr. Adams. Sorry, but Mr. Adams was out at that moment. But his message was urgent and could he possibly leave a note in his rooms? Of course, the proprietor made a show of his hesitance, but Hamilton never went wrong by underestimating the honor of the average citizen and a simple coin or two gained him entrance.

A thorough search yielded little he did not already know about Adams' doings (the old radical could even teach him a thing or two about craftiness it seemed!), but he did find an old black traveling bag pushed far back beneath the bed. Pulling it out, he saw that it held the initials "J.S." on its front. Unless Samuel Adams had taken to signing his name differently these days, it did not take Hamilton long to conclude who the bag's owner really was: Jonas Singer. How in the world it had come to rest beneath Sam Adams' bed was another matter entirely, one that impressed the young Hamilton to no end.

Eager as he was to steal away the bag right then, he knew he could never chance being caught as a thief. Instead, he pushed the bag to its place beneath the bed and left the room.

He had Adams' watched all that day with instructions that he was to be informed the instant the New Englander left his rooms again with evidence that he would be gone for some hours. Earlier that evening, the notice had come and Hamilton left his home with a hireling he had come to rely upon from past business relations. In the alley outside the Black Horse Tavern, the man he had set to watch Adams assured him that the old radical was still out and on such a cold night, was grateful to be relieved by Hamilton himself.

An hour passed, then two. At last, all was quiet and every light had been extinguished in the tavern and still no sign of Adams. Hamilton tapped the young man with him on the shoulder and nodded toward the tavern. In moments, the boy was gone, silent as a cat.

Hamilton replaced his snuff box somewhere within the folds of his cloak and listened. The need for secrecy passed, his hireling splashed up to the alley from the direction of the tavern, well ahead of the next passing of the night watch. In his hand, was a black traveling bag.

"Any problems?" asked Hamilton, taking the bag.

The boy shook his head. "Routine."

The New Yorker nodded and handed over a small bag of coins.

"You know where to find me," said the boy, retreating down the alley.

Hamilton smiled and lifted the bag to his face: the initials "J.S." winked at him in the dull glare of a street light. Just then, the sound of footsteps pressed him back against the wall. It was too early for the night watchman. Peering from around the corner of the alley wall, he looked in the direction of the tavern but saw nothing. Vaguely, he could hear low voices, but not what they were saying. At last, a light flashed as someone inside the tavern moved to answer the door and when it opened and the light fell on the visitors, even Hamilton had to gasp.

There, stepping into the tavern was Samuel Adams with his arm about the shoulders of John Pembridge! He had known Adams was pulling political strings in Congress and had plenty of important contacts, but to be arm in arm with Pembridge, a member of Hamilton's own select committee working on the Singer affair cast a whole new light on how Adams may have gotten his hands on the traveling bag. Pembridge was a spy, reporting directly to Adams! That meant of course, that Adams knew as much about the affair as *he* did! But why hadn't he broken the scandal to the public? It was well known that Adams would prefer to continue the armed struggle and force Britain into unconditional surrender. This sort of thing was made to order for him. Unless, of course, he saw the same political drawbacks in outright exposure as Hamilton's group did.

This all cast a whole new light on Adams' efforts to expedite Jefferson's nomination. He could not reveal the scandal publicly, but he could impede its being cleared up until the next diplomatic ship arrived from England, wrecking any treaty. How ironic that Adams was actually scheming in the same fields as was Hamilton! And to think he was beginning to suspect Adams of actually having something to do with the murder! He would not have put it past him. As a matter of fact, there was still no reason to dismiss the idea. After all, with Jefferson investigating the case, there was a possibility that he might stumble onto something; and wouldn't any murderer want an investigator out of the way? Hamilton remembered Adams' reputation and decided not to rule out anything.

Suddenly the night watchman turned the corner and called out, "Twelve o'clock and all's well!" *All's well indeed*, thought Hamilton as he slipped into the shadows.

CHAPTER TEN

"You want me to do *what*?" said Shippen, with some exasperation.

"I want you to help me dig up Singer's body," replied Jefferson calmly.

Shippen shook his head and paced over to the fireplace, then turned. "Correct me if I'm wrong, but didn't you tell me to bury him in pauper's field until you could clear up the circumstances of his death?"

"I did."

"And now you want to go and get him out again?"

"New evidence has led me to believe that the original cause of death may not have been the two shots to the torso, but poison."

"Yes you've said that but...well, explain to me again how you've come to that conclusion?"

Jefferson sighed and rose to his feet. "I measured the angle of the balls' entry into Singer's body from the holes they left in the floor. Their trajectories leave only one possibility: that Singer was already on the floor when the fatal shots were fired. If I'm right, then something else besides gun fire must have felled him. However, as you yourself attested, there were no signs of bumps, bruises, or contusions on the body. How then to explain this discrepancy? How to explain a man being on the floor prior to being shot without having been struck first?"

"He allowed himself to be shot?"

"Now how likely do you think that is? Would a man, even in allowing himself to be shot, arrange himself on the floor first only to have the fatal shots placed in his back?" Jefferson shook his head. "Too much to believe. And so, why not believe the obvious? That something else, other than a physical blow had felled him before the killer entered the room and fired those two shots merely to insure Singer's actual death."

"If he was felled before being shot."

"It is a theory I feel should be eliminated if possible."

"And you think poison was involved?"

"Believe me, John, I wouldn't be asking you for such a sacrifice if I didn't think it absolutely necessary in order to lay to rest every possibility."

"But even if it were poison, what's the point in exhuming the body? It would only confirm what we already know."

"On the contrary; if we can identify the poison and determine its source, we might then deduce the neighborhood of the man who administered it. After all, why should anyone use exotic poisons, when a more familiar variety, close to home, may be at hand?"

"Very well, I suppose you have good reason," said Shippen resignedly. "I'll get the wagon."

Once again the two men found themselves on the road leading from the hospital grounds; but this time, their route led them away from the city and toward its outskirts. Using the smaller, less traveled country lanes, they avoided any encounters with local night watchmen. An hour was spent as they creaked steadily along the narrow paths behind the big houses of the wealthy merchants until finally, the last one being passed, a light or two still burning on the ground floor, they emerged near the poor man's cemetery.

Luckily, Shippen knew of a second entrance that offered better concealment and when they had used it, stopped the wagon on the far side of a low hill spotted here and there with wooden head boards that stood out against the night sky like broken teeth. Unobservable from the road, they each took a spade and walked around the base of the hill, Jefferson reading head boards as he went: Smith, Blake, Principal, Jubal... Suddenly, Shippen called a halt along a small copse of oak saplings.

"It's just to the right of this brush," the doctor whispered.

"Did you bury him the full six feet?" asked Jefferson.

"Of course," said Shippen.

"I was afraid you'd say that."

Shippen was the first out of the copse and half walked, half crouched to the top of the hill for a look at the road on the other side. Up and down all was quiet with only the occasional creak of tree limbs in the winter wind. Shippen huddled deeper into his coat and scrambled back down the hill to his friend.

"All clear."

"Then let's not waste any more time," said Jefferson, feeling the cold himself. "At least the earth hasn't yet frozen," he said as he jumped on his spade, sinking its blade deep into the ground.

"You should've been here when I had to break through a foot of frozen earth to bury him," said Shippen.

Jefferson grinned. "Sorry about that."

"Don't worry about it, if we find what you hope, perhaps it'll all be worth it."

The two men worked on in silence for the next hour or so until the hollow thunk of a spade on wood announced the imminent conclusion of the unpleasant duty. A few minutes later, they struggled to lift the crude wooden box from its place in the ground to the wagon bed. Jefferson began to refill the hole.

After a nerve wracking return trip to the hospital, they settled down to give the corpse a second, more specific examination. Of course, by this time, despite the freezing action of nature, corruption of the body had already begun to retard its natural state. Just the same, Shippen hoped the process had not advanced so far as to prevent the identification of any poison that may have left traces behind.

Once again, the examination began with Shippen's observation of the skin. "Unless it's caused by the length of time since death," he said over his shoulder to Jefferson, "I'd say jaundice had set in." Jefferson leaned in closer to see where the doctor pointed. "See here and here? The yellowing of the skin; and though I'm not sure of the connection, there's always an accompanying reaction with the liver, which we'll examine in a moment."

"If the two correlate, will that be sufficient evidence for poisoning?"

Shippen nodded. "Yes...uh oh. Look here," he picked at the hair and plucked a few strands easily from the scalp. "This man *has* been poisoned!"

"Can you tell with what sort of poison?"

"Well these symptoms narrow things down considerably." He opened the mouth and examined the teeth, tugging gently on some.

"Looking for loose teeth?" asked Jefferson. "You don't think it's *datura stramonium*? It has some of those symptoms..."

"No, it's not that," said Shippen, undoing the work he had done in sealing up the corpse. In a moment he had verified the discoloration of the liver. "Do you remember the condition of the waste we washed off the body the other day?"

"It was bloody."

"Hmmm, and now that I remember the smell from the man's mouth..." He slammed a fist into his palm. "Why didn't I think of it before? It was so obvious the man had been poisoned."

"It wasn't your fault, William. We weren't looking for poison, so we didn't find it. Remember the point we brought up at the tavern the other night? That all facts are subject to individual interpretation; what might occur to one, may not occur to another. We came to the subject with an established set of criteria and looked only for those facts that would fit those criteria. It's in the nature of human beings to see the world through their own experiences."

"Thanks for reminding me of my own point!" said Shippen, brightening. "This incident ought to teach me a lesson in humility if nothing else!"

"So what can you tell us about the nature of this poison?"

"Well, as you recall, I took certain residues from inside the mouth of the subject when we made our first inspection and I have no doubt the poison was administered internally, probably in the man's food."

"But the type of poison...?" asked Jefferson impatiently.

"Now there, I'm going to go out on a limb and say it's *veratrum atra*, a member of the lily family."

Jefferson thought a moment. "Are you sure? The only specimens I know of are told of by seamen who've visited the Pacific coast of this continent."

"I'm as sure as I can be," replied Shippen. "Besides, it's not completely unheard of to find certain rare specimens of the plant growing in our western forests. I've heard tell of Indians in the region using the plant for ceremonial purposes."

"How much would be needed to cause death?"

"Oh not much, very little in fact. I suppose the victim could live for any length of time after ingesting it, but..."

"Could a killer regulate the length of time until death occurred by varying the dose of the poison?"

"I never thought of that before, but now that you mention it, I see no reason why it couldn't be done."

As new wrinkles in the affair seemed to open up before him, Jefferson still had the presence of mind to ask his friend: "Is there time to return Singer to his grave before dawn?"

"Will he stay there this time?" asked Shippen and both men had a much needed laugh.

Early the next morning, well before Congress went into session for the day, a small group of congressmen met in an upper room at the Black Horse Tavern.

"We're doing all we can without showing our hand," said Whitmer Stiles.

"It's not enough," shot back Adams, short tempered this morning. "Jefferson is still working on the Singer affair non-stop. I swear he must have all kinds of information he's not telling the special committee about, how else can he keep himself on the go as he has the past couple of days?"

"That's all very true, Samuel," agreed Increase Stevenson, "but the fact remains, if we press our case too strongly, Congress will suspect we may have ulterior motives..."

"And if that happens, they're sure to stall the nomination process to find out what it is," concluded Jenks Howell. "Even if it's only to keep us from seeming to get what we want while they get nothing out of it."

"Compromise, then?" asked Adams.

Howell shrugged. "How does anything else ever get done in Congress?"

"But what do we have to offer?" asked Henry Bolton.

There was a thoughtful silence for a moment until Stiles spoke again. "Perhaps we can do something with General Gates' supporters?"

"Gates?" cried Stevenson, "I thought that blackguard's name banished from the Congress!"

"Just because he's no longer discussed, doesn't mean he no longer has his supporters. After all, some names in Congress were tarnished as well as his own. Now if some resolution could come forward clearing his reputation, it could be seen as reflecting well on those political careers that threw in with him against General Washington."

"I still don't like it," said Bolton.

"I never said we had to like it, I'm merely suggesting political expediency for our real goal."

"Is compromise our only option?" asked Stevenson.

"I've noticed movement from Tench and his people in our support..." observed Stiles.

"That's true, and led by that young upstart, Hamilton, too."

"Don't underestimate the boy," warned Adams, keeping further thought to himself.

"Just the same, the New Yorkers have shown support for our initiative," continued Stiles. "I don't understand it, but I'm not fighting it."

"Then that means, really, we only need a few votes to throw the majority over to our side," said Bolton.

"Who're the holdouts?" asked Adams and following their identification, came listings of each man's interests, political ties, and what sorts of pressure could be brought to bear on each in order to convince them to vote in the desired manner. Soon a strategy had been mapped out and a general discussion had explored various alternatives.

"Say, where's Pembridge this morning?" asked Howell at last.

"I don't know," said Adams, wondering how best to explain the matter of the missing travel bag he had been shocked to find gone from his rooms the night before. "I spoke to him only last night and he was aware of this morning's meeting."

"He'd better not be having second thoughts about his role in our plans," said Stevenson darkly, "we all have too much invested in them to risk things coming apart now."

"Which brings me to my next point gentlemen," said Adams. He cleared his throat as they all turned to look at him. "I'm afraid we've already been compromised," he held up both hands to hold off the barrage of questions. "I'm not sure about the entire situation, all I'm certain of right now, is that someone who claimed to have an urgent message for me, talked Mr. Gustaveson, the proprietor, into allowing him to leave it in my rooms; and although Mr. Gustaveson insists he saw the man leave empty handed, I suspect this stranger of taking Jonas Singer's travel bag from my room. Needless to say, there was no note waiting for me. Worse still, I hadn't yet had the time to look through the bag what with all the running around I've been forced to do."

"Do you have any idea who this man might have been?" asked Stiles.

"None," said Adams frankly. "No one knew the bag was in my possession except the men in this room; which leaves the possibility that we've been watched, perhaps each of our rooms have been searched. I suggest, gentlemen, that you each make a careful inspection of your respective residences for evidence of trespass and guard your every movement. Until we have more information, we must proceed as if we're being watched."

"Might it be that Thomson suspects?" suggested Bolton.

"I don't rule out that possibility. Pembridge may have slipped up somewhere to cast suspicion on himself. It's entirely possible that the President of Congress has unleashed his spies upon us. But let's not panic. All of that is very unlikely, the reality is that the missing bag has probably been taken by the killer himself, in which case, we and our plans are in no jeopardy whatsoever."

"I still don't like it," said Bolton, "all of a sudden, our lives have become a lot more complicated."

Adams said nothing as the others filed out to attend the day's Congressional sessions, but his mind was working quickly, turning over possibilities, running down chains of logic, checking and rechecking all the facts. He had been unable to sleep the night before because of his restless thoughts and the upshot of all his ruminations led to but one conclusion, that the missing bag tied in with this morning's missing Pembridge.

At that moment, another meeting had been hastily called in the rooms of Alexander Hamilton.

"What's the meaning of this, Alexander," demanded Agamemnon Jones angrily. "I'm not in the habit of jumping through hoops for junior congresssmen, even those as well thought of as you."

"Believe me, Mr. Jones," placated Hamilton, "I have very good reason for calling this meeting; and although I'm sorry Mr. Dickinson couldn't be here, I'm sure you'll agree to its timeliness."

"The only thing I'm concerned about right now," said Desmond Tench, "is the vote in Congress to nominate Mr. Jefferson. Things are moving a lot more smoothly than I could've hoped for."

"It is curious that the New Englanders support us on the issue isn't it?" asked Hamilton.

"Damned peculiar I say," emphasized Tench. "What the hell do they have up their sleeves? What is it exactly that they want?"

"Perhaps the same thing we do?" suggested Hamilton.

"To get rid of Jefferson and botch his investigation? To scuttle any peace treaty that doesn't have the western lands in it? I doubt it."

"Don't be too hasty in your judgment, sir," said Hamilton. "Gentlemen, let me introduce Mr. John Pembridge of South Carolina."

As Pembridge stepped into the room, the others gasped and stood, not able to decide who to stare at, the newcomer or their young colleague.

"Good morning gentlemen," said Pembridge, not at all pleased with his situation. When Hamilton had confronted him earlier that morning, at the crack of dawn no less, he had summarized his precarious position perfectly. A traitor to his trust, his friends, and his honor, if Hamilton chose to denounce him as publicly as he threatened, there would have been no recourse for him but self-destruction. Even now, standing before these men, with the realization of the enormity of his situation fully before him, the urge to run and do the unthinkable was almost too much to bear. A single bead of perspiration trickled down his cheek; he brushed it away. And worst of all, he knew he had become a creature of Hamilton's; to do with as he pleased for he had the power now to destroy him in every way a gentleman most feared.

"What's the meaning of this?" Jones finally stammered.

"I think the particular circumstances of Mr. Pembridge's presence here are of little importance, what is important is the sort of service he can render us." Hamilton poured himself some tea. "You see, gentlemen, not only is Mr. Pembridge a member of Congress and my own special committee for the investigation of the Jonas Singer affair, but he's also the member of a sort of counter cabal to our own little band." He nodded to Pembridge.

Pembridge cleared his throat. "When Increase Stevenson arrived from Massachusetts a few weeks ago, he brought with him Mr. Samuel Adams who promptly organized an informal group of congressmen of like mind with the specific intention of coordinating resistance to any peace treaty with Great Britain that did not include the western lands as American territory. It was only luck that I, a member of the discussions, was chosen to be on the committee to investigate the Jonas Singer murder. Realizing the unique opportunity we had to destroy any peace treaty in scandal, I was persuaded by Adams that it was my patriotic duty to keep him and the group informed of the progress of the investigation. We soon decided that it would be in the best interests of the country to hamper the investigation and leave things as they stood until the diplomatic envoy arrived from England. To that end, we decided that Mr. Jefferson would have to be taken off the case." Pembridge breathed a sigh of relief when Hamilton interrupted.

"So you see gentlemen, Adams' own group has been seeking the same ends we have."

"I knew it," said Jones, "things were going too easily."

"But now with Mr. Pembridge offering his kind services to us..."

"Just how is it Mr. Pembridge is offering those services?" Tench wanted to know, his eyes narrowing and watching Pembridge with keen interest.

"I think, gentlemen," said Hamilton smoothly, "that the reasons for his coming to us are of little matter. Suffice it to say, that you asked me to investigate Samuel Adams and this is one of the results of my inquiries." The two older men looked upon their younger colleague suddenly with more respect and even a hint of nervousness. His cool resourcefulness in so short a time made them uneasy. If Hamilton ever decided his interests did not lie with theirs, he would make a formidable adversary. "In the meantime, I'd suggest that our plans for Congress should be a little easier to implement with such a valuable asset in hand."

The others could only agree and left the apartment for Congress. Alone with Pembridge, Hamilton spoke more freely. "I trust you understand your position clearly Mr. Pembridge?"

Pembridge nodded.

"You are in a most curious position," Hamilton couldn't help repeating. "A traitor to the committee, a traitor to Congress, a traitor even to your own friends in the Adams' group and ultimately, a traitor to your constituency. You're quite a disreputable fellow, Mr. Pembridge."

"No need to rub it in!" Pembridge could not help blurting, and immediately regretted the show of anger.

"It's good to see that you're not completely devoid of a sense of the enormity of your situation; as a matter of fact, I wouldn't be surprised that you might even have the courage to do the only right thing about it." He smiled. "But not, I hope, before I'm finished with you."

Not for the first time, it occurred to Hamilton that there was very little difference between the accusations he had leveled at Pembridge and his own position. A fact that Pembridge had wasted little time in pointing out but one quickly defused after Hamilton asked him how he thought he had been discovered. Calling the congressman's bluff, Hamilton said he had been exposed by a fellow member of his own cabal. It was not true of course, but Pembridge did not know that and it did offer a most convincing explanation of how he had been discovered.

Hamilton's last words were all Pembridge could take as he spun on his heel and headed for the door. There was no order to stop, and he soon found himself on the street where the world went on exactly as it always had; but for him, it would never be the same, with its history measured only against his own endurance of an intolerable situation; a situation whose real enormity, Hamilton could only guess at.

Back inside, Hamilton dropped the curtain and walked away from the window, immensely satisfied with the work already done. As he judged the situation coming more and more under his control, he felt more relaxed than he ever had since coming to Philadelphia. Recently wed to a beautiful girl he adored and a father-in-law both rich and powerful and now a delegate to Congress, he believed anything was in the realm of possibility; and with this first taste of power and intrigue, he knew his appetite for it would only grow.

He reached into a pocket and pulled out a crumpled piece of note paper, slightly torn with a return address of the Cobbler's. He had found it in a secret sleeve inside Singer's travel bag the night before along with other unimportant papers that were undoubtedly taken by Adams when he searched the Tory's rooms. Because it was written in code, he hadn't had a chance to decipher it before now, not with his early morning visit at Pembridge's rooms and this recently concluded meeting.

He looked at it now though. It was only about the dozenth time he had done so, and for the dozenth time wondered at the curious code employed. Whoever had written the message must have been one of two things: a military man or a scholar because the code was one that was not unfamiliar to Hamilton. As a matter of fact, he had used it himself as an aide to General Washington. It was the old Rosicrucian cypher, quite simple really. He sighed, but no time to work on it right then. After all, he was due in Congress himself.

CHAPTER ELEVEN

Jefferson dashed his feet into the bowl of cold water and stretched with pleasure. A few minutes later, after noting the day's weather and temperature, he called for his long time, personal slave, Jupiter, to help him with his toilet. When that was done, he asked him to prepare his horse for use in an hour's time.

Breakfast was Mrs. House's usual fine and filling repast consumed in the company of his fellow borders. Conversation revolved around current affairs and the Congress until Mrs. House brought up the subject of Jefferson's daughter.

"And how's that darling little Patsy?" she asked.

Jefferson was always pleased to talk about his children and so answered quickly; "Quite well actually, Mrs. House. She's spending a good deal of her time with her studies these days. As you know, my life at the moment is more than merely uncertain, and no definite plans can be made, so it's especially difficult on poor Patsy who has no idea where she'll end up in the months to come, but she bravely marches on; a real soldier!"

"So she's quite preoccupied? She's gotten over the death of her mother?" It was not a forward question, but one whose tone denoted genuine concern.

"As well as we all can expect. Her studies keep her mind off such things I'm sure. Since I will be taking her with me to France should I be chosen to go, I've given her a strict regimen of study to prepare for the adventure, the French language being of the highest importance."

The conversation ended there, as Mrs. House continued to move about the breakfast table, having a bit of something to say to each guest in turn. That suited the Virginian as he continued with his interrupted meal while ruminating over the confirmation that poison after all, was the first cause of death for Jonas Singer. Which brought up a number of interesting questions.

With the use of such a deadly poison, it would have been a simple matter to kill him outright at the time he ingested it, why such an inadequate dosage that would allow him to not only walk away from the killer, but into the very halls of Congress? For that matter, why not just kill him outright with a less subtle, albeit more definite, method? That was the question he had spent half the night turning over in his head. Why had Singer not been killed outright? Did the killer want his victim to leave the place where he was poisoned, perhaps to avoid any implication in the murder? But then he risked the victim exposing him before he finally succumbed to the effects of the poison. No, it would have been a good deal easier to simply dispose of the victim in the usual manner. Jefferson was sure that Singer's presence in the State House was no accident, and with Shippen's statement that the time of death could be regulated with the proper dosage of the poison, it was not too difficult to believe that the killer wanted Singer to reach the Congress before he fell dead.

But then, why the two shots in his back? Jefferson swallowed the last of his bread. Insurance obviously; but carelessly implemented.

He tried some coffee for a change of pace. Sipping it tentatively at first (making the proper tasting coffee could almost be considered a chemist's art), he continued his train of thought. He came back to the poison. After consulting the few books he had in his rooms (not for the first time, he regretted that his personal library was out of reach at Monticello), he felt he could be sure that though his first guess that *veratrum atra* or the poison lily, was native to the western coast of the American continent, it was not uncommon to find certain strains in the forests of western Virginia. Actually in this case, the land in question was disputed over by both Virginia and Pennsylvania, so the actual location was a moot point. But the fact remained that Singer's murderer could have access to the plant fairly close by; or at least closer than the other side of the continent! His books also indicated an even more specific fact, that the plant grew in only a certain valley and that the Indians of that region, needing it for one of their esoteric rituals, regarded it with more than a proprietary interest. How then, did the murderer get ahold of his specimen?

Jefferson finished his meal and dabbed lightly at his lips with a napkin. He left the room with a general good day and found his horse saddled and ready in the stables. Jupiter handed him the reins and watched his master canter off.

It was a clear, sunny, but cold winter day that made Jefferson feel glad to be alive. On such a day, it was almost possible to forget the loss of Martha. Almost. He fought down the sudden wave of depression and forced himself to pay attention to the passing scenes of the city. Soon he found himself back within the confines of the shipyards and in sight of Necessity's shop front.

Inside the old man's store, nothing had changed. Even Necessity himself seemed not to have moved since his visit two days before. He hoped the old frontiersman did not mind his coming a day late.

The old man looked up at the sound of the bell and a smile creased his leathery face. "A little later than I said, aren't ya?"

Jefferson shrugged as he came up to the counter. "I had quite a bit of business to attend to yesterday, and couldn't make it."

"Ah, in the old days, if a man gave his word, it had the force of a law. Sometimes a man's life depended on his punctuality. Why, I remember a time when..."

Jefferson cleared his throat and the old man got the message.

"But like you say, you're a busy man." He reached in his pocket and pulled out a wad of paper. Laying it on the counter, he carefully opened it to reveal the two lead balls Jefferson had pried out of the floor of the State House. "I've taken a look at these here balls. My eyes are as sharp as they've ever been, ya know. And I can say, I know everything they can tell me. Now, ask me what you wanna know about 'em."

"Well, I was hoping you could tell me all you can and that if I had any questions, I'd ask afterwards."

The old man grunted and picked up one of the balls. "Look here, young man," he said pointing an untrimmed nail at the ball. "A lead ball's got a history all its own; no two alike. Sometimes it's 'cause of the barrel of the gun it gets shot out of, but most of the time, it's the maker's marks that're different. But even if those things can't be figured out, you can never go wrong in certain generalities, if you get my meanin'." Jefferson still showed interest, so he continued. "Now with these balls, the particulars are gone; I'd say they've been fired into something hard and then pried out with none too much care." He regarded his young visitor out of the corner of his eyes.

"That's true; I had to dig them out of a wooden floor."

"Told ya so. Anyway, there's still something to be read here, if ya know how to look. Mostly there's two kinda balls. The kind made by most folks and the kind made by a backwoodsman; now I'm not 'gonna bore ya with the details, but I can tell ya with complete confidence that these balls were fashioned by a frontiersman. No doubt of it in my mind; it's sloppy, hurried work. A man defendin' himself from a charging bear or screaming savage isn't likely to get too fussy with his ammunition if you get what I mean. And this lead now," he turned the ball over in his fingers. "I can tell right off it's not the kind the Army uses, or Sunday hunters. It's crude and rawboned. Lead is mighty rare and precious on the frontier, so a man doesn't waste it. These balls," he concluded, "were either from the frontier or at least fashioned by a frontiersman who hadn't yet broken his habits." He held them out to Jefferson and dropped them into his outstretched palm.

The Virginian looked at the objects; he was no stranger to the crudities of frontier life, although he had never actually been there, so he knew there was truth in what the old man had said. "Can you pinpoint more exactly where the maker of these balls might have come from?"

Necessity rubbed the stubble on his chin and shook his head slightly. "That's a hard nut to crack, boy. It'd be easy to say something like the upper end of the Valley of Virginia, but truth to tell, these balls could've come from anywhere along the frontier. Like I said, the particulars are all gone, and without them, I can't tell ya more."

"Thank you, Necessity," said Jefferson, leaving some coins on the counter.

Outside, he looked once more at the balls before pocketing them. The frontier again! First, the *venatrum atra*, now this. The evidence seemed increasingly to point to a frontier connection. Was the murderer a frontiersman? Was the whole thing simply a vendetta, a feud carried over to the city? He dismissed that idea immediately, there were too many other things that indicated the mystery was more complicated than that. But the coincidence of the poison and the lead balls did give him a new shade to the identity of the killer. It was the base upon which he would begin to build a profile of the man's identity.

All these strange details forced him to think twice over his earlier investigations. Did he miss anything of importance in Singer's rooms the first time he was there because he had not known what he was looking for? The thought kept teasing him until he found himself outside the address on Fourth Street.

Mrs. Simms was not too happy to see him, and even less happy to let him look at Singer's room again, but another coin eased her thoughts and gained him access to the rooms. He was not quite sure what he was looking for even then, but he soon determined that if Singer was involved with something other than simple business dealings (and it was clear that he was, since he obviously had a secret meeting with perhaps his own killer before collapsing in the State House and the doubts about something or other he expressed in his diary), he may have had an unusual place to keep his more important papers. More carefully than before, Jefferson began to search the apartment for a strong box or hidden safe, but a half hour later, he had turned up nothing.

He stood in the center of the parlor and thought a moment before calling up Mrs. Simms. "Mrs. Simms," he said when she had finally finished a show of catching her breath, "Mr. Singer has taken rooms with you for a good many years, isn't that so?"

"That's correct, Mr. Singer was well pleased with..."

"You've already said that Mr. Singer had not had any guests in the days since he last came to these rooms, but has he had guests come here on previous trips?"

"No. I'm quite sure of that. Mr. Singer always said he valued his privacy and never wanted..."

"Whom did he see with any regularity when he stayed in the city?"

Mrs. Simms thought a moment. "I'm not sure. Sometimes it was a Mr. this or a Mr. that..."

"Was there anyone with whom he dealt with any regularity?" Jefferson asked again.

"Well, there was a Mr. Sparhawk, the bookseller..."

"Good heavens!" cried Jefferson, frightening the landlady with his sudden outburst. How could he have let it slip his mind? Of course! He had read in one of the letters taken from Singer's mail box a note from his business representative in the city, the bookseller, John Sparhawk! There was a good chance that if Singer had any doubts about an enterprise he was mixed up with, he would not leave incriminating evidence lying around in his own rooms, but in the possession of an unknowing third party. Sparhawk was perfect. He bid a hasty adieu to Mrs. Simms and dashed from the house. In minutes he was threading his way back to the shop district of Philadelphia.

He had no trouble finding Sparhawk's store, he had been there before and it was a very well regarded establishment. Compared with the other shops he had been visiting in the past few days, it was big and roomy with a high ceiling. Bound books (a service provided by the proprietor) filled shelves on all sides and a definite smell of parchment was in the air. At the moment, Sparhawk was busy with a customer over by the counter, so Jefferson busied himself by browsing. It was not hard to do; in fact, it was one of the things he liked to do best. A table or two sat in the center of the floor with the latest arrivals and he had gotten so involved with them, he hardly noticed when he was alone at last with the proprietor.

It was Sparhawk himself who came up to him. "Can I help you, sir?" he said.

Jefferson looked up suddenly and the first thing that came to his mind was, "How much do you want for this *History of the Present State of Virginia*?" He already owned a copy of the book by Robert Beverley, but he could always use a second copy; besides, its section on native plants might come in handy.

Sparhawk smiled and said, "A good selection sir! It may be a bit out of date, but there's still plenty of useful information within its pages." He named the price. Jefferson found it reasonable and followed the man to the counter. After paying him, the Virginian tried to broach the subject of Jonas Singer.

"Yes, I'm his business agent in the city," said Sparhawk. "Is there anything I can do for you?"

"Actually there's no delicate way for me to put this question..." No way! That was an understatement! How do you ask a man to let a total stranger look at the private papers of his employer? Especially when he was prevented from revealing that his employer was dead?

"Well, what is it?" asked Sparhawk impatiently.

"I've had some business dealings with Mr. Singer and changed my mind about certain things," Jefferson lied, "and was wondering..."

"If that's the case, I'll notify Mr. Singer and he'll get in touch with you."

"Well, that's not quite what I had in mind." Damn it! He was no good at subterfuge; lying was against his nature. "I've heard that you perhaps hold his papers and that maybe, you'd let me retrieve..."

"Look here, sir!" said Sparhawk indignantly, and who could blame him? "If you're insinuating that I break my trust with my employer, I'll have to ask, nay demand, that you leave this shop immediately!"

What could he say? It was true. Jefferson took his purchase and walked from the shop feeling as low and mean as he had ever felt in his life. Was this the price of his investigations? The sacrifice of his honor and integrity? He did not know if it was worth it. Once or twice he had come close to it in his years as a lawyer and governor of Virginia; then, he called it compromise and expediency or that the end justified the means. But each time a little piece of his soul was destroyed. More than ever, all he wanted was to get out of public life and retire permanently to his home and family, but even that was denied him because of their painful memories of Martha. Why these infernal delays in getting appointed to Europe? To get away from it all and bury himself in some foreign capital was all he craved.

Reality at last returned and the cold light of reason; he knew what he would have to do next and did not like it at all.

CHAPTER TWELVE

Even Jefferson was surprised with the quickness of the response.

After leaving Sparhawk's he went directly to the State House where he was allowed to see Charles Thomson almost as soon as he arrived. The Secretary of Congress was eager to see him of course, and he was forced to give him a recounting of his activities to date before he could broach the subject of his visit.

He thought for certain that what he asked would take some time to arrange with the proper persons, but he never imagined to be walking away from the State House with an armed contingent of Continental troops. The pressure of the potential scandal must have been weighing heavily on the minds of the committee and President of Congress for such unaccustomed action. It was his experience that the federal body under the Articles of Confederation, was a cumbersome, almost powerless organization that was over careful and considerate of the respective states' desires. The only really efficient aspect to come of the confederation was the Continental Army; after all, it was the victor of Saratoga and Yorktown. Through sacrifices and privations that would try any army's endurance, the Continentals had overcome them all, achieving victory and retaining their patriotic ardor, And the small, but professional band of soldiers he had with him now were no exception.

Jefferson viewed their perfectly maintained blue and white uniforms and professional demeanor; the cadence of their march indicated competence and the grim looks on their faces spoke eloquently of their wartime experiences. They were veterans to the last man, their loyalty to the cause unquestioned.

"Do you know the way to Sparhawk's bookstore?" asked the Virginian of the officer riding alongside him.

The man pushed his tricorn up on his head a bit with the point of his thumb and shifted the reins he held to his other hand. "I've made it a point, Mr. Jefferson," he said, "to commit the layout of the city to memory when I first received my orders to come to Philadelphia."

"So you have no resentment of being assigned to a military district with so little prospect of action?"

"I go where I'm sent sir," he said, easily. "Besides, Philadelphia is hardly free from danger. The British still hold New York not two days' good march from here."

Jefferson had heard many good things about Major Harper Laking; about his having run away to join the army for the French and Indian War and how he became one of the youngest officers in the colonial service; how he killed his commanding officer in a duel over alleged insults to the now state of North Carolina. Escaping to the frontier, he made a name for himself all over again in the bloody fighting with the Indians in the Ohio country while adding trespass to his crimes against the Crown. When the Revolution broke out, he was among the first of the backwoods contingents to arrive in Boston and from there, his natural talents and experience catapulted him to the forefront of Continental officers. Of course, that was how his friends felt about him, his enemies said quite different things.

They rode on for a little while, the crowds of people opening a lane for them as they went, until Jefferson cleared his throat. "Major Laking," he said, "although I'm sure you've been properly briefed about the delicacy of our mission this afternoon, I feel I must reiterate the gravity of..."

"You're quite correct in reminding me of its delicacy, sir," the soldier interrupted, "and though I'm completely aware of its importance, instructions from my superiors, and yours, I might add, are that I am in total charge of the affair until its completion. I don't want to seem as though I'm stepping on your toes, Mr. Jefferson, but understand that I know my responsibilities. You are to remain unobtrusively in the background until called forward. It's bad enough that I was forced to bring a whole squad with me, it's not my idea of being subtle, but Mr. Thomson insisted. But rest assured that...Ah, here we are."

They had arrived before Sparhawk's establishment and the Major wasted no time in dismounting and pushing his way into the store. The other men in the squad spread out along the front of the shop at attention, looking thoroughly intimidating to the ordinary passerby.

One of the soldiers joined Jefferson as he came down from his own horse and accompanied him into the store.

"What's the meaning of this?" Sparhawk was saying, not for the first time it seemed as Jefferson came around the display tables. Major Laking and another soldier were gently but firmly shepherding a couple of patrons toward the door while Sparhawk again repeated his question, but when he saw the Virginian, his mouth closed and his face darkened. "So, it's you again, is it?"

Jefferson refrained from speaking and remained by the door as he had been instructed. It was for Major Laking to take charge.

Testing the door to see that it was properly secured against intrusion, the Major turned back to Sparhawk, one hand inside his cloak.

"Now look here, sir," Sparhawk was saying, coming around the end of the service counter, "I know my rights. We fought a war to free us of unnecessary search and seizures and I had my fill of soldiers ordering me about when the British occupied the city..."

"Philadelphia is still under martial law and I am the duly appointed military representative of the Continental forces as chartered by the Congress sitting in behalf of the people of the confederated states; under such circumstances, it is perfectly within the rights of an officer of the military district to go wherever the Congress deems a threat to the national security may exist."

"Here?" sputtered the bookseller. Jefferson felt sorry for the man; after all, he did not have the first idea of the whole affair and never would if everything went smoothly.

Major Laking removed a paper from the confines of his cloak and handed it over to Sparhawk. "My orders, sir."

Sparhawk took the paper and read it. "So you have authority to search my store, it doesn't mean I have to like it. And I'm warning you, I have friends with the newspapers, and you can bet that some members of Congress will wish they'd never given permission for you to enter my store."

"That may well be," said the Major calmly, "but for now, you'll direct me to the belongings of Jonas Singer."

Jefferson's presence had already indicated to the bookseller what the soldiers were interested in, but hearing it spoken aloud was another thing. It made it all more real. He glanced at the tall, red-headed figure near the door and looked him up and down with contempt before turning on his heel and going into the back room.

Jefferson felt none too good in that withering glare, but also knew the real reasons behind this undemocratic intrusion. They justified the action didn't they? He was still trying to answer that question when Major Laking appeared in the door of the rear room and motioned for him to join him there. Another gesture kept the soldier with Jefferson near the outer door. A small crowd had gathered outside the shop, all straining to see through the steamy windows inside.

Laking's cloak swelled as he spun toward the rear of the room, throwing droplets of melted snow onto Jefferson's clothes. On the floor near a cluttered desk, knelt Sparhawk, fumbling with a heavy padlock that held fast the door to a safe. One of the four brass disks of the combination lock seemed to be giving him trouble. Fitted on a central spindle, each disk was incised with a series of letters randomly selected and operated by means of a keyword that contained as many letters as there were disks. According to the *Encyclopedie Methodique*, they were supposed to be easy to operate, but...there, Sparhawk sprang the lock at last and removed the heavy instrument from the safe door.

Major Laking stood aside and motioned for Jefferson to approach and receive the contents. Sparhawk none too graciously dropped a heavy pouch into the Virginian's hands and watched as he went to the desk and opened it.

It took almost an hour for Jefferson to sift through all the papers, account books, and ledgers only to find nothing of value. Of course, there were items the Congressional committee investigating the activities of Tories would be very interested in seeing, but he felt it was not correct to take anything he was not actually looking for. Thinking about it, he supposed Singer was not stupid. If he *was* involved with anything that would place his life or freedom in danger, he would not leave any evidence around for someone to find.

He began to gather the papers back together again when one of the ledger books fell to the floor. Major Laking stooped to pick it up and when he did, something fell out of it. He picked that up too and handed it over to Jefferson without looking at it. The man *was* a professional!

Jefferson replaced the ledger, opened the paper and frowned. It was filled with a series of angles and dots arranged in an obvious pattern and he guessed immediately that it was a cypher of some sort. Then Singer *hadn't* destroyed everything! But from its nature, Jefferson figured it was a mistake; somehow Singer had overlooked this particular piece of paper. As a matter of fact, just a cursory glance revealed its hurried nature. It was probably only a first, practice draft, copied afterward in final form with this one meant to be destroyed.

"Are you finished?" asked Sparhawk impatiently.

Major Laking looked at Jefferson inquiringly.

Jefferson nodded and handed the pouch back to the bookseller who replaced it in the safe.

"You people better have a good reason for all this," he said. "Because Mr. Singer isn't going to like it at all...and neither are the newspapers."

"None of this will reach the newspapers," said Major Laking with unmistakable menace in his voice. "A highly sensitive investigation is under way that involves the security of our new nation, and the Congress will not permit any interference with it. This matter will remain between the three people in this room under pain of treason, is that understood?"

Sparhawk glared but said nothing.

Major Laking motioned for Jefferson to precede him from the room when Sparhawk decided that indeed, he did have something else to say.

"And what about me? What about my reputation? You come here with your uniforms and your troops in the middle of the day making a spectacle of yourselves in front of my store; what are they supposed to think?" He pointed to the crowd gathered outside his window. "In no time, my name will be bandied about as a dirty Tory..."

"I'm sure there'll be nothing to worry too much about," said the Major. "Incidents like this are happening all over the city and most are not involving Tories. In any case, any talk will blow over and your reputation will be none the worse for wear. Come Mr. Pass."

The two men exited the store and in moments were astride their mounts and making their way back to the area of the State House. "I'm afraid Sparhawk may have been right," Jefferson said at last.

"About what? His being marked as a Tory?"

"That too, but mostly the more general effect of calling attention to the incident. I didn't like the idea of sending such a show of force to the bookseller, advertising the whole thing; my investigation was supposed to be discreet."

"I really don't think you have much to fear on that account. Sparhawk won't talk and like he said, most people will think it related to Tory activity or somesuch. In a few days, it'll all disappear."

Jefferson was not at all sure about that, but decided to drop the subject. Taking the paper from his pocket again, he opened it and studied the strange characters lining its face. It occurred to him that the cypher was one used by the Rosicrucians, a secret society of intellectuals that believed in a new order of world government based on an improbable mixture of science and the occult. But he was sure that had nothing to do with Singer's use of the cypher, after all, it was used frequently by those who had nothing to do with the Rosicrusians. But the important thing was, he was familiar with the code and with a bit of research to refresh his memory, he should be able to decypher it.

Hamilton turned from the window and picked up the drink he had set down a few minutes before. He drained it in a single gulp and replaced the glass.

Moving to the center of the room, he glanced again at the paper lying on his desk. He had had to leave the work of decyphering it when he was due for the day's session of Congress, his mind plagued by the possibilities of what it might say. But in finally getting to his rooms at the end of the day, he found himself procrastinating, doing little things, writing letters, anything but working on the note. It was as if he regretted the solving of the mystery too quickly. But now, there was nothing left to do and only the note awaited him.

He went over to the desk and sat down. He placed the note squarely in the center of the table and flattened it with the palms of his hands. On the yellowish paper, a series of hand drawn angles and dots ran across the sheet in a single line divided into four groups:

The cypher was quite familiar to him. As General Washington's adjutant, he had been privy to secret communiques, many of which were encoded with the Rosicrucian cypher that sat before him now. He knew nothing really of its origins, or even the reason why so many of the officers seemed to know of it, but was satisfied that it had been an effective method of safeguarding certain low level communications from

158

enlisted hands. The first step in solving the message was to help his memory by drawing up the key to the code. A minute later, he was finished:

A B C	D E F	G H I
J K L	M N O	P Q R
S T U	V W X	Y Z

Reading the message was simple when one knew the key. Each letter of the alphabet resided in its own certain box or partial box in the grid and the position of each letter within a box was denoted by a dot. One simply needed to find the corresponding full or partial box of the encrypted message with its twin in the grid and then note the position of the dot and compare it with the letters of the box in question. After he had finished with the operation, Hamilton ended up with the following message: "Come to the headquarters."

Hamilton leaned back in his chair and crossed his arms over his chest. He frowned at the words before him as if that might help him to understand them. A simple message obviously. Singer receives it, vanishes, and reappears a few days later as a corpse on the floor of the State House. He had obviously walked into a trap. But whoever sent the message must have had previous communications with Singer, and in the same code, otherwise, why should Singer have so easily followed its instructions or was expected to know what was meant by "the headquarters?" It was beginning to look as though the whole affair had been a falling out among thieves.

Hamilton leaned forward, elbows on the desk and held the note in front of his eyes. What had Singer been up to that forced his associates to kill him? He knew of Singer's Tory sympathies; could they have had anything to do with it? He looked at the message again and decided there was nothing in the words to help him answer his questions. Finally, he decided that any hint he could get from it was in its very use of the Rosicrucian cypher. From it, he could conclude a few things about the sender: that he may have been a scholar or scientist as Rosicrucians prided themselves as thinkers and philosophers leagued together to create some utopian world order; that he may have been a military officer, as the code was commonly used by them in various armies, or that he actually *was* a member of the Rosicrucian Order. Hamilton found it hard to believe any thinking man would have anything to do with such a preposterous organization, but he did not get to where he was by ruling out of hand any possibility. The use of the Rosicrucian code was the most solid bit of evidence he had and it suggested the most obvious next step he should take.

CHAPTER THIRTEEN

"Washington is victorious at Yorktown. Cornwallis surrenders. British movement everywhere slows. With the French firmly on the side of the Americans, the outcome is certain. What do we do now? With Clark in possession of Vincennes, the whole northwest will surely be claimed by the United States. I fear this means the end of our plans, nothing more can be done. I will continue to help our Loyalist brethren against the reprisals that will surely come as long as I can; afterwards, I shall retire to Canada."

Jefferson reread the transcribed note again for the fourth time, trying to piece it together with the other information he had. His supper lay cold on the table near his bed.

He had no real doubt that the message had been written by Singer just after the news of the great victory in Virginia had reached New York and Philadelphia and that he had felt that whatever he was up to, was negated by that action. But really, the Virginian had long since made up his mind about just what Singer and his secret allies were interested in: taking advantage of the confusion caused by the war to lay claim to land west of the Appalachian Proclamation Line.

It was personally despicable to Jefferson that men would take advantage of the life and death struggle of their brothers for mean profit when instead, they should have been taking part in the historic fight against tyranny and injustice. While good and honorable men were ready to sacrifice both their fortunes and their lives if necessary for this sacred goal, these others were willing to give up only their honor. But he was not fooling himself, Jefferson well knew the type of men these were. No generation was ever free of them. There would always be certain lawless, unfeeling elements ready to take advantage of their more sensitive fellows.

He pulled the drawer out from his desk and took the envelope that lay far in the back. He pulled out the surveyor's map inside and unfolded it. Unfortunately for him, Singer's agent, Issac Invernol was a clever man, he left no indication of just where the map fit on a larger scale in the lands it was supposed to represent. Jefferson turned the map over until it was upside down, then onto its side. Nothing. He simply could not recognize it. From Invernol's measurements, it was not high ground, nor mountainous. It was located at the confluence of two rivers and he had reported that the Indians in the area were amenable to bribery but not which tribe they may have been. Jefferson had studied Indian culture for years and had collected a sizeable native vocabulary of every tribe in the east and could actually speak a bit of it, so any hint of the tribe's identity could have helped him identify it, but there was no clue.

Suddenly an idea struck him: the lead balls that had killed Singer had come from somewhere to the north of the Valley of Virginia; the poison had been taken from a plant that grew wild only in a particular area of the frontier, the hunting grounds of the Delaware; could Invernol's map illustrate a portion of the same area the balls and the poison came from? The more he thought about it, the more logical it seemed that the next phase of his investigations must lead him to the frontier. He was sure that if he could find Invernol, he would get the information he needed to conclude the whole business. But how old was Invernol's letter? A quick look at the envelope and message gave no hint but their soiled nature indicated that they had been on the road for a good long time. With this new avenue opening before him, he began to worry about Invernol's whereabouts. Was he still in the area of the map? Or had he moved on? With Singer dead, was he now in the employ of Singer's unknown acquaintances?

For the first time, Jefferson felt as though he had a real chance of finishing the business and wanted to move as fast as possible before the trail disappeared. Time, he felt, was his most precious commodity.

He had a late meeting with Thomson's committee and decided to take all the material he had found so far. Perhaps by sharing it with the others, possibilities he had not thought of might be suggested by them.

Paul Huntington slowed his horse when he came into sight of the Hudson River again. He had been riding for almost two days and thought he would make New York in record time, but now he was not so sure.

He had left Philadelphia with the messages from the Cobbler's with a stiff breeze at his back and clear sunny skies, but in the two days since, clouds had rolled in until the sky was a featureless gray that threatened snow again. The countryside on Manhattan was drab and colorless this early in the winter; the trees were bare and black against the sky and hordes of browned leaves carpeted the ground where patches of early snow had not covered them.

After being ferried across the river, he thought he would have been in the city in an hour, and although he had expected no easy time, he never thought things would be as difficult as they turned out to be. The land between the mainland and the city was still mostly a neutral ground between the American and British lines. In it, only the lawless of both sides prowled about and the traveler had to be constantly vigilant. At least the British soldiers who scoured the countryside for farm goods usually left civilians alone; it was the American "skinners" as they were called, who felt no allegiance to either side that preyed upon civilians and soldier alike. He was warned by the ferryman that the skinners had been especially active lately, probably sensing that with the end of hostilities would come the end of their lawless opportunities, and to be extra careful. The warning served its purpose as Huntington was able to avoid certain incidents, the last, only by a wild chase through the barren woods.

He looked over his shoulder but saw nothing. His pursuers, whom he never saw too clearly, had suddenly given up the chase only a few minutes before and he had begun to congratulate himself on his wonderful bit of riding when he saw the real reason for their having abandoned pursuit. He had just rounded a bend in the road when he came into sight of a British mounted patrol. His heart leapt involuntarily to his throat as the lead figure raised a hand in signal for him to stop. He did.

In a moment, a few more soldiers had joined the first, the red uniforms spotless, pistols in their free hands and their mounts nervous. "Come forward," commanded the lead figure, "slowly." Huntington did as he was bid and in moments was surrounded by the little group. One man cantered farther up the road and stopped. "State your business, rebel," said the leader with ill disguised contempt. Huntington sensed that it would give the man great pleasure to run him through with his sabre right then and there.

"I'm a postal rider from Philadelphia," he said, patting his pouch. "We have permission to run the mail through during the truce."

"Don't be too sure of that," said the soldier, eyeing him up and down.

"He doesn't look like a skinner," said another from under his hat.

"No, he's too clean. Open the pouch."

Huntington never considered for a moment to protest and handed over its contents. The soldier looked through the small set of notes and letters, even opened a couple, but luckily seemed bored with the duty and never gave them more than a cursory look. Nothing striking him as subversive, he gave them back saying, "On your way, rebel."

Huntington did not need to be told twice and rode off gladly. When he looked back, the soldiers were gone. Were they "cowboys," British soldiers that robbed from local farms, or a real patrol? He decided that like him, they were too clean to be. The rest of the way to New York was free from further trouble except for the last guard station just before the city that ruined any chance he had for a record time.

New York was hardly recognizable to him after being occupied and under martial law for so long. It was not so much physical change as one of the feelings. Because of the occupation, it was a Tory town and many of the people he saw had the haunted look that came when one had no idea of one's status. Would they stay or would they be forced to move? Could they take their possessions with them, or would they lose everything? Did they pick the losing side? And if so, what would the winners extort from them? Would the British honor their loyalty and not abandon them? Where would they go? Their entire lives were here. Huntington imagined every eye boring into his back as he rode by the weathered houses. Soldiers were everywhere and he could see the forest of masts that poked up behind them from the harbor. This enemy, he concluded, was not yet defeated. From the rejoicing in Philadelphia, it had been easy to think that the British were beaten, but they still had thousands of troops and scores of warships here. They did not look anything like a defeated army to him.

Huntington looked at the address on the first envelope he took from the pouch and decided it was not too far away and headed in that direction first. Minutes later, he was knocking at the door of a nicely painted town house and wondering what sort of tip he could expect from Mr. Bolling.

The door opened and a man stood before him. Huntington decided the man was in his thirties even though his hair had already begun to recede over his forehead. "What can I do for you?" the man said.

"Personal message for Mr. Simon Bolling," said Huntington, holding the envelope up as proof.

"I'm Mr. Bolling." He was handed the note and looked at it with disapproval.

"It was opened by the officer of a British patrol outside the city, sir," Huntington hastily explained.

Bolling nodded and grunted in a disgusted way and slipped the letter from the envelope. The corner of his eyes wrinkled and a smile creased his face when he read from whom it had been sent. Huntington smiled too. When the recipient was in a good mood, it meant a good tip. He was not disappointed. It was a happy messenger from the Cobbler's that remounted his horse and moved on to his next stop.

Bolling had not heard from Thomas Jefferson since the occupation of the city; at least not personally. He had heard the regular news about his governorship and his

166

being nominated for a position in Europe, but the military situation had an annoying way of disrupting old friendships. He tucked the letter back into the envelope. Jefferson's requests did not seem too difficult to follow up. He turned back into the house, closing the door behind him.

———

"Let me see if I have this right," said Hamilton, placing his fingertips onto Thomson's desk where Jefferson had spread out all the material he had gathered so far in the affair. "You suspect Singer was killed because of his involvement with land speculators?"

Jefferson shifted his weight from one leg to the other and cleared his throat. Put that way, it did sound too simple, but this young Hamilton had a way of using words to twist meanings about...and to put his finger on the crux of a matter. "Put simply, yes. Land speculation is nothing new, but the late war has created unprecedented opportunities for unscrupulous elements..."

"Not that you Virginians have never taken opportunities for land speculation..." Hamilton insinuated.

"There's nothing wrong with pure land speculation within the law," said Jefferson, "and land companies have always been a business staple in Virginia. I believe that without it, our country could not have progressed so rapidly as it has. Why, one needs only to look at those territories claimed by Spain to realize that..."

The Virginian continued on for another few minutes making a well reasoned argument for land speculation, and Hamilton had no real objections to it, in fact he agreed with it. He noticed Madison's silence, but that was to be expected as his relationship with Jefferson was much like that of his own with General Washington. It was Pembridge's silence that was interesting to him. The man seemed remote and distant and up to now, had not taken part in the meeting at all. The New Yorker vaguely enjoyed that, after all, it was his secret influence on the man that kept him quiet. On the other hand, if he did not act his normal self, people would begin to take notice.

"...and so, you see, the entire advancement of civilization in the New World has depended on our appetite for western lands," Jefferson concluded.

"Gentlemen," said Thomson before Jefferson could catch his second wind, "I think we've wandered from our subject."

"Of course, Charles," agreed Hamilton. "I think Mr. Jefferson's discourse on land speculation did have some effect in clearing up the discussion. Mostly by making the point that possession of the western lands is crucial to control of the continent. The long term economic interests of the United States are irrevocably tied up with its control. The Mississippi River must be made an international waterway."

"If our western counties are prevented from free navigation of the river and access to facilities in New Orleans, there will always be trouble on the frontier," added Madison. "Thank God Clark's taken Vincennes!"

"We're all agreed on the importance of the west," said Thomson, "but what could Singer have hoped to accomplish during the war that he couldn't have before or after? Why all the secrecy?"

There was silence a moment, even from Hamilton, until Jefferson spoke. "I think there was more than mere land speculation at work here. The letter from Invernol suggests Singer was interested in specific sites for speculation. The area on the map shows a prime location at the forks of two rivers and the building of a trading post, but what more could they have expected after the war when the land would have still been under the control of either Britain or the United States?"

"We know Singer was a Tory," said Madison, "perhaps there's more to it we don't know about. Were they working in secret for British interests and only making these plans for the west when it was time to claim their reward?"

"These speculations are getting us nowhere," said Thomson. "Thomas, do you have any further plans for your investigations?"

"Actually I do, after one more visit here, I'd like to head for the Valley of Virginia."

There was astonishment on the part of the others.

Hamilton was not too surprised at the statement, but he was more concerned with what Jefferson's absence from Philadelphia would mean to his own plans. At first he had been as anxious as his associates that Jefferson not solve the murder and thus hopefully scuttle any preliminary treaty that may not have provisions for the western lands. But as time went on, he had begun to think on the ramifications of Clark's possession of Vincennes and what that meant for the United States' interest in the west. With the fort in American hands, the whole northwest question had become moot. Whether the British liked it or not, the United States had every right to expect its annexation at the conclusion of hostilities. Hamilton may have been more than efficient in the cause of his own interests, but no one could deny his patriotism. The welfare of his country would always come first to him. And so, he had begun to see the wisdom of clearing up the Singer affair before the scandal could wreck any treaty and give the British an excuse to continue the war. He remembered Dickinson and the others and mentally shrugged. He would handle them when the time came.

"I'll need money and supplies for at least two weeks and a squad of continentals for my security," Jefferson was saying.

"Do you really need to go to the frontier?" asked Thomson, who never expected for things to go this far when he had summoned Jefferson.

"Unless my last enquiry here bears fruit, I don't see any other way to go."

"And what is this last enquiry?" asked Madison.

"I prefer not to say," said Jefferson.

The others looked at one another until Thomson demanded, "Why not?"

"I don't like to say this, Charles," sighed Jefferson, "but I suspect there may be someone in this room who is not completely trustworthy."

There were the usual protestations of innocence and declarations insisting on the honor of all those present, but none of it impressed the Virginian. "The fact remains that no one outside this room has had information concerning Singer's death and yet Singer's rooms were broken into and papers taken, including a travel bag..."

"But that's hardly proof of betrayal," said Madison, "it was most likely the murderer..."

"That's probably the case, but if I'm going to be entering the wilderness, I'll be a great deal more vulnerable, especially if the area I find myself in is still in the hands of the enemy. From this moment on, I don't want to take any more chances. I want knowledge of the whole investigation to be as limited as possible."

The others did not like the insinuations on their honor, but agreed to abide by Jefferson's desires.

As the group filed from the State House, Hamilton would have liked to speak to Pembridge and warn him of his suspicious behavior, but did not dare while the others were about. Besides, he had things to do.

CHAPTER FOURTEEN

Two days later, Jefferson found himself approaching the small town of Lancaster, southwest of Philadelphia. After almost two days in the saddle, even the botanical interest he had in the local varieties of flora was beginning to pale.

It pained him to think that he could not trust the committee to keep its secrets, but he knew with his projected trip to the west, he would be more exposed than ever. There were a hundred ways to die in the wilderness and not all of them were natural. In any case, he hoped the preparations for his expedition would be completed by the time he returned in a few days.

He took a deep lungfull of frigid air and exhaled slowly, watching his breath steam out before his face. He was riding leisurely along a well packed road that wound through open pastures of browned grass dotted by the occasional wide branching tree and stretches of forest that spread over rocky, untillable ground. Occasionally, he would stop and collect a few samples of the plants he passed: leaves, twigs, grass, or nuts. The wide array of plant life in the United States continued to astonish him, even after years of study. It was one of his passions to disprove current European attitudes that somehow, everything in America was an inferior version of the original found in Europe. He took particular exception to the ideas expounded by the French naturalist, Georges Louis Leclerc, Comte de Buffon.

Buffon believed in the absolute fixity of species by reason of their biological grouping according to physiological characteristics, habitat, and survival of the fittest, but when all was said and done, those species found in Europe were still inherently superior to those in the New World. A position Jefferson took strong exception to; strong enough in fact, to spend months researching, studying, and writing his *Notes on the State of Virginia* where he specifically refuted Buffon's assertions. Quite a daring enterprise at the time for an unknown scholar in America to so openly challenge one of the most respected minds in Europe. But Jefferson had felt he was on solid ground because of his great knowledge of native flora and fauna and of the array of facts he could marshal against Buffon. Satisfied with his arguments, he only wished he could crown them by sending Buffon a genuine sample of the New World's fauna in the form of a stuffed moose or elk, but that was only a dream at the moment.

His horse snorted and he saw the road straighten out ahead. He really did not expect to find anything of importance at Ephrata, the name of the Rosicrucian lodge in Lancaster, but he felt he could not leave such an obvious connection unexplored. With the common use of the Rosicrucian cypher, one did not need to be an initiate to know about it. After all, *he* was familiar with it and he did not have the slightest connection with the order.

Suddenly the trees in front of him parted and he made out the first few buildings leading into the town. As he approached, he kept an eye out for the path he had been told about that would lead up a slight rise to the big house where the Rosicrucians kept their lodge. Spotting it, he reined in alongside, and waited to see if anyone was about before spurring his mount into the close cropped shrubbery lining the path.

He was not sure what line he would take when he arrived. He had vaguely decided to try to seek membership and pursue events from there.

He ducked beneath a long, hanging branch just as the path took a sharp turn revealing the south face of the house. Jefferson pulled up and backed his horse slightly into the concealing underbrush, spying the house from among the branches. All seemed quiet. The house was large, with two stories and a wide veranda that circled it on three sides. Big double doors opened on a gravel drive that led from the path to the front of the house. He dismounted and was about to take a step into the open, when a voice stopped him.

"I should have known you'd be here."

Jefferson whirled in the direction of the voice while trying to calm his surprised horse.

Hamilton stepped out from the concealment of the underbrush, his black cloak and hat blending perfectly with the shadows; behind him, Jefferson could just see a jet black mare nibbling at some dried grass.

"What are *you* doing here?" the Virginian demanded.

"The same as you no doubt," said the New Yorker, smiling.

The two men stood face to face, one still young and self assured, the other older, but wiser. Both men were tall, but physical differences ended there: one was black and calculating, the other simple and open. Jefferson was already a giant to some in the panoply of the new nation, while Hamilton only held the promise of greatness; but somehow, each took the measure of the other in a glance and knew he was in the presence of someone equally as formidable no matter their differences. In the years to come, issues and events yet unforeseeable would rock the new republic to its foundations and test its mettle in the crucible of party politics as each man found himself locked in ideological combat with the other to determine what course their country would follow. But that was in the future, for now, each man sensed the mettle of the other and admired what he saw.

"What do you mean by that?" asked Jefferson.

Hamilton decided the time for subterfuge had passed. "Bring your horse over here out of sight." When Jefferson had complied, he continued. "Suffice it to say, that while you've been investigating this whole affair, I have not been content to merely stand aside and do nothing. I've been doing a little looking around myself." Jefferson said nothing, so he continued. "You recall, of course, your report of Singer's missing travel bag?" Jefferson nodded, eyes narrowing. "Well, I found it."

"What!" exclaimed the Virginian, unable to contain himself. "You've found the bag? Where...?"

Hamilton held up a hand and continued. "For reasons of my own, I'd decided to keep watch over Samuel Adams, in the course of which I discovered that it was he who was in possession of the bag..."

"Adams? Why should he have the bag...and more, how did he get it? What's *his* connection with this whole affair?" Jefferson was getting rapidly confused with this sudden revelation. Could Adams be involved with the murder? He knew of the Yankee's reputation, but never considered him to be completely ruthless. But the fact remained, he had the bag.

"I've reason to believe that Adams has been moving behind the scenes in Congress to manipulate your investigation and wreck any peace treaty that might be signed..."

"Why would he want that?"

Hamilton shrugged, he had not planned on revealing too much, especially his hold on Pembridge; after all, some of his practices could in no way be considered ethical and he wanted Jefferson to have nothing to use against him in the future. "I don't know, personally, I don't trust him, he's too hot blooded; his brand of radicalism has become an anachronism unsuited to our nation's changing situation. In any case, I managed to get ahold of the bag..."

"How did you do that and why didn't you say anything about it before?" Jefferson suspected there was a good deal more to Hamilton's story, but decided it would serve no purpose to insist upon it here.

"I don't think that matters right now," the young man replied coolly. "What does, is that I found a message hidden in the bag written in the same Rosicrucian code you found on the note from Sparhawk's. When I saw that, I decided to..."

"Why didn't you tell me any of this before now?" Jefferson reiterated. "Why didn't you inform the committee?"

"Frankly, I doubted your abilities to do any good in the Singer affair from the start," said Hamilton truthfully. "That's why I've been doing some work on my own. My coming here was just the next step; but when I saw you coming up the hill, I knew this was as far as I was going to go on my own. That, and I've finally admitted to myself that you've been a great deal more resourceful than I thought you'd be. Will you accept my apologies?"

Although Jefferson still did not fully trust the man, this frank admission and request for forgiveness touched him. He sensed that indeed, there was truth in the man's statements despite the things he obviously decided not to tell him, but there was enough for Jefferson to feel that nothing related to the Singer affair had been held back. He extended his hand.

Hamilton took it and shook firmly, the respect he had felt growing in him for the Virginian, seemingly justified.

"Were you able to decypher the note you found?" asked Jefferson afterwards.

"Easily. It read simply: 'Come to the headquarters.'"

"That's all?"

"Yes."

"And you figured this headquarters could be Ephrata..." he lifted his chin in the direction of the house.

"Is that what they call it?" asked Hamilton, looking over to the house himself.

"Anything else?"

Hamilton shook his head. "That's all I've been able to find out. I was hoping the master of the lodge would be able to help me... By the way, how were you going to proceed in there?"

It was Jefferson's turn to signal uncertainty by shrugging. "By seeking membership."

"Then what? Ask if they keep murderers on the books?"

"I'll worry about that when the time comes. Do you have any better ideas?"

Hamilton laughed and clapped the Virginian on the shoulder. "By heavens, I think I'm going to enjoy working with you!" Then, "No, I had the same intentions you did."

"Then perhaps we'd better stop loitering out here and get on with seeking out the mysteries of the lodge?" suggested Jefferson smiling. Hamilton extended a black-gloved hand in invitation for the Virginian to lead the way and the two men walked the rest of the way to the top of the hill.

The first thing they noticed was how deserted the property looked. There was no sign that anyone was around. They stopped at the foot of the steps leading to the front door and looked up at the house, expecting some sign of life at their approach, but nothing stirred. Jefferson led the way up and knocked at the door. A glass mosaic filled the upper half of the door and in its center, made of pieces of stained glass, was the image of a cross with a single red rose in its center.

"Do you think anyone's at home?" asked Hamilton rhetorically.

Jefferson was about to answer, when the door creaked and opened wide. "Can I help you?" asked the tall, thin man standing in the doorframe. Behind him, a darkened corridor stretched toward the rear of the house where details were obscured.

Hamilton looked at the Virginian with a half comical grin and crooked his head as if to say, "Go ahead, tell him we want to join!"

"Is this the main lodge of the ancient and mystical order of the Rosy Cross?" Jefferson asked instead.

The tall man bowed slightly and replied. "The Rosicrucian order in America, yes. I am Joseph Klaus, master of the lodge."

"Yes, well, my name's Mr. Pass," said Jefferson, "and this is Mr..."

"Lancer," said Hamilton quickly, inclining his head.

"Mr. Lancer and I have come to enquire about membership in your order," concluded Jefferson.

A look that could only be translated as complete understanding passed over Mr. Klaus' face. "Well then, such serious intentions should not be discussed out of doors gentlemen." He stepped back, opening the door wider. "Please come in."

"Thank you," said Jefferson stepping inside. Hamilton followed, doffing his hat.

Their host closed the door behind them and led the way to a parlor just off the corridor. The small party arranged themselves about the room and when they were comfortable, Mr. Klaus spoke again. "You say you're interested in joining our order?"

"Yes," said Jefferson. "We've heard quite a bit about it and when we learned you were only a couple days ride from Philadelphia, decided to come down and find out more."

"The interesting tenets of the order are peculiarly compelling to us," said Hamilton crossing his legs. His comment earned him an ironic look from Jefferson.

But Mr. Klaus smiled and rose. "I'd like to discuss our order in more detail before we go on to the formalities of initiation, gentlemen. Allow me to fetch us some tea before we begin."

"Certainly, that's most kind of you, sir," said Jefferson. As soon as their host left the room, he turned to Hamilton. "You didn't have to go that far..."

"I didn't think it would do any harm to flatter the man."

"Just the same, I think it best to let Mr. Klaus do the talking."

"I've no objections." There was no more time to talk before Mr. Klaus returned with the tea. Jefferson figured he must have already had it prepared to serve it so quickly.

They were sipping their tea, waiting for Mr. Klaus to speak again. "Are you gentlemen aware of our order's history?" he asked.

"Not enough to feel confident about it," said Jefferson.

"Well then, you must know of the ancient lineage of the Rosicrucian Order; how the first temple was founded in the Pharaoh's Egypt but later destroyed. In fact, it wasn't until the founder of the modern temple, Christian Rosenkreutz, made his astounding journey through the Middle East more than two centuries ago that the order was revived with all the force and vigor of the original."

"Wasn't Rosenkreutz a monk?" asked Jefferson.

Mr. Klaus nodded. "He left the monastery in order to travel to the holy land; but along the way, he lingered at different places, learning all the wisdom of the east and only returning to Germany many years later. At home again, Rosenkreutz gathered a number of disciples to himself and began to teach the wisdom he'd found in the east. At last he died and was buried but with instructions that his tomb was to be opened again fifty years following his death." His voice assumed an air of great reverence that Hamilton and Jefferson found difficult to understand. "When the allotted time had passed, the small band of Rosicrucians opened his grave and do you know what they found?"

Jefferson shrugged, and Hamilton said, "No."

"Nothing!" said Mr. Klaus, leaning forward in his chair, the tea sloshing in his cup. "Rosenkreutz was gone and in his stead was found a total of twenty books encompassing the complete knowledge of Rosicrucian lore."

"Well that hardly constitutes nothing…" began Hamilton before Klaus, oblivious to his point, cut him off.

"The most important book however, was *The Chymical Wedding*, in which Christian Rosenkreutz, using an allegorical tale divided into seven days, each representing a different alchemical principle, outlined the secret truths of the Rosicrucian Order. Each day revealing a different truth culminating in the seventh day's ultimate revelation."

"And that revelation?" asked Hamilton, becoming interested despite himself.

Mr. Klaus leaned back and smiled. "Ah, that wasn't revealed."

"But why not?"

"Rosenkreutz never said, but it is assumed that when the order lives out the principles outlined in *The Chymical Wedding*, the truth will be made manifest to us. Anyway," he continued breezily, "it was the great Francis Bacon, Imperator of the order in Europe…"

"Francis Bacon was a Rosicrucian?" Hamilton interrupted again.

"But of course," said Mr. Klaus, "All the greatest minds of Europe were members. Our order knows no cultural or national boundaries. Newton, Hume, and Diderot were members. And here in America, Benjamin Franklin and Thomas Jefferson..."

"Thomas Jefferson is a member?" asked Jefferson incredulously. This was a surprise!

"Of course," said Mr. Klaus blithely.

"But..."

"What about Alexander Hamilton?" asked Hamilton not without a trace of jealousy.

"Who's he?"

Hamilton was about to list all of his best qualities when he was interrupted by Jefferson, who was rapidly losing patience with the whole subject. "You were explaining the order's history..." he prompted.

"Yes, well, Francis Bacon ordered a lodge formed in America and in 1694 the first members reached Philadelphia (which they named, by the way)," this was news to Jefferson, "and immediately laid the foundations to almost every cultural, artistic, and scientific establishment in the country." By this time, Jefferson could see that Hamilton had had enough foolishness and only wanted to get out as soon as possible and decided to try a gracious way to make their exit, but he still needed to know if Jonas Singer had any connection with the order, which he now doubted more than ever!

"Mr. Klaus, membership was recommended to us by a Mr. Jonas Singer, and I was wondering if he himself was a member in good standing..."

"Well, I really can't say, Mr. Pass..."

"Is there some rule of confidentiality?"

"Oh no, members have nothing to hide," said Mr. Klaus confidently.

"Then what...?

"Gentlemen, our order is venerable and well respected. Our members see no need to proclaim their membership on the housetops like other, less serious groups. Just who is and who is not a member is self evident, we keep no roles, no records..."

"You mean you don't know who the members are?" asked Jefferson, completely at his wits' end.

"That's correct," admitted their host.

Hamilton was nonplussed. "Then how can you be sure Jefferson is a member? Or if Alexander Hamilton isn't for that matter?"

"Why it's common knowledge. One can always tell who our members are by the way they write their public papers, by how erudite and concise they are, by their brilliance and wit..."

"Let's get out of here!" said Hamilton suddenly, rising to his feet and jamming his hat on his head.

Jefferson was right behind him but managed to retain his accustomed graciousness to stop at the parlor door and say to the astonished Mr. Klaus, "You'll pardon our abrupt exit, sir?" and bowed.

Hamilton was waiting impatiently for him outside. "That was the most ridiculous balderdash I've ever heard!" he stormed.

"I'll admit it was..."

"Mythical men disappearing from their graves, Egyptian temples, hidden truths, secret histories, and unknown memberships! This was a waste of time."

"Are you sure you're not more upset because you weren't assumed to be a member?" said Jefferson, poking fun at Hamilton's self image.

Hamilton snorted. "This group is just too ridiculous and the Singer affair too serious to think these Rosicrucians had anything to do with it."

"I wouldn't dismiss them too easily, Alexander," said Jefferson, assuming the air he did with his close friend, James Madison. "Despite what we heard inside, the Rosicrucians were once an organization that many brilliant men sought desperately to join. It was more out of pride than anything else; but a brilliant man still has as much common sense as any other man and it can be fooled just as easily." He laid a hand on the younger man's shoulder. "I'll tell you what, there's a tavern back along the road to Philadelphia, why don't we stop there for the night and treat ourselves to a big supper?"

Hamilton smiled and led their horses out onto the path. "After today, I could use a pitcher of rum!"

CHAPTER FIFTEEN

It was almost midnight before Hamilton could have his fill of rum; and when he did, he placed his mug on the table with a hollow thud and leaned back in his seat.

He and Jefferson had managed to reach the Trailside Tavern just past midway from Lancaster to Philadelphia not an hour before, but when the proprietor learned who the red haired stranger was, they could not have stopped him from fixing them a meal if they wanted to. Just now they were alone in the big, low ceilinged common room of the tavern where the fire from the hearth had been reduced to a pile of glowing cinders and the only light they had was the candle sitting on their table.

The two men occupied a booth near the hearth, managing to soak up the residual heat from the dead fire and making up the difference with a bit of wine and a liberal amount of rum. The candle flame and the glow from the hearth cast a strange light upon their faces and the lack of occupants in the room allowed them to speak freely.

Jefferson rubbed his head where he had bumped it against a hanging lantern when he first came in. The beams that crossed the ceiling were so low that he was obliged to walk at a slight stoop when moving about the room.

"Your height can be a disadvantage my friend," said Hamilton, who had never been regarded as short himself. "Hardly the characteristic desired for the discreet snooping you've been called upon to perform in this affair."

"Not only for this," said Jefferson. "I've never been regarded as a man of action, least of all by myself, where one's height adds to one's air of authority. Thus it has ever given me a quality of unintentioned intimidation or awkwardness."

"I should say! I can just picture you turning a step or two with the ladies!"

Jefferson laughed. "Now you strike too close to home, sir. Why, when I was younger, I was regarded as a fine dancer. Now with you, I'd say it was mode of dress."

Hamilton picked at his cloak. "This color? Merely my own form of studied intimidation. I've found most people expect certain things of me, and I rarely wish to disappoint them. So I dress the part."

"Why do you feel the need to live up to others' expectations of you?"

"It's not for them, it's for me. By nurturing a certain image, I place others on the defensive, they expect a formidable figure in me and I give it to them. That gives me the advantage in any situation."

"But from what I hear, Alexander Hamilton needs no artificial image to enhance his reputation."

"And what have you heard?"

"That he was a protege of General Washington and is greatly loved by him; that he is a brave, resourceful soldier; a patriot; well connected with a bright political future ahead of him..."

"You flatter me, Thomas. Surely there must be less savory talk?" In fact, he knew there was plenty.

Now it was Jefferson's turn to lean back. "Very well. You're said to be ruthless, cold, calculating, zealous in the cause of our recent struggle and sometimes brilliant in political and philosophical endeavors."

Hamilton crossed his arms. "I don't know if that was any less flattering, but it's probably closer to the mark." Then in a rare moment of confidence, he said, "Not that I like it, mind you. I've had a difficult time getting where I am; I've had to claw my way up every step of the way and am justifiably proud I think, of my accomplishments. My sometimes abrasive qualities have prevented many men from becoming true friends."

Jefferson sat quietly, listening. He knew of the man's unfortunate background: that he was a bastard and mostly self-educated. He had been taught the business end of the mercantile trade from a young age and came to America in the same capacity as an adolescent. When the war broke out, he joined the Continental army and because of his intelligence and administrative experiences, found himself a member of Washington's staff. It was due to his wartime position that he was able to meet his wife, whose father, against the prevailing gossip over the young man's birth, not only accepted him wholeheartedly, but from what Jefferson heard, had actually become a sort of disciple to his brilliant son-in-law. When Hamilton had finished speaking, Jefferson nodded understanding.

There was a pause in the conversation then, with each man concerned with his own thoughts until the proprietor returned to clear away the remnants of their meal. Then Hamilton leaned onto the table and said, "So, any ideas where we go from here?"

Jefferson shrugged and sighed. "Nothing except my plans to go west." He chuckled. "This little expedition turned out to be a waste of time, didn't it?"

Hamilton snorted. "I'll say."

"What was it your note said again?"

Hamilton reached inside his waistcoat and produced a tiny slip of paper. Unfolding it, he read: "'Come to the headquarters.'"

"'And that's all?'"

"Nothing more. Like I said before, the only thing I could get from it, was deduced from the code itself, and we both know where that led."

"Still, I keep wondering about this 'headquarters,' it seems to have some kind of official ring to it, not the sort of thing applied to some cave or cabin..."

"The Headquarters, you say?" said a new voice from behind them. They both looked up suddenly and saw the proprietor's head as it peeked over the high back of Jefferson's seat where he was cleaning up the next table.

"Yes," said Hamilton hesitantly, "do you know of it?" He glanced at Jefferson, whose eyes were firmly fixed on his.

The proprietor came over to their table, wiping his hands on his apron. "I heard you say you were looking for the Headquarters?"

"That's right," said Hamilton again, controlling his impatience.

"It's not hard to find," said the man. "Just ride up the road a piece until you're just a few miles shy of Philadelphia. You can't miss it; it's a big, beautiful place with columns and lawns and everything. It's become quite an attraction since that blackguard, Benedict Arnold used it for his headquarters while he was military governor here. Why, the talk that went around after the fancy masked balls he had there, some say with Tories..." He did not have time to finish before both men were on their feet and shrugging into their cloaks.

Jefferson threw some coins on the table. "Thank you my good man, you've been a help to us." When he turned to leave, he saw that Hamilton was already through the door.

Outside, the clear winter sky was filled with a powdering of stars but no moon and the street was empty of traffic except for a lumbering cart approaching them from the south.

Hamilton halted on the steps leading down from the tavern. "I think it's worth a look," he said.

"So do I," agreed Jefferson. "But I feel like a fool for not thinking about it sooner."

Hamilton waved a hand in dismissal. "Forget it. I guess it was just too obvious."

For the second time in less than a week, Jefferson wondered at the phenomenon first raised by Dr. Shippen at the City Tavern and how he blamed himself for missing the evidence of poison used against Jonas Singer: that sometimes an observer might miss important facts simply because he was not looking for them. And now, here was Hamilton doing the same thing. How many facts had he himself missed in the process of investigating the whole affair? He shivered in the folds of his cloak and watched absently as the cart made its way up the street, the occasional flick of the driver's whip keeping the horses awake.

While talking, they had moved a bit farther out into the street and began walking toward the makeshift stables to the rear of the tavern where their horses had been taken. "If we start off now, we could be at the Headquarters by..." The sudden loud crack of a whip and the thunder of driving hooves and rattling harness broke the quiet of the night and the train of Jefferson's thoughts.

When he turned to look, he was confronted with the sight of the charging cart; the once dull looking nags were now steam-snorting demons driven to fury by the vicious licks of the whip. And they were hurtling directly at him!

Hamilton was the first to react, his reflexes at self-preservation still sharp so soon after leaving the army. He threw himself to the ground and rolled clear of the charging wagon, regaining his feet as smoothly as a cat. But when he looked up again, he saw to his horror that Jefferson had not yet moved! He stood in the path of the barreling wagon as if frozen to the spot. Without a thought, Hamilton ran and threw himself at his new friend, catching him squarely in the side and throwing them both clear of the flying hooves and spinning wheels. A second later, still swathed in the dust of the passing vehicle, the New Yorker pulled a pistol from inside his cloak and fired it after the wagon. Shooting high, his arm bucked at the discharge, but he saw no slackening in the speed of the wagon. In another few seconds it had disappeared down the road.

He was already busy reloading his firearm when Jefferson said, "You saved my life, Alexander."

"And if I didn't, where would our investigation be?" Hamilton said, finishing with his pistol and replacing it on his person. "Seriously though, what was I supposed to do? Let you get run down?"

"You have my thanks, sir. I don't know what came over me. It's not like I've never seen a runaway cart before."

"More likely, you never saw one deliberately aimed at you before. I've seen it happen more than once in the army; when some country boy, familiar with guns all his life, suddenly freezes up when confronted by one that has him as its target."

"Then we're of one mind, that the cart was meant to kill us," said Jefferson.

"I think the cart was meant to kill *you*," amended Hamilton. "As far as anyone knows, my involvement with the Singer affair goes no farther than my membership in the special committee. You, on the other hand, are the special investigator and have been poking around for days. That, and the fact that the driver never bothered to come back to see if we were all right after his team 'lost control.'" He turned to Jefferson. "No, I'm sure you were the target."

"Then we must be getting close to something to force the murderer's hand this way."

"It surely wasn't the Rosicrucian business."

"No, but the murderer must feel that by eliminating the possibilities, I'm getting too close to the truth."

"Come on, I think we'd better be moving along," said Hamilton, urging his companion toward the stables, guiding him by his elbow. A number of people had gathered on the street as a result of the disturbance.

A few minutes later, they were relieved to be leaving the village behind and heading to the traitor Arnold's previous address and wondering what dangers lurked for them there.

Hamilton did not mention it, but there could be reason for his life being in danger as well. His use of Pembridge could be a double edged sword. If his treachery had been discovered by Adams, it was more than possible that the old radical could try something desperate to save his own plans from ruination. And not for the first time, he wondered if even Adams was capable of murder?

Adams had done some checking and found that the wily Hamilton had left Philadelphia, most likely to go back to New York, but he could not be sure. In any case, it was the perfect opportunity to confront Pembridge about certain suspicions he had been having about the South Carolinian.

It was Pembridge who had kept him out late the night that Adams discovered his rooms had been searched. And the very next day, he failed to appear for a scheduled meeting of their group. That coincidence was more than enough for Adams' conspiratorial instincts to surface. The very next day, he had spoken to Mr. Hersey, the proprietor of the Black Horse Tavern where Adams kept his rooms, and with a little inventive arm twisting, managed to get the man to admit to his perfidy and describe the person to whom he had allowed access to Adams' rooms. The description matched no one better than Alexander Hamilton. Adams grinned. At least one good thing came of the matter: he now had Mr. Hersey under his thumb in case he had use of him later. After all, how much business could an innkeeper expect when word got out that he allowed strangers to search his customers' rooms?

In any case, the only conclusion he could reach by the facts at his disposal, was that after Hamilton had searched his rooms, he had somehow employed Pembridge to delay him that night while a second visit had secured Singer's travel bag. Pembridge's absence from the meeting the next day only served to signal Adams that something was wrong. Making discreet enquiries, he had discovered Hamilton's absence from the city and decided to confront Pembridge that night.

Even now, he could hardly contain his mounting rage at Pembridge's betrayal. How much had Hamilton learned? Were all his political schemes hopelessly compromised? He knew what he felt like doing to Pembridge, but decided it would be more profitable to turn the tables on Hamilton and use the South Carolinian as his own controlled double agent. After all, he could always publicly expose him later, after his usefulness was over. To a gentleman, death would be preferable to the resulting disgrace.

The light was on in Pembridge's room when Adams reached his boarding house. He managed to slip past the parlor unobserved and mounted the stairs. The landing at the top was empty and he knocked lightly at the door. No answer. He looked down and saw light shining from beneath the door. He knocked again with the same lack of response. He tried the door and found it unlatched. Slowly, carefully, he pushed it in, then swiftly squeezed through, closing and barring the door behind him.

When he turned, even he was shocked at what he saw. Suspended from a beam across the ceiling, a rope around his neck, was Pembridge. A stool lay kicked aside beneath his feet. Adams recovered himself quickly; in his position, Pembridge took the only logical way out. Adams was only disappointed at the lost opportunity to turn Pembridge against Hamilton. Now he would have to continue to worry about how much the New Yorker may have known about his plans.

Turning his back on the grisly sight, Adams began to search through the desk and highboy; then the clothes worn by the dead man, careful not to put too much additional weight on the rope. Finally, he gave up, frustrated at finding nothing. He was about to leave when he noticed the odd smell in the room. He shrugged and stepped through the door again, never noticing the open bottle of wine on the night table or the glass with the pinkish residue alongside it.

CHAPTER SIXTEEN

The house was every bit as impressive as the proprietor of the Trailside Tavern had indicated. A seven foot wall of brick surrounded the property and a heavy gate barred the only entrance. As the two men brought their horses up to it, they could easily see the house perched on a low hill that rose up almost two hundred yards inside the walls. A graveled drive wound from the gate around the edge of the hill and up to the colonnaded veranda that exposed the brick faced, two story structure. A well manicured lawn sloped down the hill to where trees and shrubs, unnatural to this part of Pennsylvania, clustered in artificial patterns. It was a few hours after dawn and as the sun climbed into the sky Jefferson, an architect himself who had fashioned and built his own home at Monticello, could appreciate the classic lines of the building's design.

"Quite impressive," he said at last.

"Just the place if you're in the mood for conspiracy," replied Hamilton, standing up in his stirrups and craning his neck to get a better look. He sat back down and said, "Arnold was never a man to settle for second best."

"You knew him?"

"Only slightly. But he was an extremely vain man, easily insulted. He was wealthy and successful in private life and yearned for military success as well. When promotions didn't come his way, he felt it a personal insult. Some said he spent more time battling imagined slights than the enemy; although when he did fight the enemy, he was one of our ablest soldiers." He shook his head. "It's too bad."

Jefferson tried to understand what his companion was saying, but just could not muster the strength. After Benedict Arnold had betrayed his country, he leant his services to the British crown and led an expeditionary force into Virginia while Jefferson was governor of that state, ravaging, burning, and plundering the entire tidewater, including the capital culminating in an episode that cast aspersions on Jefferson's honor. To this day, he was hounded by political enemies who still used the incident to disparage him, never allowing the cloud to leave him. For that alone, he could never forgive or understand Arnold.

"This gate's locked," said Hamilton. He had moved up to the gate and was tugging at it with his hand.

"There's a groundskeeper's house over there," said Jefferson, pointing. "Let's see if anyone's home."

They dismounted and tethered their horses to the gate. Walking in the direction of the house, they came to a wooden door in the wall almost hidden by creeping vines and knocked. There was no response so Hamilton took out his pistol and struck the butt against the door. That received an answer. In moments, there was the sound of a key in the lock and then the door was pulled open. A young man stood inside a neat little courtyard that opened on to the cottage behind him. "Can I help you?" he asked.

"We were wondering who lived in the house up there," said Hamilton, inclining his chin in the direction of the hill.

The groundskeeper looked over his shoulder and back again. "No one right now, sirs. The house is for rent."

"For rent?" said Hamilton, disappointed.

"You see sirs, ever since the traitor Arnold stayed here, Mr. Abner has found it very difficult to rent..."

"Is Mr. Abner the owner?" asked Jefferson.

"Yes, sir."

"But when was the house last rented?"

"Mr. Principal was the last tenant, sir. But he left six days ago."

"Well, I guess that's all..." Hamilton began to say when Jefferson cut him off.

"I'm looking to rent a house in this area. Is it possible for you to show me the premises?"

The man's face brightened with the prospect of presenting a tenant to his employer. "Why certainly sir," he stepped aside and held the door open wider. "Won't you come in? And mind your step there."

When the two men had entered the courtyard, he closed and locked the door behind them. "This way sirs."

They passed the little cottage that displayed an unmistakable feminine touch and stepped onto the gravel drive that led to the house.

"Can you tell us anything of this Mr. Principal, Mr..."

"Smith's the name, sir."

"Mr. Smith," finished Jefferson, his mind going over the events of the last few days and deciding that Mr. Principal vacated the premises the day following Singer's murder. He watched Hamilton as he walked briskly a few yards in front of them, his head cocked to one side, ostensibly surveying the house, but obviously listening.

"Not much to tell, sir. Mr. Principal kept very much to himself, except for when he'd have his visitors. I never saw him leave the property, although my wife says she has, but then he never needed to. He had a servant who ran his errands for him and a series of visitors who came at all times of the day. There was plenty of coming and going and sometimes, all these people would be here at the same time."

"Can you describe any of these people?" For some reason, the name "Principal" seemed oddly familiar to him. Where did he hear of it before? "And what was Mr. Principal's full name?" he added suddenly.

Smith seemed to think over which question to answer first, then made up his mind. "Isaac Moresly Principal," he said at last. "The third. At least that's what his servant told me. Mr. Principal only used the number when he signed his name. And you know, every time someone called him by name, I got the feeling he was laughing at them. I don't know why, but that's the way I felt. My wife never felt comfortable around him, thought there was something not quite right, but you know women..." He looked at Jefferson as if seeking reassurance that he and his wife's uneasiness was purely imaginary.

Jefferson never let on that hearing Principal's full name sounded more familiar than ever and kept him from fully concentrating on what Mr. Smith was saying.

"He was a tall man, almost as tall as you are sir," Smith continued. "His hair was graying and I'd say he was at least in his mid forties. He didn't have an accent at all. You know with the war and all, I've had the opportunity to hear men from all over the colonies speak and I've never heard so many sorts of dialects in all my life, but Mr. Principal didn't seem to fit in any of them! But he must have been well educated, because he used a lot of words I never heard of. He..." He stopped talking as Hamilton reached the veranda of the house. Jefferson hardly noticed as he was deep in thought, trying to follow a mental trail back over the past few days to the spot where the name Principal might be found.

Smith climbed the steps, and inserted a key in the lock of the front door. The inside of the house was just as impressive as the outside: big rooms filled with tasteful furniture, painted walls and ceilings lining the main corridor, and a wide staircase that rose from the entrance hall before branching to either side giving access to the upstairs. It was easy to imagine the house filled with laughing guests in gaily colored costumes dancing the night away. Fires had not been lit for days so it was almost as cold inside the house as it was outside, but it was warmed a bit by the great beams of sunlight that fell inside through the tall French windows lining the front rooms. Their voices echoed slightly in the cavernous spaces.

"The house was built for Mr. Abner, but after it was complete, he found that it was impractical for him to be so far from his shipping offices in the city, so for now, he rents it." Smith stepped into the parlor and the others followed. They were not exactly sure what they were looking for, but examined the room carefully anyway. "When the British occupied Philadelphia, it was used from time to time by a Captain Andre for balls and masques that were always well attended by the King's officers and loyalists."

"*John* Andre?" asked Hamilton.

"Yes, I believe that was his name."

Hamilton grunted.

"Does the name mean anything to you, Alexander?" asked Jefferson, momentarily distracted.

"Yes. Capt. Andre, later Major, was Arnold's contact with the British before his perfidy was discovered by Washington," said Hamilton. "It was the capture of Andre by local highwaymen while in civilian garb that uncovered Arnold's scheme to betray West Point to the enemy."

"Now I remember," said Jefferson. "Andre was later hung for his role in the incident."

"While Arnold escaped in the nick of time."

Smith, wide eyed, had apparently never made the connection between the gay cavalier and master of elaborate entertainments he had known and the sinister espionage agent later involved with the young country's first great villain.

"Mr. Smith," said Jefferson, after a brief pause, "would you mind stepping out of the room a moment? My colleague and I wish to discuss our impressions of the house in private."

"Oh," replied Smith, startled from his new-found revelation. "Certainly, sir."

When they were alone, Hamilton said, "See anything?"

Jefferson shrugged and looked around. "I don't think so. But if this Principal person is connected with the affair, there's always the chance of there being something he overlooked."

"Did you notice that he left the house the day after the murder?"

Jefferson nodded. "Which isn't much to go on. However, his name does sound familiar to me, if only I could remember..."

"Mr. Smith," called Hamilton. When Smith returned, he asked him, "Can you show us the study?"

"This way, sirs." In a moment, they were in a small back room whose walls were lined with an excellent selection of books. "These are some of Mr. Abner's books," said Smith.

The room was neat and clean without a scrap of paper out of place. Hamilton wandered about the room running his fingers over the furniture and his eyes over the books. Jefferson sat in a chair, deep in thought.

Smith was getting visibly impatient with them when Hamilton pulled one of the drawers in the desk open. Jefferson had already done it but found nothing. Out of curiousity, the New Yorker took out the blank sheets of paper he found there and held the top sheet to the light.

"Have you got something there?" asked Jefferson, getting up.

"I don't know," said Hamilton, putting the sheet flat on the desk top. "Our spies in the army used to tell me about some of their tricks. One of them was that sometimes when a person wrote a message on a piece of paper, an impression of the writing could be left on the sheet immediately beneath it." He did the same thing to another sheet, and another. At last, he said, "Look here, can you see it, the faint lines in the paper."

Jefferson squinted and saw something. "Do you have a bit of gunpowder on you?"

Jefferson spread the sheet on the desk top and crumbled Hamilton's powder over the paper. Even Smith was curious enough to approach and observe the operation. Presently, the Virginian blew over the paper and Smith gasped. Figures were clearly visible in what remained of the powder.

"I can make out the letters NGER," said Hamilton.

"Singer!" exclaimed the excited Jefferson.

"It must be! Then there *is* a connection between Principal and the murder."

"Murder? What murder?" asked Smith, backing away suddenly.

"Nothing to be afraid of, Mr. Smith," soothed Jefferson hurriedly. "We're not house hunters, but members of the constabulary investigating a murder. Nothing to worry about." He hoped the man would not ask any more questions. "But I must ask you not to repeat anything you hear or see here. In fact, you must regard us as never having even been here." He hoped the man did not ask for identification!

"Mr. Smith," said Hamilton quickly. "Who can we speak to regarding more information on Mr. Principal? Could Mr. Abner help us?"

"Why yes, sir. Mr. Abner could tell you all you need to know."

"Let's not waste any time," said Hamilton replacing the blank sheets of paper in the desk. He pushed the drawer shut but something prevented it from going all the way back. He reached a hand to clear the obstruction and pulled out another, crumpled sheet of paper. Opening it, he found it was blank except for a preprinted heading. "Look here, Thomas! Congressional notepaper!"

Jefferson examined the sheet and looked up. "Do you know what this means?"

"It means one of my colleagues is in league with this Principal blackguard!" roared Hamilton, entirely ignorant of the irony regarding his own surreptitious activities.

After that, they made a closer inspection of the house and, finding nothing, took their leave; they were both eager to return to the city and look up Mr. Abner for any information he might be able to provide.

It was almost dusk as they approached the outskirts of Philadelphia, their throats dry from long discussion regarding the whole Singer affair. Suddenly Jefferson cried out, "Good Heavens!" and reined in his horse.

Hamilton brought his own mount to a halt and turned around to face his friend. "What is it?"

"This cemetery!"

"Pauper's field," confirmed Hamilton, coming alongside the Virginian.

"This is where I saw the name Principal!" It was all coming back to him now.

"What do you mean?" asked Hamilton, confused.

"I came here almost a week ago with Dr. William Shippen..."

"The mad-house doctor?"

"...when we exhumed Singer's body for additional inspection."

"Yes, you informed the committee of the whole..." But before Hamilton could finish what he was saying, Jefferson had urged his mount past the entrance of the cemetery and into the burial ground. When he reached the Virginian, he was swinging his horse about first in one direction, then the other. "What's wrong?"

"The last time I was here, we came in at night and from the rear," said Jefferson. "I'm not sure which direction Singer is buried." At last, he made up his mind and galloped off toward a stand of trees. He was already off his horse when Hamilton rode up.

Along the edge of the trees were arranged a short row of head boards and the New Yorker saw his companion examining each one in turn. At last he stopped and straightened.

"Here it is," he said.

Hamilton walked up to the marker indicated, and in the fading light, read its inscription: "Here lies Isaac Moresly Principal III, 1719-1758."

——— —— ——

Hamilton handed Jefferson a glass of wine. The last thing in the world he ever expected to do was to be entertaining the Virginian in his own rooms, but here he was! Was it only a few days ago he was planning ways to get rid of him?

"Very good," said Jefferson after tasting his drink.

"I should hope so," said Hamilton, "its run the blockade from France to get here."

"That's one thing I must look into if I ever get to Europe," said Jefferson, "check out the continent's famous vintages."

"So," said Hamilton, finding a chair, "you think the meeting went well?"

They had retired to Hamilton's rooms right after a late afternoon meeting of the special committee in which Jefferson had given its members as complete a picture of the investigation as he could. But with Hamilton already in the know and Pembridge absent, it amounted to almost a personal briefing with only Thomson and Madison to speak to.

"I think it'll prove to be a smart move not informing the committee of our working together," said Jefferson. That was another matter they had thrashed out before the meeting. "The attempt on my life has demonstrated how dangerous the waters we find ourselves in can be. We have to at least try to keep the murderer thinking that I am his only threat. With luck, the driver of the cart that tried to run me down the other night will not have recognized you or at least won't bother to report your presence to his master."

"You still don't trust the committee?"

"I was right not to before, wasn't I?" said Jefferson, smiling.

Hamilton smiled too. "All right, so your instincts were right in regard to me! But I mean a serious threat." He still had not told his new found ally about Pembridge's connection with Samuel Adams. For one thing, he wanted to keep the South Carolinian to himself for future use; for another, he did not want to spoil Jefferson's trust of him by uselessly informing him of his own subterfuges. Besides, he needed an absolutely safe avenue of information for himself, free of what the Virginian might decide to tell or not to tell him. He felt a brief twinge of guilt at the thought, but forced the unprofessional attitude down.

"The fact that an attempt was made on my life is enough for me to suspect everyone," said Jefferson, "We must keep the information we have on the affair to as limited a group as possible, that way, if anything is discovered, it'll be that much easier to decide how it escaped. Meanwhile, with the killer's attention focused on me, you might have a freer hand in your own investigations."

"Then you still refuse to allow me to accompany you west?" He had tried to convince Jefferson to let him go by pointing out the fact that his military experience had saved his life once already, but the Virginian remained unconvinced.

"Absolutely. I'm certain that there's still more to be found right here in Philadelphia." He finished his wine. "After I've gone west, you'll visit our Mr. Abner about his recent tenant and continue keeping an eye on Mr. Adams. Also, I told you I'm expecting information from my friend, Simon Bolling, from New York. But most important of all, is to keep as low a profile as possible. Although I'm hoping to draw the attention of the killer with me out west, there's still a chance he'll have agents in the city."

Jefferson was sure now that Singer's death represented much more than a simple crime of passion.

Hamilton nodded. "If he does take the bait, are you sure you'll be safe?"

Jefferson smiled. "Even though I don't have your military experience, Alexander, I'm still not helpless. I'm an excellent horseman and more than just a good shot. Besides, with Major Laking along, I'm sure there won't be much to worry about."

"You trust him?"

"I have no reason not to. After all, not everyone is mixed up in this mess!"

"Well, I've asked about, and the general opinion of the Major is that he's a very dependable man to have with you in a tight spot."

"I gathered that when I went with him to Sparhawk's," agreed Jefferson. "Very professional." He rose and straightened his waistcoat. "Well, it's late enough and I have an early day tomorrow."

"When exactly are you leaving?"

"Four o'clock in the morning, that way there'll be few people about to see the expedition off. But just in case, the Major and his men will leave without me and later, I'll meet up with them outside the city. I don't know how long we'll be gone, but until then, I hope you can make the best of your time." He held out his hand and Hamilton grasped it warmly, genuinely sorry to see him go.

"Good luck," said the New Yorker, "and watch your backside!"

"You can trust to that, my friend!" And in another moment, the door was shut between them.

***

The door had no sooner closed than Hamilton's thoughts turned to something that had been bothering him since the committee meeting. What happened to Pembridge? His absence at the meeting worried the New Yorker. He was caught between the desire to keep the South Carolinian under his power and the fear of playing with fire. If Pembridge decided to talk to any number of people, Hamilton's own reputation would be irreparably destroyed. He had to know the reason why Pembridge missed that day's meeting, even before he went to work on the Singer affair. That night was a long and troubled one.

——— —— ——

Samuel Adams sat alone in the recently vacated upper room in the Black Horse Tavern. The table was still littered with the empty tankards and pitchers of the meeting just concluded. But thoughts of politics and strategy were not uppermost in his mind at the moment. It was his discovery of Pembridge's body the day before and what it meant that dominated his thoughts. If, as he suspected, Pembridge had been turned by Hamilton, then he could easily see the sort of future the Carolinian had to look forward to; and if Hamilton had already demanded too much for his honor to support, then self-destruction would have been his only option. But what had Hamilton asked? Certainly to spy on him and his little group but that still did not seem enough to force a man like Pembridge to take such an extreme step. There must have been more to it, and, he decided, things had gone far enough. The death of a good man cried out for action, for confrontation, and he decided to give Hamilton just that.

CHAPTER SEVENTEEN

From far above, the land looked like a wrinkled bedsheet or a frozen ocean; in the west, the mountains receded to the horizon in an endless series of ridges that eventually dissolved into a blue distance. An impenetrable carpet of green covered everything, from the scrub pines of the upper reaches to the lush cane breaks in the valleys. A soft mist rose from the surrounding countryside as warm air moved from the east into a region still chilled with the nearness of winter. A hawk circled lazily in the sky.

Slowly, the sky overhead whitened until it seemed as if a blanket of snow hung suspended over the land. No wind stirred the lower forests and soon, even the lone hawk had disappeared. Over all a great quiet lay. The air, pregnant with anticipation, waited for the next act in nature's drama.

Soon the whiteness of the sky in the east seemed to thicken and grow dark, like a smudge of smoke against a cloud. The shadowy mass continued to grow and resolved into great piles of foamy clouds as they crowded one atop another, filling the sky and pushing the neutral white aside. Soon, the atmosphere was filled with black, boiling clouds, still moving in utter silence, and the land beneath was thrown into gloomy semi-night. Suddenly the darkened landscape was illumed by a flash of stray lightning that edged everything it revealed with the sharpness of a knife. The world seemed to hold its breath for the expected crash that would signal the end of the calm before the storm. When it came, the boom of thunder struck like the voice of God at the dawn of creation: it cracked like a living thing, like a fist slammed onto a table. The ground shook and the forest trembled at its fury. Stones were shaken loose from the heights of the mountains and running waters leaped in agitation.

Immediately, the rain followed, a freezing rain that lashed the land mercilessly, drowning it in a deluge every bit as complete as any waterfall. Streams filled quickly and lakes overflowed their banks leaving whole stretches of forest submerged and creating acres of new swampland. Rocks and mud slid in great waves from off the sides of the mountains and choked the passes trapping the hordes of animals, crazed at the excess of nature, that ran blindly through the maddened forest. Trees that had stood for longer than any man could remember, fell amid the loosened soil, their great roots thrown into the air. A crack and roar like rolling thunder filled a valley and in an instant, a thousand acres of woodland slid from the face of the mountains, crashing into a splinter of shattered trees and rubble at the base of a gorge that had taken the stream at its bottom ten thousand years to carve.

At last the worst of the storm seemed to pass; the lightning stopped and the blast of thunder became only a distant booming beyond the farthest hills. The rain continued to fall, soaking the land and erasing the fresh wounds incurred by the storm. In a day or two, the sun would shine again, the birds would return, and new plant growth would begin to carpet the mountains.

Daniel Boone stood at the top of a high ridge watching the distant storm. From where he stood in the cold sunlight of winter, he could see the stormfront as it passed before and away from him. Leaning against his musket, he sniffed the air and found that the rain had scrubbed it clean of any scent save that of soil and pine. It would be a while and at lower altitudes before he could expect to pick up the smell of any worthwhile game.

He looked in the direction of the storm again and saw the sides of mountains scraped clean of forest. Not for the first time he wondered if some higher purpose could ever be found in the normal cycle of life where living things were born, grew old, and died, some to aid inanimate nature and others to become part of the food chain. There seemed to be some pattern there, but none that he could find in the catastrophes of nature: fire, flood, or earthquake. Was nature good or evil?

He had decided long ago that it was worse than good or evil, it was indifferent. Chance, and the various random forces of nature that govern the world determined who or what was to live and die. The Indians had their own ways of dealing with the problem; usually by complicated and esoteric rites, acknowledging and appeasing certain spirits in nature. But Boone had long since concluded that there could be no way to forecast these natural catastrophes and that any supernatural help he needed from his God was summed up in the conviction that God helped those who helped themselves. To survive, especially in the raw, Indian infested country of the frontier, men had to adapt to its merciless laws or perish. And to adapt was to become as much one with the rhythm and flow of nature as it was possible to get. The farther he removed himself from direct contact with nature, from the enemy, the more difficult the rapport between the hunter and nature. He had found that to survive in this wild, random environment, he had to slough off the accoutrements of civilization, to become a new man, a new kind of being, somewhere between the Indian and his own kind.

Often in the past, he had worried about this transition; that this new state of being was driving him too far from his roots. More than once, he had left his wife and children for some longhunting in the Kentucky country before it was settled and had lost track of time. When he had returned home with his collection of pelts and furs, he had found that years had passed and that he had been taken for dead. But he found the wilderness as powerful a mistress as his wife and it sometimes took all his strength to keep from submitting completely to its lure. He smiled. Even now it called to him from over the mountains. Had he not just been censured by the Virginia legislature for never attending its sessions? It was final proof to him that he could never go back to living the sedentary life of a propertied man, or at least nothing more than planting the stray crop of tobacco now and then.

He hefted his musket and began the steep descent of the ridge, returning to the place where he had tethered his mules.

⸻

Hamilton awoke to a pounding at his door.

Irritably, he dragged himself from bed and looked out the window. It was still early and he had had a short night; no wonder he found it hard to shake the sleepiness from his head. Finally, he managed to drag his legs from beneath the covers and place his feet in contact with the cold floor. Naked, he went to the door and asked, "Who is it?"

"It's Madison," came the reply.

Hamilton opened the door a few inches and peeked around the edge. "Madison! You never struck me as the excitable kind; what's so important that you have to come pounding at my door..."

Madison would have stepped inside rather than speak from the corridor, except that he could see Hamilton's bare shoulder and guessed the man's state of undress. "It's Pembridge! He's dead; suicide they say!"

"What!" cried Hamilton, shocked; he had almost flung the door open. "Are you sure, man?"

"Absolutely. A contact I have at one of the newspapers informed me about it. In another hour, the whole city will be talking about it."

For once, Hamilton could hardly think straight. What did this new twist put on his activities? Did Pembridge leave a note? Did he tell anyone anything before he died? Had his subterfuges been discovered by other parties? And what effect would Pembridge's death have on his plans? Guilt ran side by side with regret from the loss of a controlled agent in Hamilton's brain. All those, however, were but the thoughts of a moment. "Wait downstairs," he said to Madison. "I'll be right down."

He dressed as quickly as he could, letting his cloak hide any evidence of his haste. In a few minutes, he had joined Madison by the front door and together, they made their way the short distance to their colleague's residence.

No wonder Pembridge had not attended the committee meeting last night, thought Hamilton as his mind began to arrange itself into some kind of order. He remembered how Pembridge looked and acted during a prior committee meeting before he left for Lancaster and his teaming up with Jefferson. Pembridge had been quiet and morose, even drawn and haggard looking, as if he had not slept for days.

He should have guessed something more was wrong with Pembrdige than merely fear of giving himself away if he spoke too freely in the company of others. Hamilton slammed a fist into a palm that caught Madison's attention.

"Anything wrong?"

"No, I was just angry with myself for not noticing before this that something was wrong with Pembridge," said the New Yorker, not untruthfully.

"I know what you mean," said Madison.

Hamilton glanced quickly at his colleague, aware of his close ties with Jefferson.

"I felt the same way at the last committee meeting."

Hamilton relaxed.

A large crowd had already gathered on the street outside the boarding house where Pembridge had his rooms and when the two men approached, some people recognized them and shouted their names.

Questions came from all directions after that with Madison trying to answer them but Hamilton ignored the mob and shouldered his way single mindedly toward the entrance to the boarding house. He had to force his way inside, as Pembridge's fellow boarders had been deputed to keep the curious from coming in.

"Let me in there," said Hamilton in his most authoritarian tones. "I'm Alexander Hamilton, a member of the Congress."

"Colonel Hamilton!" said someone from inside. "Let the man in!"

In seconds, Hamilton had abandoned his companion to the mob and was standing in a small circle of white faced men. A heavy set woman was sitting and sobbing quietly just inside the parlor.

"Colonel Hamilton," said one of the men, extending a hand. "I'm Sheriff Horner, I served with you at Yorktown, sir."

Hamilton took the proffered hand and shook it. "Good to see you again, Horner," he said. "Mr. Pembridge was a colleague of mine and a good friend," he continued blithely. "When I heard the news, I couldn't help associating it with the way he behaved during a committee meeting we shared a few days ago. This sad news comes as a great shock to me, but in retrospect, perhaps it's not so surprising."

"I'm still investigating the circumstances surrounding his death," said Horner. "But I see no reason not to consider it simple suicide. Would you like to see the body of your friend, Colonel?"

"By all means. And I'd like the privilege of informing his family of their great loss."

"You can gladly have *that* duty, Colonel."

They reached the top of the stairs and walked to an open door at the end of the landing. Inside, the early morning sunlight streamed unchecked from the single window and Pembridge's body lay on the bed, draped in his cloak. Horner gestured him in for a closer look, and though Hamilton was not a stranger to ghastly death nor even the peculiar horror of the hangman's noose, the familiar distortions of the facial features were still unnerving. It was Pembridge all right.

"Did he leave any final message?" he asked.

"Nothing," said Horner.

"Were you expecting something?" said another voice.

Hamilton turned in its direction, and Horner said, "I'm sorry, Colonel; this is Mr. Samuel Adams, also a close friend of Mr. Pembridge and a great patriot."

It was a day for surprises as Hamilton shook Adams' hand, wondering furiously what the old schemer was really doing there. But "I've heard a great many things about you, Mr. Adams," was all he said.

"I'm sure you have," replied the Yankee, smiling.

The more he thought about it, the less he liked it. What was Adams doing here? Of course Pembridge was his informer on the committee and he was the man's friend, yet that did not seem enough of an explanation for Hamilton. The way the man had asked his initial question, the way he smiled, his whole knowing manner put the New Yorker on guard. Despite his earlier boast to

Dickinson and the others that he was not impressed with Adams, the old radical was still the only man who had managed to keep him constantly on edge. And if there was one thing Hamilton did not like, it was not being in complete charge of any situation.

"I was asking, Mr. Hamilton," said Adams, "if you were expecting a note?"

Hamilton shook his head. "Not especially; although most suicides do leave notes behind." He did not say it, but he had his suspicions about a suicide without a note.

"Are you saying this was no suicide?" said Adams, again smiling.

That damned smile was driving him mad! Were Adams' words mere innocent questions or did he know more than he was letting on?

"Of course not. The lack of a note means nothing." He hoped his words would throw Adams from that line of thought. But what if...and this was a new thought, what if Adams had had something to do with Pembridge's death? It would not be the first time he had wondered how far the Yankee would go. Although he had dismissed the wild stories connected with the man, maybe they had some basis in fact. He looked again at the slightly roly poly figure before him, his thinning gray hair and mannered behavior. It was difficult to connect the man with his reputation but Hamilton well knew that appearances could be deceiving.

"I think we can discuss anything further downstairs, gentlemen," said Horner from the door. "No use in keeping such morbid company."

The men filed from the room to Horner's "Death by self destruction, and nothing more..," but just as Hamilton was leaving, he noticed the open bottle of wine on the table near the door and the empty glass beside it. Quickly, he took the glass and slipped it carefully into the large pocket of his coat.

Downstairs, the three men discussed the affair further, Adams and Hamilton relating what they knew of Pembridge's attitude and movements until Horner decided that there was nothing left to learn. Eager to leave, Hamilton wasted no time in slipping from the house and rejoining Madison outside. They had just cleared the curious crowd when Adams approached from the opposite direction.

Hamilton halted in his tracks, dumfounded. How had he gotten there? He was positive he had left the house well ahead of the Yankee and yet here he was, smiling and strolling along with his hands in the waistline of his breeches and not even breathing hard.

"Ah," he began, "it's fortuitous that I was able to run into you, Mr. Hamilton."

Madison, of course, recognized the man immediately and looked at Hamilton with a questioning look on his face.

"Mr. Adams and I met inside," explained Hamilton, jerking a thumb back in the direction of Pembridge's rooms.

"I was wondering if Mr. Madison would mind if I could accompany Mr. Hamilton in private. There are some...matters, I'd like to discuss with him." He smiled.

Madison was as sharp as Hamilton and immediately sensed there was more to the man's smile than simple friendliness, but decided there was little he could do without being rude. "Please do," he said to Adams, "I have other business to attend to." Then to Hamilton, "I'll see you at the State House?"

Hamilton nodded and when Madison was gone, turned to Adams and suggested breakfast in his most courteous manner. Adams, of course, smiled and agreed.

Alexander Hamilton and Samuel Adams walked easily along the street; it was still early in the morning, but the few people who were outdoors, if they bothered to notice, could tell that there was something about the two men that kept them apart, indeed, forced them apart. Like the law of nature that dictated the behavior of magnets, that opposite forces attracted one another and like forces repel, the two men could never come completely together, even if they wanted to.

They were too much alike for that, although both would never admit it. Their subterfuges had become so much a part of their lives that they could not even imagine that it was not normal in other people. In short, they did not trust each other and never would.

So busy were they, keeping on their guard, that they never noticed what a fine early winter day it was. The air was so cold, it was like every impurity had been brushed from it during the night (it was still too early in the day for the stench of the city's markets and open sewers to assert themselves). The sky was so blue it hurt the eyes to look at it and the only sound was the soothing clatter of the occasional coach.

The two men did not say a word in the whole time they walked together, there was no need to. At last they reached the shipyards where a number of dockside taverns plied a brisk business without ever bothering to ask anyone questions. Hamilton stepped into one and looked around for a secluded table. He found one in the back and headed for it, hearing Adams' footsteps close behind him. They hung their things on a peg board nearby and sat down. A serving wench came by to take their orders as they made themselves comfortable in the anonymity of the booth. Hamilton noticed that Adams had ordered milk to drink instead of wine. He had a weak stomach; well no wonder! A man who had lived on the edge as long as

Adams had, was entitled to it. A lesser man would have broken down long since.

They ate their meal in silence and when they finished, with the remnants taken away, Adams spoke at last.

"I've been wanting to meet you for a long time, Mr. Hamilton."

"Is that so?" replied Hamilton, sipping at his wine.

"Yes, you've had an interesting career and have made some even more interesting friends."

"Well, I admire you too, Mr. Adams."

"Oh?"

"The ease with which you move from one world to another; from the rarified atmosphere inhabited by the likes of Hancock to the more sordid one of the streets. I particularly liked the way you manipulated Mackintosh and Swift to your purposes."

In Boston, Pope's Day, or Guy Fawke's Day as it was known in England, was celebrated every November by two factions; each would build elaborate platforms with effigies of the Pope and haul them through the streets of the city in loud and raucous parades. Eventually, the two groups would meet, and under the leadership of toughs like Mackintosh and Swift, would inevitably disintegrate into violent street fights in which people would be beaten near to death and a great deal of community property destroyed. Adams had taken this uncontrollable force and redirected its anger in the direction of the crown appointed governor and British soldiers stationed in Boston. Soon, any relation to the gunpowder plot of 1605 faded until the festivities became purely political.

Adams smiled.

"But what I find difficult to understand," continued Hamilton, "is how you reconcile these sordid activities with the purer ideal of our sacred struggle?"

"The end justifies the means," said Adams. The faith of his puritan ancestors still burned strongly in his breast and he resented the insinuations Hamilton was making. How dare he? A bastard himself, the product of illegitimacy! He resented even sitting here speaking to the man. "But then, Mr. Hamilton, you should know about that."

"How do you mean?"

"I'm speaking about Pembridge of course," said Adams easily. "His death wasn't a surprise to you was it?"

Hamilton reared back. "What are you saying sir? If you're trying to do me dishonor, then come out and say it!"

"Take your hand from your pistol, sir," said Adams. "You had Pembridge turned and we both know it."

"What do you mean by that?"

"You know exactly what I mean. Now if you don't want to speak frankly, I'll just pay Mr. Horner another visit and tell him about the late night meetings you've been having with Pembridge lately. It won't exactly be proof, but in some respects, the appearance of guilt will be enough to finish your career before it starts."

"And what's to stop me from doing the same to you? What business do you have in the city, meeting clandestinely with members of the Congress and with Pembridge running from the committee to you and back again?"

Adams leaned back, finishing his milk. "So, it seems I was right. You *have* turned Pembridge; or at least you *did*. What did he tell you? Never mind; I'll tell you. That I've been hosting a certain group of congressmen who've been trying to expedite Jefferson's nomination and voyage to Europe to keep him from solving the Singer affair. And, I suspect, that's the same objective Dickinson and his wealthy friends want too, isn't it?" Hamilton said nothing. "Well, if we're agreed on the ends, why not the means? I'm offering to work together on this, sir. The British will never agree on giving the United States the western lands, that's why we have to stop any damn treaty until we can more firmly establish ourselves on the Ohio. Vincennes is a good beginning, but it's simply not enough. Now it's your turn. Tell me how you turned Pembridge and took the bag."

"It was simple. I was deputed by certain...colleagues..."

"Dickinson and his friends."

"...to find out what you were doing in the city. While doing that, I saw Pembridge meet you late one night. Later, I confronted him with his perfidy and managed to convince him to work for the both of us so to speak."

"No wonder he hung himself," said Adams.

Hamilton said nothing, although he had always thought self destruction a cowardly act.

"And the bag?" asked Adams.

Hamilton had hoped the Yankee would forget about that part of it. He was willing to give him his Pembridge connection, but if he wanted to remain effective in the investigation of the Singer affair, he had to maintain his distance from it. He decided to put on his best theatrical airs and bluff his way through. "What bag?"

"You know very well what bag!" said Adams, losing patience for the first time. "Singer's travel bag, the one I took myself from his rooms."

"*You* took it! Jefferson told us he suspected the murderer; how did you get there so quickly?"

"Never mind that," said Adams, wondering for the first time, if Pembridge had had the fortitude not to tell Hamilton everything he knew. Besides, he counted himself an excellent judge of men and Hamilton's surprised response cast a shadow of doubt in his mind. After all, anyone could have answered to the description given by the proprietor of the Black Horse Tavern. Maybe he was wrong.

Hamilton carefully kept the look of innocent shock on his face. It was working, Adams had fallen for his bluff. He congratulated himself on that; the man was not infallible after all. Two could play at that game, it seemed.

Adams decided to cut his losses; there was plenty of time to think further on this. "Well, I'm glad we were able to clear up this Pembridge business, sir. Perhaps, together, we can finally get Jefferson out of the country."

"Agreed," said Hamilton, getting their cloaks. "You know," he said as they made their way to the door, "I half suspected you might have been involved in Pembridge's death..."

"Oh, come now, me?"

Outside, Adams reiterated his desire for the two of them to work together to destroy any premature treaty and Hamilton was mildly surprised at his own feelings on the subject. The very same position he had held only days before, now sounded wildly radical and even dangerous.

"By the way, Mr. Hamilton," said Adams as he was about to leave, "I still don't trust you. We'll talk again."

Hamilton watched the roly poly figure with the graying hair walk away and found it difficult to believe the man had such a formidable reputation, but he shook off the feeling with a mental sigh of relief. He had held the crafty patriot off for now, and given himself more time to work on the Singer affair; but for how long?

———

Hamilton plucked a pocket watch from his waistcoat and judged that it was late enough in the morning to pay Mr. Abner a visit. Following the instructions given to him by the groundskeeper, Mr. Smith, he soon found himself on Market Street, just east of Sixth Street. It was the well to do neighborhood of the city; Mr. Abner kept himself in good company it seemed, what with the wealthy congressman, Robert Morris living on the same street with his famous house guest, General Washington.

The houses along the street were all singularly grand, and Abner's was no exception. Finding it, Hamilton stepped up to the door, admiring the small panes of stained glass that framed it on either side along with the two huge pots holding evergreen shrubbery. A gold plaque on the door read "Hannibal Abner" with a gold knocker immediately beneath it. He took the knocker and let it fall twice.

Presently, the door opened revealing a young woman in servant's attire who inquired politely, "Can I help you, sir?"

"My name is Mr. Lancer, I'd like to see Mr. Abner on the matter of a rental property he has out on the Lancaster Road."

"Will you please step inside, Mr. Lancer?" said the girl, standing back and opening the door wider.

Hamilton stepped in and as the door was closed behind him, was waved to a sitting room just off the corridor. "Please be seated, sir, while I inform Mr. Abner of your presence."

"Thank you." Hamilton remained standing however and entertained himself by examining the room's many strange artifacts collected from around the world by Abner's fleet of trading vessels.

"Mr. Abner will see you now, sir," said the girl suddenly, and Hamilton followed her along the corridor to the rear of the house where she held another door open for him.

This next room was dominated by the smell of paper and seemed darker than it was due to the black wood paneling its walls. Sound was curiously muffled due to the bookcases that surrounded the room and the thick rug that covered the floor. Abner was standing behind his desk with a hand extended. "How do you do, Mr. Lancer?" he said.

Hamilton grasped his hand. "Thank you for seeing me on such short notice, sir."

"No problem," said Abner. "Won't you sit down?" He reseated himself after he saw that his guest was comfortable. "Now, Henrietta tells me you're interested in my property out on the Lancaster Road?"

"Yes..."

"I assure you, my rates are very reasonable and I never hound..."

"I'm afraid you misunderstand me, sir. I'm not interested in renting, but in information regarding your last tenant." At this news, Abner's face made his disappointment plain as he realized his guest did not represent a financial increase in his fortunes. "You see," said Hamilton, rushing forward, "I've come a long way to meet Mr. Isaac Principal and was informed that he was staying at your house on the Lancaster Road. But the groundskeeper, Mr. Smith, told me that he left rather hurriedly some days ago and I was wondering if you might be able to tell me where he'd gone."

Much of the animation had left Abner's voice when he replied. "I don't know and I don't care. All that mattered to me, was that Mr. Principal paid his rent on time and in cash. Do you realize how difficult it is to get cash these days, Mr. Lancer, what with the war and all?"

"Mr. Principal was a wealthy man then?" Hamilton hoped Abner did not notice how someone who was supposed to be an associate of Prinicpal did not seem to know much about him.

"I'd say. Like I said, he always paid cash for his rent and he hired a full staff of domestics, plus he had a phaeton that would do a Hancock proud."

A phaeton was a huge, well built carriage, more a work of art than craft and almost always imported. If Isaac Principal, or whoever he was, was still traveling about the country in such a vehicle, it would make finding him so much the easier. Pheatons were so expensive that they could only be afforded by the very wealthy. But as he learned more about the man, Hamilton realized that Principal's wealth alone ought to narrow the field of suspects considerably. "How would you describe this phaeton, Mr. Abner?"

"Oh, a grand thing sir, grand. It was all white with gold trimming and even had a top over it that could be put up or taken down as you wished and it could easily hold six passengers..."

"Easy to spot, eh?"

"Of course...say, what's the meaning of all these questions? I thought you said you knew the man?"

"Not personally; only through business dealings in the mail. But the mail has been unreliable of late; the war, as you said." Abner seemed satisfied with that. "So there's nothing you can tell me about his whereabouts? He left no forwarding address where he could be reached?"

"Nothing, sir." He began shuffling some papers. "Now, if you'll excuse me, I have work that must be done."

"Of course," said Hamilton, standing. "Thank you, sir, for your time." Henrietta appeared and showed him to the door. Outside, he replaced his hat. At least the trip had not been a complete waste. He should be able to do something about tracking down the phaeton, but first, he wanted to see Dr. William Shippen about a dirty glass.

Inside, Abner ignored his papers and instead, ordered his carriage out.

CHAPTER EIGHTEEN

Jefferson could tell they were nearing the frontier when he saw the mutilated corpses impaled on stakes by the side of the trail. Actually, they were still days from the old Proclamation Line that marked the *official* frontier, but during the late war, Indian raiding parties, armed and inspired by the British and led by such able leaders as Simon Girty and Joseph Brant, had been making attacks on settlements farther east, until the outer zone of safety from their raids lay only a hundred miles of the eastern seaboard.

The small party of Continentals that formed Jefferson's expedition, had halted suddenly at the grisly discovery and everyone sat their horses along the crowded path. All at once, their imaginations peopled the surrounding forest with murderous savages. Every chirp, every snap, every call was a calculating foe inching his way closer to them until, within striking range, they would spring from concealing underbrush with their blood curdling howls to butcher them without warning. Nerves were completely shattered, even Jefferson's, when Major Laking's voice cut the stillness, silencing the normal forest sounds and reminding the soldiers that the only thing they ought to fear was their superior officer.

"Pull over there! Out of my way!" the Major was shouting, as he forced his way forward from where he had been inspecting the baggage train. Horses snorted in protest as his big roan forced its way along the narrow trail. He rushed past Jefferson to where the lead soldiers had stopped, their pale faces bright in the forest gloom. The Major hardly glanced at the terrible sight as he confronted the soldiers. "What's the matter here? Haven't you ever seen corpses before? I know you've seen worse at Saratoga..." He stopped then, seeing something in the men's eyes that he knew no horror of open battle could put there. These corpses, they knew, were not the result of simple warfare, where a man knew the risks and took his chances; these were deliberately mutilated in ways that would have kept the person alive for hours before finally expiring. It was not warfare, but butchery. "All right men, I know. Take them down and we'll give 'em a decent Christian burial."

The men worked in silence over the next few hours at their heartbreaking task (one of the bodies turned out to be that of a woman, the entrails torn from her body), until six graves lay alongside the path. As Major Laking read from his Bible, everyone there knew that in a few weeks, it would be impossible for anyone to ever find the makeshift burial site. The victims' identities would probably never be discovered; merely six more names to add to the hideous toll taken on the frontier by white and red men alike. But Jefferson knew that would not stop them. The border people had become a new breed of men. Hardened by over twenty years of constant war with the Indians, a kind of war hardly ever experienced in the history of the world, they had developed a kind of acceptance of fate, as if the sudden attack of a war party was nothing more than an act of nature, and just as useless to rail against. For years, they were a timid, fearful people, always complaining that the army was not doing enough to protect them and the army in turn complained that they were cowards, unable to hold their own. Then the king drew a line on the map he called the Proclamation Line that ran along the watershed dividing the settled east from the western side of the mountains, hoping to end the bloodshed by keeping the settlers and the Indians apart. But no invisible line could keep the frontier people penned up. By the end of the French and Indian War, a war fought with exceptional ferocity and unspeakable cruelty, a new kind of people had been forged from the timid stock that had first ventured west.

It was the wilderness they liked, the hardship it represented, but the freedom too. When the soldiers burned them out to enforce the Proclamation Line treaties, they simply moved to other locations. The war and its atrocities developed in them an abiding hate of the natives, whose utterly alien ways they could never hope to understand. They were rude, violent, bitter, cruel, and remorseless and would shoot an Indian on sight as they would any dangerous beast. Their children learned to lift a scalp before they learned to read while their men felt as comfortable in the wilderness as any Indian. Twenty years of war had created a hard core of veterans who became accustomed to it, they could not live without it; they wandered the forests, pushing their homesites farther and farther west, inciting new wars and new dangers. But it was these remarkable people more than any other that gave the force to the new country's argument for its possession of the western lands. They were there; living, hunting, farming. Where were the British, except for the handful of its troops huddling in scattered forts on far flung rivers?

"Mr. Jefferson? We'll be moving on now," said Major Laking, releasing Jefferson from his thoughts. "It's pretty late in the day now, so I think we'll only go far enough to put this spot behind us and camp for the night."

As Jefferson watched the party remount, he found it hard to believe that it had only been a week since they started off. They were headed for the fort at Winchester at the head of the Valley of Virginia, one of the oldest and so, one of the most thickly settled areas on the frontier. The Indians of that region, as he had discovered in his researches, used *veratrum atra* for certain religious ceremonies. Being the only area on the continent outside of the western coast of America where the plant could be found and coupled with the frontier configuration of the balls found in Singer's body, Jefferson thought it was at least a good guess at where he might find "Mr. Principal's" trail again. Luckily, the Indians in question, the Delaware, were split into two factions: friendly ones living in their own towns and shepherded by Moravian missionaries, and hostiles living on the western side of the old Proclamation Line. It was with the friendly ones that he hoped to acquire information about "Mr. Principal" or his agents.

A tree branch swung in his face, stinging his eyes. The path they had been following for the last few days, days and nights, it seemed, spent in the saddle, had regressed from a fairly roomy one in the beginning, to hardly more than a trace now. The thick underbrush of the forest crowded it on both sides with new, first growth birch and pine already towering over their heads where older trees had once been hacked down to clear the original trail. Luckily, it being winter, the trees and shrubs had lost most of their foliage, allowing the nervous party, with their muskets across their knees, a less obstructed view into the forest. Winter also meant that they could expect fewer braves on the warpath as the natives needed to range farther afield to find adequate game to feed their families. Unfortunately however, the discovery of the mutilated bodies along the trail indicated that not all the Indians were taking part in more peaceful pursuits.

"The damned British must be supplying the savages with food," grumbled Major Laking from behind him, as if reading his thoughts. "Otherwise, raiding parties wouldn't have the time to come this far east."

"Do you think it may have been an isolated incident?" said Jefferson over his shoulder.

"Not this close to the settlements. A war party coming this far into hostile territory would need to clear out as quickly as possible after an attack; no time for hunting. It'd take days at least, maybe a week to get back to their own hunting grounds from here. Besides, this sort of warfare has all the earmarks of that damned ingrate, Joseph Brant."

"Brant? Wasn't he raised by William Johnson, the Indian Agent for the crown and educated in the east?" Jefferson's interest in Indian languages had led him to study all aspects of their histories, including the lives of their leading men.

Laking spat. "Yes, he taught him everything he knew, treated him like a son. I suppose," he temporized after calming down a bit, "he joined the British side in the war because of that. After all, he did owe them everything. He even went to Europe too, I understand." Then his manner changed again. "But you'd think after years of living with whites he'd have learned about our way of fighting wars. But he obviously didn't; he's been one of the main leaders of war parties in the east, and his band treats their victims, men, women, and children, no different than any other savages. For that alone, I'd like to flay him alive!"

"But wouldn't that lower you to the level of your enemies?" asked Jefferson not unreasonably.

"What difference does that make? It's the only kind of warfare they understand. Listen, do you know what an Indian's greatest weapon is? Terror. Pure, undiluted terror. And the way he creates it is by what we just saw back there along the trail. The most important thing to an

Indian on the warpath is to force his enemies to fear him. To him, it's like a kind of magic. Simply killing a man isn't enough proof of a warrior's skill in combat. The most satisfying way for a warrior to justify to himself and his fellows that he's the greatest warrior who ever lived, is by making his enemy aware of it by the use of protracted terror. Torture, mutilation, and the Indian's devilish genius at creating new ways to kill have pretty much succeeded in terrorizing the frontier."

"It's the standard by which they measure their fighting prowess; how better to get the message across to them that our magic is greater than theirs?" He looked around the forest. "We'll make of ourselves their greatest nightmare. Anyway," he said, shifting mental gears so fast, Jefferson had a hard time keeping up, "we'll be getting to Braddock's Road by tomorrow evening."

"Is it in better condition than this one?" asked Jefferson, plucking a withered leaf from a passing tree.

"Well, it's not what it used to be, but it is better than this one. You have to understand, that in the last few years, with all the raiding back and forth in this country, travel between the east and the frontier has slowed considerably."

"But not completely as I understand."

"Mr. Jefferson, westward travel will never stop, I can't stress that enough. There's a new breed of people here who aren't just looking for land, they're looking for freedom, just like their brothers in the east; but the freedom they seek is total..."

"But that sort of freedom is impossible, it's a nice dream to have, but to possess it in real life..."

"Of course, but it's that dream that keeps them going, it's the reason why they'll never stop. There'll be plenty more fighting with the Indians, clear across the continent, but unless they can stop the unstoppable, the Indians are doomed. Behind every longhunter is a settler and behind him, a farmer and behind him, civilization; but they come all too quickly for the longhunter, and so he pushes on. I hear that somewhere beyond the forest lies a great desert where no man can live; or at least no white man. Maybe that'll be the natural barrier where settlement will finally stop. Maybe the Indians can find a home there, but I doubt even that. But as for the westward movement coming to a halt? I doubt it." He spurred his horse forward at a signal from one of the lead men and Jefferson was left with the same convictions that he had held for some years.

The native way of life was doomed, he realized, and that friction between red men and white would always be until the Indian was gone forever. That is, unless something was done for the Indian to train him to adapt to the white man's way of life. Jefferson had always thought that the way to do that was to set aside certain lands for the Indians, supply them with the tools and seeds they needed, and teach them the art of farming. Eventually, they would be civilized and be able to live side by side with their white neighbors. But the essential thing was that they needed to be given the time and space to do it.

Suddenly the column drew up in a little clearing and the Major ordered camp to be set there for the night. In minutes, the horses were picketed and the brush was pushed back from the perimeter of the clearing as much as the men were able to do it. The Major had decided against the building of a fire and each man tried to make himself comfortable with his saddle and bed roll and a piece or two of dried meat. Two men would stand guard at two hour intervals through the night. Jefferson was no exception. He insisted on doing his part and was rewarded with the last watch of the night.

As usual, it was difficult to sleep in the cold and while lying on the hard ground, so it was with general relief that the sun at last began to peek through the trees the next morning. With no sign of trouble during the night, the mood of the men rebounded as they looked forward to their arrival at the town of Winchester that evening.

Once again, the small group of men rode on into the almost trackless wilderness. Jefferson's annoyance at the soreness he had developed in his backside over the course of the trip was mitigated by the unparalleled beauty of the early morning forest. The low lying sun cast its nearly horizontal rays slashing through the trees and branches of the woods casting everything in a golden glow that Eden must once have sported. For the first time since they started out, Jefferson took some time to pick and study different specimens of the forest's flora and began filling one of his saddle bags with his growing collection.

Finally, near mid-morning, the land on either side of them began to rise. Great outcrops of rock and loosened boulders dotted the landscape until soon, the formation of a great ridge began to make itself apparent in the gloom of the forest floor. To be sure, they had already passed their share of the foothills of the Alleghenies, but this portended something more definite. They all felt that here at last, was the first sign of the coming watershed; on the western side of which, all streams flowed west instead of east and where the longhunters called themselves men of the western waters.

The ridge was passed, but now they could tell that they were to be permanently in the grip of the coming mountains. The terrain over which they crossed was continuously rocky and uneven and covered with every manner of crawling and low lying plant. Old growth forest, with its huge, ageless trees, split the stone formations with their relentlessly digging roots and now at last, between breaks in the trees up ahead, they could see the blue silhouette of the main part of the Allegheny range.

Nervousness seemed to have crawled back into the hearts of the men almost unnoticed as the trail continued to sink between slopes that rose to higher ridges on either side. The features of the land were mostly masked in the thick woods so it was hard to tell just where wrinkles in the land around them rose and fell. Then they were in a narrow defile between two walls of stone and Major Laking ordered everyone to loosen up and string themselves farther apart in case there was an ambush. The whole world, to Jefferson, seemed to slow so that it seemed to take days to cross the short defile. But at last, they emerged safely on the other side and he could actually see the men's shoulders begin to relax.

The column closed ranks again and continued along the narrow path, leaving the defile behind them. It was as they were descending a shallow slope with the forest opening up on their left to reveal the Valley of Virginia in the hazy distance that the Indians struck.

A ragged volley of shots sputtered on the right as the soldiers' horses panicked. A few of the men were thrown from their saddles while the others dismounted quickly and sought cover in the underbrush. Some of the lead soldiers who were still mounted, tried to dash farther up the trail but were met by more shots from across the path that knocked one man from the saddle and frightened the others from theirs. All Jefferson had time to see before he jumped wildly for the patch of thorn bushes to his left, was the half score puffs of gun smoke rising from the shrubbery across the path that marked the position of the enemy.

Major Laking was shouting something, but Jefferson could hardly make it out over the screeching and howling of the savages all around them. Feeling somewhat secure in his thorn bush, he found that he had had the presence of mind to retain hold of his musket. Dragging it to his shoulder, he waited until a shot was loosed from across the path and aimed at the identifying puff of smoke and fired. The gun bucked against his shoulder, but he could not tell if his shot had been successful. Ignoring the pain the thorns were giving him in every part of his body, he carefully reloaded his gun for another try. There was a crash and a thud by his side and his heart went to his throat. Fully expecting a painted, wild eyed savage ready to cut his throat, he was relieved to see that it was only Major Laking. He had lost his hat and had a nasty gash across his forehead where a ball had almost brained him.

"We've been ambushed," he said unnecessarily. "A perfect L formation." He pointed across the path. "They've got about ten warriors facing us across the path there and a few more blocking it and facing back at us farther up the trail. I figure there can't be more than fifteen of them, but there might as well be fifty as they've got us pinned here but good."

"Have there been any casualties?"

"Two. That gives us eight men in all. Not good odds. But I'm betting this here's part of the war party that killed those settlers we passed. If so, they can't afford to hang about here for too long. We're too close to Winchester and they probably don't have enough food with them. They're going to have to finish us soon."

"Then what do we do, try to hold on as long we can?"

"In any other scrap, I'd say yes; but with these devils, it's a big risk. No one can slink through the forest as well as they can. They'll have us outflanked in a bit and then we'll be in real trouble. The only chance we've got, is to wait for that movement, then, while their forces are split, charge the far side of the path and hopefully take them by surprise. I still don't like our chances, but at least we'll take a handful of the devils with us!" He slapped Jefferson on the back and rose to a crouch. "Watch your flank, Mr. Jefferson!" Then he was off to the next man in line as a few shots followed his racing figure.

As the day progressed, Jefferson found himself less and less satisfied with his position. His powder was running down, despite his trying to save it, and he kept hearing sounds to his rear as if someone or something were trying to creep up behind him. Earlier, he had dismissed it as nervousness, but now, he was not so sure. He found himself wishing that Major Laking would give the word to charge and get the whole thing over with. He was not a fighting man and readily admitted it. He had done his share of hunting as a boy, but when childhood friends expressed interest in a military career, he had found the world of ideas to be much more alluring. And when the great opportunity came to fight, he found himself governor of Virginia instead of an officer on Washington's staff. Something whizzed past his ear, not for the first time, but this time it came from the opposite direction than across the path!

Then, before the order had been given to charge by Major Laking, a blood curdling yell that chilled Jefferson to the bone was heard from somewhere to the rear. It seemed to ululate and echo forever amid the canyons of the forest and he imagined the painted, bloodthirsty savage whose throat it must have come from. Then a shot was fired followed by two and three more. With his imagination running at full tilt, he hardly needed Major Laking's order to charge that came an instant later.

With a thousand painted devils to his rear, Jefferson surged forward; in seconds, he had crossed the trail and plunged into the underbrush on the opposite side, ignoring the puff of smoke that filtered from the brush almost directly in front of him. Then he was past the initial trailside thicket and into the more open space among the trees beyond. Movement caught his eye there and he swung, firing his musket from the waist, then he was thrown to the ground by the hurtling form of an Indian, hatchet in hand, ready to bury itself in his brain.

With his musket knocked aside and weaponless, he grappled with his fearsome antagonist. The hatchet came down, missing his ear by inches and he took the opportunity to grasp the man's other wrist and force him up and over, using his own awkward position to unbalance him. The Indian's wrist twisted and he was forced to release his hold on the hatchet where it remained impaled in the earth. A series of snorts and grunts filled the air and Jefferson was not at all sure if they all belonged to his adversary. They rolled along the ground, the crackling leaves that blanketed the forest floor almost the only sound. He felt the savage's hot breath on his cheek as each struggled for a hold on the other's wrists. Suddenly, Jefferson jerked and accidentally dug a knee in the other's groin that weakened his grip allowing the Virginian to roll free in the neighborhood of the hatchet. He took it and leapt to his feet just as the Indian regained his own and it was then he noticed the trickle of blood that seeped from the man's side. He could see it pulsing out and for the first time, he realized that the ground where they had fought was liberally sprinkled with the red fluid. The Indian took a few steps toward him, murder in his eye, and then fell flat onto his face. In a few more moments, all signs of breathing halted. The hasty shot fired when he first broke through the underbrush must have found its mark after all!

Jefferson breathed a sigh of relief, but the continued shooting reminded him that he was still not safe. He retrieved his musket and reloaded it, slipping the hatchet in his belt. As he cautiously made his way back to the path, he noticed that what firing there was began to recede.

What had happened? Did the Indians win? Was he the last of his party? Or did their desperate attack succeed? He could not see a thing through the surrounding forest. Instead, he slowly followed the smell of gunpowder in the air back to the trail. There, he carefully parted the brush and peeked out.

The body of an Indian lay across the path and farther along, he could see the legs of a horse protruding from some flattened brush. Then the distant firing stopped and he began to hear voices calling, and one of them was calling him! It was Major Laking! He stepped out of the bushes and cupped a hand to his mouth. "Here I am!"

A few seconds later, Major Laking came down along the trail followed by a handful of the Continentals and what looked like an Indian prisoner.

"Am I glad to see you!" said the Major in an unaccustomed display of emotion. There was even a smile on his face.

"Not any more than I am to see you!" returned Jefferson.

"Any trouble? Are you hurt?"

"I had a scuffle with one of the enemy back there, but I'm all right; if you could call being nearly torn to ribbons by a thorn bush all right."

"Better than losing your scalp!" said the Major more in relief than in jest.

Smiling a little himself now, Jefferson gave closer inspection to the prisoner, deciding after a bit that he was not an Indian after all, but a white man. His skin was tanned so dark, that at a distance, he could pass for a native and his style of dress was the usual for the frontier: buckskin shirt and leggings and Indian style moccasins on his feet. A rather worse for wear slouch hat sat on his head and the musket cradled in his arms was protected in its own buckskin sheath. "Is this a prisoner, Major?" he said at last, inclining his chin toward the newcomer.

The Major laughed and said, "On the contrary, Mr. Jefferson, this is the man who saved our lives."

Jefferson was surprised to hear that; after all, no one helped him with the savage who almost took off his head!

"The savages did exactly as I thought they would," continued Major Laking. "They circled around us, hoping to catch us between them; I was just about ready to give the order to attack across the path, when Boone here..."

"Daniel Boone?" asked Jefferson, amazed.

"The very one. Oh, that's right. Mr. Jefferson, may I present Mr. Dan'l Boone. Dan'l, this here's Mr. Thomas Jefferson."

"I'm mighty pleased to be shakin' your hand, Mr. Jefferson," said Boone.

"Your pleasure can't be as great as mine at this meeting, sir," said Jefferson, taking the proffered hand. "I've followed your exploits for years and regard you as one of Virginia's noblest citizens."

Boone smiled and leaned on his musket. "I feel the same about you, Mr. Jefferson as does everyone on the frontier. Why, if it weren't for you, George Clarke wouldn't have had a single barrel of powder with which to fight the damned British and their savage friends. Things have been mighty grim in Kentucky for the past few years, mighty grim. And what little help we got came from you. The people of the frontier ain't forgetting how you risked the safety of Virginia in order to send us all the supplies you could."

"But how did you happen to be able to save us, Mr. Boone..."

"Dan'l, if you please, sir."

"Well, Daniel, how did you...?"

Major Laking spoke up again. "Like I was saying, Mr. Jefferson, just as I was about to give the order to attack, Dan'l came up on the flankers and gave a scream that froze the blood and drew the savages' attention to himself. At that moment, believing we were under attack ourselves, I gave the word to charge. It was beautiful, as spirited an attack as any troops I saw at Saratoga! We crashed through the Indians' without losing a man. Most of the savages up and ran off and when I turned to see to our backsides, I discovered the Indians there had run off too. I found out after that Dan'l here, heard our firing earlier and came down to see the Indians creeping around our flank. It was his yell we heard first..."

"His?" said Jefferson, surprised. "It sounded as frightening as any Indian's!"

"Comes with spending years with 'em, Mr. Jefferson."

"That's right, you'd been kidnapped and adopted by a tribe and lived with them for almost two years didn't you?"

Boone nodded. "They're a lot more complicated people than most folks give 'em credit for being."

"Anyway," said Major Laking, trying to finish his explanations. "Dan'l spooked the flankers so much they weren't able to support their friends on the other side of the path. Without their fire at our backs, our attack worked. Dan'l saved our lives all right," he reiterated.

"Sir," said one of the soldiers, saluting. "We've buried Clay and have Sylvester on a travois."

"Good, I'll be anxious to get to Winchester after all this excitement," said the Major. "Will you be accompanying us, Dan'l?"

"I'll be glad to, Harp," replied the longhunter, throwing his musket over his shoulder.

Jefferson sat in the yellow pool of light cast by the dingy room's single beeswax candle. Although the earthen floor and rough log construction of the building he occupied with Major Laking was the best Winchester could offer; it was difficult to think of the tiny settlement as a town in the proper sense of the word. Nevertheless, situated as it was at the head of the Valley of Virginia,

Winchester was strategically positioned for it to have become the starting point of two great westward movements. The first occurred when it became the head of Braddock's Road, British Major General Edward Braddock's invasion route to the west during the French and Indian War. Unfortunately, the Road led Braddock directly to a military disaster that soon developed into a titanic struggle for empire. The second was its unique position as a staging point for the settlement of the fertile Valley of Virginia that pointed like a dagger directly at the Kentucky country beyond. Slowly, the Valley filled up, with the line of settlement pushing ever southward until Daniel Boone and other early pioneers breached the mountain barrier and the Proclamation Line to start the trickle that would become a steady flow of frontiersmen into the land of bluegrass and canebreaks. But even with all that, Winchester was a far cry from what anyone would call a bustling community.

A clearing in the forest that hosted a score of rude log cabins and a fort dominating a bit of high ground to the north was about all there was, except for the people, about a hundred in all, scratching out a living from the soil. Surrounding the town lay newly cleared farmland, now empty, but in the late summer and autumn, green with acres of corn. Animals of every kind ran loose in the muddy streets and children played close to home under the watchful eyes of their mothers. Women who, as a result of the hideous toll taken in the constant warfare with the Indians, might be on their second or third husband. Indeed, there was not a man or woman in the community that had not had some member of their family horribly killed by Indians. Though the war was over for most people, here on the frontier, the wild, uncontrollable forces set loose by the British during the revolution, still continued. Angered by the ceaseless encroachment onto their land by the settlers, the various tribes of Indians refused to halt their depredations. And though the people of the frontier hated them, their hate was more like that for a dangerous animal than human beings; they saved their real anger for the British who kept the Indians supplied, paid them for scalps and urged them on, even leading them against white settlements. That, they could not abide and it was their worst nightmare to be abandoned to the British and Indians by any peace treaty signed by the new United States. A concern that the people of Winchester lost no time in making known to Jefferson almost from the moment he arrived in town. Rumors had been flying for months about secret negotiations that would guarantee the British dominion over the western lands, and when Jefferson demanded to know who was spreading such stories, no one could say, except some trader here or a land agent there.

"Can't you see that it would be in that sort of person's interest to foment discontent among you?" argued Jefferson. "A trader or land agent would have everything to gain by keeping law and order out of the territory. With the end of the war, the fate of our new nation hangs on the disposition of the western lands; I guarantee you, your representatives in Philadelphia and even Europe know this and are fighting to preserve it as a part of the United States. In the meantime, it's to the advantage of certain unscrupulous people to breed discontent among you, to keep you and we in the east apart and distrustful. It's that sort of intrigue we must guard ourselves against. I see a great and glorious future for our nation with both sides of the mountains equal partners in every respect. Believe me, you have not been forgotten."

It was this new learning experience that solidified in the Virginian certain ideas he had been thinking about that would revolutionize the way empires were created. In the old model of England and France and Spain, colonies, as Jefferson had known firsthand, were almost always treated with disdain by the mother country, their people as second class citizens, breeding resentment and rebellion. He saw the same elements here on the frontier, and if the new central government did not do anything about it, they would go their separate ways just as the thirteen colonies did. To avoid that, he was thinking about the continuous creation of new states to be added to the originals, each with an equal voice in the central government. He sensed how radical the plan would be, but also how it could save the west for the United States against the machinations of forces trying to wrest it for themselves.

The seriousness of the situation was further impressed upon him when he finally reached the fort and met its commanding officer, Colonel Todd Stevens. Stevens told him of the appalling weakness of the Continental garrison in the area. Mostly stationed further west at Fort Pitt under the command of Brigadier General William Irvine, the force was so weak with lack of supplies, food, and just plain ill health, that there was no way it could offer any real succor to the suffering settlers. In fact, most of the fighting in the area was done by the frontiersmen themselves under the command of local officers. As a result, the past year had been the bloodiest, most discouraging twelve months in the entire history of the west. It was a miracle there were any white men still living west of the Proclamation Line. Finally, there was evidence of a number of agents working in the area trying to convince the people to separate themselves from the east and to ally themselves either with the Spanish or British, and there was enough discontent for it to work.

More than ever, thought Jefferson, suddenly feeling older than he ever had before, he had to conclude his business here as quickly as possible. The danger to his country was even greater than he guessed. It was clear to him now, that whether Singer and others like him were mere land speculators or Tory plotters, their rumors and subterfuges would have the catastrophic effect of sundering the new nation right down the middle and setting up an intolerable situation where it would find the borders of two hostile world powers surrounding them on three sides!

Jefferson's gloomy thoughts were interrupted by a knock at the door.

"Come in."

The door was pushed open and Boone stooped inside the musky cabin.

"Heard you wanted to see me about somethin' Mr. Jefferson."

"That's right Daniel. I haven't even been in Winchester a full day yet and I'm convinced that what's happening out here will be crucial to the survival of our new nation. The rumors the people have told me about are not coincidental or haphazard. There's a pattern to them; they're deliberate and they're working."

"I won't argue with you over that, sir," said Boone. "I know fer a fact that there're people out here doin' their mightiest to stir folks up. Why there's even talk from some about settin' up our own country and the first thing to do would be to push the Spaniards out of St. Louis and open up the Mississippi for our produce."

"Then the situation is as grave as I thought. Listen, Daniel; I don't know where your loyalties lie in this matter. All I know is, you fought the Indians and the British both..."

"I reckon I can see where this talk of western independence is goin'. And I don't like what I see. We can't survive on our own, and I'll be damned if I see Kentuck join up with them murderin' British after the heartache they've caused. What is it I can do for you?"

In response, Jefferson reached into his waistcoat and pulled out a thin, leathern pouch. Opening it, he withdrew a yellowing piece of paper and unfolded it. Flattening it out on the table, he gestured for Boone to take a closer look. "This is a surveyor's map of a region somewhere in the western country. By the surveyor's description, Isaac Invernol's his name, it's located at the confluence of two rivers that give easy access to the Ohio and then the Mississippi..."

"Not just easy access," interrupted Boone, taking the map and turning it around. "It's right on the damn river. Look here, there's hardly a single elevation over a few thousand feet for miles around and the way this river flows, I'd say it's got to be the Scioto and where it empties is the Ohio itself. That's Shawnee country, far enough for the savages there to take some money and forget about helping their red brothers in the east." The longhunter straightened, brushing his unruly hair against the ceiling of the cabin. "It's damn good country and anyone with a trading post there, would stand to make a fortune from river traffic and the fur trade. Who did you say this surveyor was? Invernol?" He rubbed his chin. "Sounds familiar. Is he a Britisher?"

"His master was a Tory."

"To be workin' in Indian country that way, he must be pretty friendly with 'em. Workin' out of Niagra or Detroit maybe, but those forts are still mighty far off. You know, the more I think about it, the more I think he's around here somewheres. I'll ask around." He turned to go.

"Wait," said Jefferson. "Have you given any thought to guiding me to the Delaware town as I asked?"

"I'll take you, sir. There was no need to worry on that score. We leave first thing in the morning." He stepped through the door again, leaving the Virginian with the loneliness of his thoughts; thoughts that in moments of stress, usually turned to his departed wife. He cradled his head in his hands and wondered again how he would get along without her.

"Oh, Martha..."

CHAPTER NINETEEN

Jefferson was lying on his belly just inside the tree line as Boone approached the stockade. Sweat rolled down his side despite the chill of the season. At the top of the stockade, he could see a dozen guns pointing at the longhunter and he knew that the men holding them had every reason in the world to shoot the white man on sight.

Mintokeeharie was once a peaceful Delaware village made up of Christian Indians converted by Moravian missionaries. Over the decades, the Moravians had been successful in establishing a number of such villages along the Tuscarawa River, turning the Indians from their warlike ways to those of peaceful farmers living in the style of any white man. But with the recent escalation of savage fighting between British inspired natives and maddened settlers, all restraint on the part of the latter vanished, making them incapable or unwilling, to differentiate between hostile and friendly Indians. In a series of brutal reprisals, and with the Continental presence too weak to protect them, the settlers took it upon themselves to lash out against their tormentors. Unfortunately, the nearest Indian settlements were those on the Tuscarawa and after a while, they had all been attacked and wiped out, culminating in the horror of

Gnadenhutten. Now Mintokeeharie, the last Moravian town left, had managed to ring itself with a stockade in an ironic imitation of their white enemies. In the future, positions would be reversed, it would be white men besieging a fortified town held by Indians.

There was movement near the base of the wall, a door opened, and Jefferson saw a dark clothed man step through the opening and begin to walk toward Boone; the guns on the wall remained steady. Jefferson remembered the disappointment suffered the day before, when Boone had discovered that Isaac Invernol was dead; killed by a patrol of settlers in the Ohio country some months before. It seemed Invernol was known all along the frontier as a British agent, once being sighted with a war party on a raid at Harrodsburg; killing him had been a great pleasure. So Jefferson was denied whatever information the surveyor could have given him, making his visit here at Mintokeeharie all the more important.

Suddenly, Boone was calling him. He rose carefully from his place of concealment, making sure his gun was pointed to the ground. As he neared the two men before the fort, he could see that the black suited figure was a white man and assumed immediately that he was one of the Moravian missionaries. He stopped before them and Boone spoke.

"Mr. Jefferson, this here's the Reverend Zeitz; he's in charge of the mission."

"A pleasure to make your acquaintance, Reverend Zeitz," said Jefferson.

Zeitz smiled weakly, the weariness of months of siege on his face. "And I you, Mr. Jefferson. Even in the backwoods, we've heard and drawn comfort from the words you've written in our Declaration of Independence. Would that its fine sentiments were bestowed on the country's native population as well."

"Oh, but the Congress fully intended it so..."

"I'm sure it did," replied Zeitz. "Unfortunately, good intentions and reality sometimes don't see eye to eye. Despite what our leaders may intend, the situation is, the Indians will never acquire their rights until they've seized being a menace to the white man's settlement of the frontier. Only then might they be trusted enough to be accorded their due."

"You're right of course." Jefferson could not help thinking of a plan he had once conceived that would have had the entire Indian population removed beyond the white man's area of settlement to prevent just such strife.

"Well, what can I do for you?" asked Zeitz.

Jefferson looked at Boone in puzzlement.

The longhunter cleared his throat and leaned more heavily on his musket. "The Reverend here says that any talkin' we do's got to be done outside the stockade on account of the Indians' fear of lettin' any white man inside the town."

"I'm afraid Mr. Boone is correct," confirmed Zeitz. "Any goodwill we managed to instill in our Indians, has all but disappeared with Gnadenhutten."

"Well then," said Jefferson, "I've come to Mintokeeharie all the way from Philadelphia to seek information." Even Zeitz had to express surprise at that. "Specifically, what I'd like to know is, do the Delaware under your guidance know anything of this plant." He handed the missionary an illustration of *veratrum atra*. "It's a member of the lily family, very rare on the eastern portion of this continent, but has been known to grow in the these parts. I have information that tells me that the Delaware used this plant for certain of their tribal rites. That is, before they were converted," he added quickly.

Zeitz looked carefully at the illustration and said, "You came all the way from Philadelphia simply to find out if this plant grows here?"

"Actually, I know it can be made into a deadly poison; and speaking confidentially, has been used thus to the detriment of our new nation." Jefferson felt safe in his belief that anything Zeitz might repeat of their conversation could never reach Philadelphia quickly enough nor in any kind of ungarbled fashion to jeopardize his investigation.

"So you also wish to know the qualities of this poison?"

"That's it; and also, if possible, if there's been any interest by white men in using it for such purposes."

"I can assure you that the Delaware would never tell..." He stopped. "Just a moment." He turned quickly and reentered the stockade, the door closing to behind him with its bar sliding noisily into place on the other side. The guns continued to point at the two visitors and the only sounds were those of birds in the nearby trees. Jefferson could see them clearly as they crowded the naked branches. Then he heard the bar being lifted and the door opened.

Zeitz walked up to where they stood and handed the illustration back to Jefferson. "Yes," he said, "the Delaware say the plant does grow on their ancestral hunting grounds, but they haven't seen or used it for many years. They refused to tell me how the poison is manufactured, but have allowed me to tell you about Esau Freundler..."

"Esau Freundler..." said Boone, "The Brooding Panther?"

"You know him?"

"He's a traitor!"

"What are you talking about?" asked Jefferson. "Who's this Esau Freundler?"

"Esau Freundler," began Zeitz, "was the son of a German settler and one of our mission's greatest disappointments. He was kidnapped and adopted by one of the still hostile tribes of Delaware after a raiding party had killed the rest of his family. He lived the first nine years of his life with the Indians until he was ransomed by the Rev. Heckewelder, another of our missionaries, over thirty years ago. The child proved remarkably intelligent, learning both English and German in the first three years he stayed with us. After that, Rev. Heckewelder decided the child deserved a better education than he could provide and sent him to schools in the east that included Harvard. We lost track of him after that, he always was most peculiar that way; his Delaware name, translated as Brooding Panther, was quite illustrative of his dual nature; quiet and thoughtful at times, and at others, violent and efficiently warlike. In any case, we had no news of him until only recently, when we learned he was once more on the frontier, but in the Cherokee country around the Carolinas or Georgia as a general in the Continental armies."

"We knew of him on the frontier all right," added Boone. "He was in charge of the largest military force in the Cherokee country, but never left camp; always claiming he didn't have enough supplies. The men I knew swore he was no coward, but if so, why didn't he ever move?" He shrugged his shoulders in answer to his own question. "We never found out one way or 'tother, 'cause one day, he disappeared; just vanished. Deserted. Took his army's entire payroll with him and, it was discovered later, profits he made selling government supplies to the Indians. He must've changed his name along the way, 'cause we never heard of him again, and if we did, every man on the frontier I ever spoke to has sworn to take his scalp first chance they get."

Jefferson rubbed his chin. "So this Esau Freundler probably knew about the poison."

"Most definitely," said Zeitz. "While he was a member of the tribe, he was privy to what every boy aspiring to become a warrior was taught."

"Say, Mr. Jefferson," said Boone. "If you're interested in Freundler, I can take you somewhere's with only a little detour on the way back to Winchester."

Suddenly, Jefferson was only interested in getting back to Philadelphia as quickly as possible, but said yes to Boone anyway. Thanking Zeitz, the two men turned once more to the forest, leaving Jefferson frustrated at the helplessness he felt in the face of human nature. There was nothing he could do in the immediate future to help these Indians against white depredations; all he could do was to vow to himself that if he ever achieved an office high enough to make a difference, he would do whatever he could to ease the lives of other Indians in other places.

———

Shippen removed the glass from under his nose and handed it back to Hamilton. "It's the same all right. *Veratrum Atra*; the same damnable mix that dropped Singer in his tracks. Where did you find it?"

Hamilton set the glass down on the counter, wondering whether he should tell the doctor any more than he needed to know. After all, he had just confirmed something that was already making the New Yorker's mind spin with its ramifications. The same poison used to kill Singer is found in the wine of a man who was supposed to have hung himself but that now seemed most definitely to have been murdered, or at least Pembridge may have discovered he had been poisoned and decided to end his life in his own way. In any case, the fact remained that the same person who killed Singer, had very likely been involved in the death of Pembridge as well. But what was the connection between Pembridge and the killer? Was the timing of Pembridge's death significant? And more importantly, could Pembridge have already been involved with the murderer before Hamilton managed to turn him? For that matter, was Pembridge a spy for the killer in addition to his activities with Adams and the congressional committee itself? If so, the implications were monstrous. Every move Jefferson made and reported to the committee, must have gone directly to the very man he was trying to find! In addition, everything he and Adams schemed had also been compromised. If his suspicions were true, the unknown killer had been one step ahead of them all the whole time. Now Hamilton remembered the close call he and Jefferson had had that night on the Lancaster Road. They had probably been spied on right from the start and when "Principal" decided they were getting too close, tried to put a stop to them permanently. Then a new thought came to him: were his and Adams' backdoor attempts to rid themselves of Jefferson performed less on their own initiative than as the result of "Principal's" informed, behind the scenes manipulations? The idea was frightful if true. Suddenly, Hamilton's face reddened in anger and humiliation, an action that had not gone unnoticed by Dr. Shippen.

"Is something wrong, Mr. Hamilton?"

Hamilton managed to control his emotions enough to reply. Suddenly, everyone was suspect. Jefferson was right when he decided not to trust the committee or anyone else. The fewer people who knew what they were up to, the better. "I'm sorry Doctor, but I can't tell you anything about it and I must insist that you tell no one about it either, or even of my visit here."

"What am I to tell? I don't know anything!"

It occurred to Hamilton that Shippen's life may well have been in danger; after all, Jefferson had informed the committee of his dealings with him. For a few seconds, rival emotions warred in his soul until he came to a decision. Not a good one, but a decision nonetheless. "Dr. Shippen. I can't tell you anything more except to say that the poison in this glass has a bearing on the Singer affair and even Mr. Jefferson's safety..." He held up a hand to ward off Shippen's spoken desire to help his friend. "The best way to help Mr. Jefferson, is to help yourself. Doctor, I have reason to believe your life may be in danger. If there's any way for you and your family to leave the city for a while until this affair is cleared up, I strongly suggest you do so. I can't say any more. Just heed my advice in the deadly serious nature it is given."

After that, Hamilton left as quickly as possible. If he had stayed to discuss the matter more, his warning would be diluted and he would have revealed more about the affair than he wanted to. Besides, he had to pack his own things and abandon his rooms as quickly as possible.

———————

The underbrush in this part of the forest was thicker than usual, even in early winter. The ground had long since frozen solid and the sky had become a featureless sheet of gray that was already spewing a dusting of snow that thickened with distance until it seemed as if a light mist obscured the more distant trees.

Jefferson shivered against the cold as he eyed the surrounding forest, his head turning from side to side in a constant lookout for hostile Indians. In front of him, making enough noise it seemed, to wake the dead, Boone hacked and chopped his way through the clinging brush that choked their path.

"How much longer, Daniel?" asked Jefferson when the longhunter had stopped to catch his breath.

"Should be around here somewhere's," said Boone. "As a matter of fact, all this choppin's a good sign. Means no one's been around here for a long time. We won't be disturbed."

He started to work again, but in minutes, a clearing opened up before them and in a few seconds more, they were stooping their way beneath a small cluster of conifers. At last, they emerged on the far side and straightened up. Before them stood what was once a homestead. A single room cabin stood against the far side of the clearing, its roof crushed amid a splintering of blackened timbers. New trees had grown out of the field of old stumps that dotted the clearing before the cabin and over all the unstoppable growth of the forest had almost obliterated any evidence that a man had ever tried to carve a home for himself in the wilderness.

They walked slowly around the trees growing from the stumps and approached the cabin.

"Look," said Boone, pointing.

Jefferson looked where the other indicated and saw unmistakable signs of three graves. Wooden headboards stood nearby, but they were illegible and almost completely rotted away. "Who were they?" asked the Virginian.

"This here's the homestead of Esau Freundler's folks," said Boone.

Immediately, Jefferson's mind was filled by the horrific details of what he had heard an Indian raid on a white settlement was like and grieved for the long since departed family that lay buried alongside their cabin. Boone was over by the doorway and he joined him there. Looking inside, all he could see was a few rude pieces of shattered furniture, all no doubt made by the homesteader himself. A crib sat almost untouched by the door, completely surrounded by fire-blackened walls. "It was a miracle the baby survived," he said almost to himself.

"Was it?" asked Boone, grimly.

The homestead did not give Jefferson any more information than he already had, but it did make his quarry more human and less the elusive force he was beginning to think he was.

Wordlessly, the two men turned from the sad scene and made their way back in the direction of Winchester.

The festivities had just peaked at the home of Governor Dickinson when Hamilton decided to step outside for some fresh air. He needed it more and more lately as the revelation of Pembridge's allegiances slowly came to dominate all of his activities.

As soon as he left Dr. Shippen's hospital, he lost no time in packing a bag with essential items, paying his board a good three months in advance, and vacating his rooms for new lodgings in another part of the city. Leaving in the early hours of the morning and out the back entrance, he crossed over to the property immediately behind his lodgings and made his way to the opposite side of town where he found a single room over a barrel maker's. It was a good deal less comfortable than he was used to, but he could rest assured that he had lost himself to any prying eyes. From his new address, he continued to attend Congress and his daily affairs, but when leaving and returning, he made absolutely sure he was not followed. More than once, he returned to the neighborhood of his original rooms and suspected that the premises were being watched. It maddened him to think how his circumstances had changed. Where days before, he had been the hunter, he now found himself the hunted! Furthermore, he was finding his search for "Principal's" phaeton useless. Of course, he did not expect the man to ride it about the city, but he did think that some mention of it would surface; or even someone's recalling seeing it around.

He stepped down from the portico and onto the driveway that stood crammed with the carriages and tethered mounts belonging to Dickinson's guests. A small knot of coachmen sat together near the walk that led to the kitchen, eating their meal. Suddenly, he had an idea. Why had it not occurred to him before? Shrugging off the cold, he went over to where the coachmen were gathered. The two or three who were sitting, came to their feet at his approach.

"Enjoying your meal?" he asked them, receiving a jumble of positive replies. "Good, good. I was wondering if you boys could give me some information?"

They looked about at one another nervously until someone answered, "If we can, suh."

"Good. What I'd like to know is, have any of you seen a big phaeton, white with gold trimming anywhere around town? It's big enough to hold at least six people and might have a removable top on it. There's a gold sovereign in it for the man who leads me to it."

He could see that mention of a reward had started them thinking hard, until one of them finally spoke up.

"I seen one like dat, suh."

"You have? Come forward there. Where did you see it?"

"At Mr. Desmond Tench's, suh."

The name shot through him like a red rocket. At Tench's! A cold fist seemed to tighten its grip around his heart. First Pembridge, now Tench. He felt like a puppet being jerked along by its strings. Had he been manipulated from the start? He felt his face redden again, in direct proportion to the anger and frustration he felt. He hardly noticed when he pulled the pistol from his cloak and began fingering it. His honor demanded a gentlemen's brand of justice, and justice demanded a murderer's due.

It was only the silence that had fallen upon the little group of coachmen that reminded him of where he was. He saw that their eyes were fixed on his pistol. He put the piece away and tossed the sovereign to the man who had given him the information he asked for and walked away.

Lights still shone brightly from the windows of the mansion as Hamilton rode out the front gates, his black cloak flying and his hat shading his eyes from the harsh moonlight.

Minutes later, he stood in the street off the property of Desmond Tench, studying the house. All was quiet. Not a single light burned anywhere. Tench must have given his help permission to retire early while he had gone to Dickinson's. Well, if things fell the way the New Yorker expected, Tench would have an interesting reception once he returned home.

Purposefully, he strode across the street and into Tench's driveway, the gravel crackling underfoot. Shielded from the house by towering shrubbery, the carriage house lay like a squat toad in the rear of the property; a pair of wide, green painted doors stood closed before him. Reaching out, he undid the latch and swung them wide, surprised at their well oiled soundlessness. Inside, one stall was empty, but the other was filled with a bulky form, its exact shape masked by a big sheet of old sailing. Moonlight fell in from a high window in the rear peak of the carriage house. Hamilton found a hurricane lamp hanging on the wall, lit it, and brought it close to the covered form. Then, in a single sweep of his arm, he threw back the sailing, revealing the white and gold phaeton beneath.

He sighed and stood back; but that was all he had time for as a voice from behind him chased every thought from his mind.

"I'm sorry you had to see that, Alexander."

Hamilton spun and faced the barrel of a pistol. Desmond Tench was not smiling as he jerked his head in the direction of the house.

CHAPTER TWENTY

Jefferson pushed the piles of records aside, leaned back and rubbed his eyes. He glanced out the window for the first time in hours and noticed that night had already fallen. Had it been a whole day already? He looked around the empty room; all was dark except over the table where a sputtering candle covered him in a precarious pool of light. Dimly, he could see books lining the walls and a portrait whose subject he had forgotten.

The long journey back from the frontier, although filled with anxiety, had proven an uneventful one as the truce with the British finally took some hold among the Indians. Why, he had even heard that Americans were already fishing in Lake Champlain!

The first thing he did upon reaching the city, was to pay a visit to Hamilton; but when he reached his rooms, he found that the New Yorker had not been to them in over two weeks. His fears were somewhat abated when he later learned that he had been attending his duties in Congress regularly up until the Virginian's arrival in the city. But his unvisited rooms still troubled Jefferson. It was obvious to him, Hamilton had taken new rooms elsewhere; and the only explanation he could think of was that he had not only been discovered as cooperating with the Virginian, but that he had felt his life was in danger. So how were they to come together? Jefferson had decided to loiter about the State House and run into him there during that day's session but even though others reported having seen him in attendance at Governor Dickinson's ball the night before, Hamilton never appeared. Jefferson shook his head. Such questions, he decided for the second time that day, had to wait; at the moment, there was nothing he could do save sift through the records that lay before him.

And he had spent the day doing just that. He had forgotten how quickly even an infant bureaucracy like that of the United States could collect official papers and correspondence! When he had asked Thomson to allow him to go through the Commissary General's military records, he never dreamed he would be entering such a morass. With the dual misfortunes of a war to fight and the absence of a filing system, he had been forced to spend the whole morning just searching for the proper records; the rest of the day, up until only a few minutes before, were spent in actually reading and collating what he had found on General Esau Freundler.

Knowing Freundler's age, he was able to talk with a number of his contemporaries in Congress who had actually attended school with him at Harvard and other lesser institutions, and they were able to confirm the man's brilliance and rapid rise through the halls of learning that earned him a scholarship to greater schools in England itself. Through it all, there was more than a hint of the man's brooding, driven nature that prevented him from ever calling any man friend.

Freundler returned from Europe with every accolade, but before he could make use of his education, the revolution broke out and he was able to obtain a commission through the good offices of General Horatio Gates. Assigned to the southern sector, he began assembling an army of over five thousand men near the frontier with orders to combat the Indian threat to Georgia and the Carolinas. Curiously, as Boone had said, his army never broke camp except for an occasional scouting party into the wilderness. Later, he was implicated in the Conway Cabal. Exasperated at his lack of initiative, Congress ordered Freundler investigated, but the day before the inspectors were to arrive, he vanished. When the inspectors showed up, they found an army in near rags who had not been paid in months and nearing starvation, subsisting only on what game they could shoot with their dwindling supply of powder. Mutiny was at hand. How Freundler could have kept such a volatile mix together long enough to rob them and the Congress blind, was a mystery, but do it, he did. Estimates on the loss ranged anywhere from one to three million dollars worth of supplies that were sold to local Tory leaders and certain shadowy figures that were guessed to be Spanish agents. The villain took only gold for his wares, depositing it somewhere safe no doubt, then disappeared without having been seen since. It was all old news, but Jefferson could not help the anger he felt at the base treason of the man! Why, he had been governor of Virginia at the time, relying for the security of his state on Continental forces to the south! He remembered how he had stripped the state bare to support military efforts further north and wiped his forehead in nervousness even now at the thought of how vulnerable such action had left it.

Jefferson shook his head in a vain attempt to clear his thoughts and picked up his notes. But all that did not help him to find Freundler now. Why did he kill Singer? What did he plan to do with the millions he stole? The bits and pieces Jefferson was able to gather together, all seemed to point in the direction of the frontier: Freundler's relationship with the hostile Delaware; Singer's man Invernol and his map of Ohio; Freundler's stolen millions and how some of it was channeled to some of the southern Indian tribes; his mysterious dealings with the Spanish, who controlled the lower Mississippi; his desertion and apparent Loyalist sympathies; Singer and his connections with New York Tories.

He threw the notes onto the table and got to his feet. He had spent enough time here. What he needed was a good night's sleep and maybe in the morning, he would be able to make sense of it all.

He came down to breakfast the next morning with no more idea of what to do next than he did the night before. The other guests noticed his unaccustomed reticence and kept to themselves. Even Mrs. House seemed to sense his melancholy and merely served him his breakfast with a closed mouth. By the time he had finished his meal, everyone else had gone and he decided to go over to the State House and see if Hamilton would show up at last. Just before he left the house however, he was stopped by Mrs. House, who handed him a message.

"This came for you last night, Mr. Jefferson."

Jefferson, desperate for any kind of information to break the mental block from which he seemed to be suffering, took the envelope and saw that it had been sent from New York. His hopes rising, he tore it open and read the message. His eyes scanned the scribbled lines with a sinking heart. Bolling had found nothing of real value in New York; Singer had been a well to do and respected figure in the city before he declared for the Crown in the late war. Among his associates, most were Tories like he was, except one:

Desmond Tench, a wealthy furrier with extensive interests in the west (he was owner of the Trans-Mountain Fur Co.). Despite Tench's patriotism and Singer's Loyalist sympathies, the two men continued to see one another and, according to local patriots, still had extensive business connections. As Jefferson probably well knew, Tench presently sat in Congress as a representative from Connecticut.

Jefferson hardly had time to fold the paper and slip it into his waistcoat when there was a knock at the door that proved to be James Todd, the same boy who had summoned him the evening he first learned of Singer's death.

"What is it, Mr. Todd?" he asked.

"Mr. Thomson, sir," said the boy, panting. "He says to come to the State House quick."

Jefferson wasted no time in obeying the request and in a little while, found himself brushing the snow from his shoulders in Thomson's office.

"Glad you could get here so quickly, Thomas," said the Secretary.

"What is it you wanted me for?" Was there a bit of impatience in Charles' voice? He usually tried to repress such outward signs of emotion, but the Singer affair was beginning to affect him in ways Jefferson did not like.

"The diplomatic ship from England is coming in!"

Jefferson froze. "Are you sure?"

"Absolutely! One of our naval ships came in this morning and ran the news up to Congress only an hour ago."

"The treaty...?"

"It's definite; the preliminary treaty is aboard. But Congress will only be presented with it after the British consul has received the courier. But that's not the worst part Thomas, I know you've been out of the city for a few weeks and only just returned, but while you were gone, rumors began to fly about a scandal in Congress..."

"How...?"

"I don't know how! How do these things usually get out? We had Continentals at Sparhawks' for God's sake! Samuel Adams has been in town for almost two months now; who knows what deviltry he's been up to? And after Pembridge's suicide..."

"Pembridge is dead?" asked Jefferson, shocked.

"You didn't know? Well, I guess that's to be expected. He hung himself in his rooms almost right after you left. Hamilton went over and met Adams there. I heard they had a good talk together afterwards, although nobody's been able to figure out what it involved. As if I didn't have enough to worry about, without those two getting together."

Hamilton and Adams together...followed by Hamilton's disappearance...did the two have any connection? "But the ship, Charles. Is there anything we can do to stop it?"

"Stop it? Why, that could ruin things as easily as any scandal."

"But there must be some way... What if we sent that navy sloop back out to tell them there'll be some delay before they can enter the harbor? Maybe a scuttled ship or rumor of pestilence..."

"No, it would be too easy to find out later that there was no such thing; but maybe we can delay them and use the excuse of a bureaucratic mix up later on."

"That's a good idea."

"But it won't last long," said Thomson hurriedly. "A couple days at most, maybe even less. Can you get this Singer affair cleared up by then? I know it's too much to expect of you, but you're our only chance. If the treaty is scuttled because of this scandal, it may mean the end of our Republican dream. With our defeat, men will say the common people are unable to govern themselves, and kings will use the excuse to extend their powers."

"I know the dangers," said Jefferson, thinking hard. "Just delay the ship from entering port as long as you can." He had only one slender lead and he hoped he could make something of it in the impossibly short time he had left!

———————

A short time later, the American sloop *Congress* slipped from the Delaware River and into Delaware Bay where it approached the British diplomatic fleet and halted within hailing distance of the *Thunderer*. Messages were exchanged that resulted in the British fleet lying to while harbor officials in Philadelphia ironed out certain legal difficulties in allowing the foreign ships into port. The British admiral fumed at the delay. These back water bumpkins intended to rule a nation?

———————

"*Mon seigneur*," said the aide, "*l'Americain et ici.*"

The slight emphasis placed on the word "American," told Luzerne that the man was no ordinary visitor but the very special native informer he depended upon to keep abreast of Congressional affairs.

"Show him in," he said.

The aide bowed himself out and returned a moment later with the American spy.

"It is about time you report," said the French minister after the aide had left the room. "The whole city's in an uproar!"

By the "whole city," Luzerne was actually referring to the small group of Congressional representatives, the diplomatic community, and those politically connected enough to be privy to the actual goings on in Congress, not to the average man in the street.

Since his interview with Admiral de Grasse, what had merely been suspicious activity had grown solid enough to create real frustration in his efforts to keep the Americans alienated from Britain and trusting in the advice of Vergennes.

First, there was the sensational news of the suicide of John Pembridge, the representative of North Carolina to the Continental Congress. Although the local authorities claimed there was nothing to indicate the reasons behind his death, Luzerne was able to piece together from various sensational newspaper reports and some knowledge of his own not available to the editors of the local tabloids, that Pembridge had been a member of a select committee within the Congress whose purpose he had never been able to discover.

Second was the curious episode at one of the city's most well known book sellers. In that incident, a man identified only as a "Mr. Pass," but whom Luzerne knew to be Thomas Jefferson, an eccentric but wealthy landowner, former governor of Virginia, and past member of the Continental Congress, had been personally escorted by a troop of Continental soldiers to the bookstore where business was conducted while the public was kept out of doors.

Both incidents would have been highly suspicious by themselves, but taken together, they only drove the French minister's concerns to a bothersome peak. And what made the situation all the more bothersome was the fact that he had had very little hard information available upon which to base his surmises as his sources of information had not been reliable in the past few weeks.

For which reason, Luzerne looked balefully upon the well dressed man before him.

"Well?" he asked.

The man frowned and said, "Don't take that attitude with me, minister. I'm risking my neck running you information, and especially in coming here personally as I have."

Luzerne willed himself to relax. *Damn these American peasants!* Even those sympathetic to the aristocratic order of Europe showed the insolence toward their betters that seemed to infect anyone who lived in this colonial backwater! More than ever, the minister found himself anxious to be relieved of his duties and ordered home.

"Yes, yes, of course I understand the risks," admitted Luzerne. "But I have been virtually blind for the last few weeks and I'm certain there is something important going on behind the scenes in Congress that I need to know about."

His visitor smiled. "And I think I have the information you're looking for. I've just found out from very credible sources that the British vessel *Thunderer* has arrived off shore carrying the preliminary treaty approved by Parliament and the American negotiating team in Europe!"

"What? So soon?" Luzerne was so stunned, he had to sit down again. Suddenly, his mind was filled with a dozen possible courses of action he would need to take...all of them he felt quite sure, useless if the news was true. And of that he had no doubt. Information brought to him from this agent had never been faulty before.

"But that's not all," continued the American. "There's been a glitch somewhere, and the *Thunderer* has been ordered by the Philadelphia harbor master to stand off until some bureaucratic paperwork can be cleared up."

Luzerne shot up from his chair. "Held back!" What did that mean? Why should the Americans risk angering the British over such a transparently obvious ploy to delay receiving the treaty? It didn't make sense.

"And I hear the British consul is in a rage over the incident," continued the American. "He's vowed there'll be no treaty at all if the matter isn't cleared up soon."

This news alarmed Luzerne who dismissed the American, ordering him to see his aide over the matter of payment. Certainly, his government did not want to see a continuation of the war; although it was apparent that they had succeeded in prying its colonies away from Britain, in the process, France had lost a number of its own possessions to the island nation. On the other hand, Vergennes did not want to see an independent United States reestablish strong ties with England and most especially, did not desire the new nation to grow strong and offer proof that rule by any other than the aristocracy was possible.

Suddenly, for the first time in his diplomatic career, Luzerne was at a real loss as to how to proceed in such a situation.

CHAPTER TWENTY ONE

Jefferson stood across the road from the home of Desmond Tench; he did not know it, but in the same spot Hamilton had stood a few nights before. Light shone from the windows on the first floor and a thin wisp of smoke curled from the chimney in the frigid air. The snow that had begun to fall earlier in the day, continued to come down until he could feel the inch or so of it crumple beneath his feet when he crossed the street.

Despite himself, he felt the urging of desperation begin to claw its way at his brain and he fought to keep the feeling down. If Tench turned out to be a dead end and not the link that would finally lead him to Freundler, all his efforts over the last month would come to nothing. The British envoy would enter Philadelphia, learn of the scandal, and feel obligated either through pride, uncertainty, or loyalty to those Americans who stood by the Crown in the recent struggle to hold back submission of the preliminary treaty until he could receive new instructions from London. And from all the reports sent by John Adams and Benjamin Franklin, His Majesty's government's decision to deal with the Americans was achieved only by the slimmest of margins. This sort of thing would certainly sway the crucial votes in

Parliament, throwing the two nations once more into war; a war the United States was too exhausted to continue. With these thoughts in mind and the realization that his own republican dreams were on the brink of being shattered forever, he knocked at the front door.

A servant replied, took his name, allowed him to wait in the anteroom, and disappeared in search of his master. A moment later he returned and showed Jefferson to the drawing room where he saw Tench standing by a blazing hearth. There was another man in the room with him, a big man whose identity surprised him and yet disturbed him at the same time. Just why, he could not say. But Bartholemew D'Estaing's presence there stretched coincidence too far.

Big and powerful looking, but not overweight by any means, D'Estaing wore an immaculately powdered wig and was dressed fashionably in clothes that had obviously been tailored in Europe. His face was broad with clearly defined features that told of many years of exposure to the elements. He stood by one of the wing backed chairs with an air that suggested to Jefferson that he had just risen upon the Virginian's arrival.

"Mr. Jefferson!" Tench was saying, straightening. "To what do I owe this pleasure?"

Jefferson, his mind racing, was about to reply, when a second voice interrupted.

"Don't play his game, Thomas; he knows very well why you've come."

Jefferson spun to face the wing back immediately at his elbow and saw to his amazement that Hamilton had been sitting there all the time, hidden from him by the very nearness of the chair. "Alexander!" he cried. "What are *you* doing here? Where've you been? I've looked all over for you..." Then, like a thunderbolt it all hit him. He looked up at the one man in the room whose presence he could not account for. "Esau Freundler, I presume?" he said icily.

D'Estaing smiled a dangerous smile. "That man is dead, Thomas. As you know, my name is Bartholemew D'Estaing." He bowed.

"Are you sure 'Bartholemew D'Estaing' is not dead too? His name on a headstone somewhere?" asked Jefferson.

D'Estaing laughed. "You're as amusing as ever, Thomas."

"You've taken a chance showing yourself around the city as you have," said Jefferson. "You're a man wanted for desertion and theft. Aren't you afraid someone will recognize you?"

"But no one has. Simply a judicious use of actor's paints and putty to alter my appearance enough to throw off suspicion. Keeping my distance and my back to the light has done the rest. Something I've had practice with the last few years; that, and cultivating a completely separate set of acquaintances among members of the Philosophical Society."

A cold dread spreading over him, Jefferson turned once more to his friend. "How did you get here?"

Hamilton glared at Tench. "I discovered that 'Principal' owned a distinctive sort of phaeton and began to look for it and found it in Tench's carriage house. Tench surprised me while I had my back turned. Even though he was supposed to be at Governor Dickinson's fete that night, it was an unforgivable error on my part to be so careless."

"We'd been expecting either one of you for some time now," said Tench, moving over to a tray with a decanter of wine and some glasses.

D'Estaing inclined his head. "You were more resourceful than I gave you credit for, Mr. Hamilton.

We'd completely lost track of you when you vacated your rooms."

"It was only luck that I'd noticed you leaving Dickinson's house to go outdoors," continued Tench, pouring some wine in the glasses. "I managed to get up close enough to hear your conversation with the coachmen and then beat you back here."

"I trust you've enjoyed our hospitality?" asked D'Estaing.

"If that's what you'd like to know, step over here within reach of my arm, and I'll..."

"I wouldn't recommend such a move," interrupted D'Estaing with a definite air of menace in his voice, the sort of voice Jefferson had never heard from the man in the entire time he knew him as a member of the American Philosophical Society. As a matter of fact, he had never really thought much of the man at all. He had come highly recommended for membership by acquaintances in Europe and the Society had taken him at face value. This revelation of D'Estaing's true colors had shaken Jefferson's confidence in himself; could he now trust any of his conclusions? "I've broken better men than you with my bare hands..." continued D'Estaing.

"That's it," said Jefferson unthinkingly. "We don't need to stand around trading threats! Come Alexander, we'll report these two to the proper authorities and..."

Hamilton did not even make to rise as D'Estaing stepped away from the wing back he had been using to hide his right arm. A pistol appeared in his hand, leveled at Jefferson's chest. "I'm afraid I can't allow you to leave, Thomas. You see, Mr. Hamilton has been our guest for the past few days, only so long as you remained free. But now that you're here, please accept our hospitality until the British envoy has had time to come into port."

D'Estaing sat down in the chair he had been leaning on, still keeping the pistol aimed at Jefferson. He accepted some wine from Tench and sipped. "No need for self reproach at your ignorance, Mr. Hamilton. You're still a young man yet, with plenty to learn in the arts of subterfuge and manipulation. I'm only sorry that you won't live long enough to find any consolation in that however."

"Such 'arts' are hardly honorable traits in a gentleman," said Jefferson reluctantly taking a seat.

D'Estaing shrugged and looked at his drink. "That's quite true, Thomas; but wouldn't you say that certain...sacrifices...to one's honor must be made when the stakes are high enough?"

"What could be so high?" demanded Jefferson, thoughtlessly.

"Your new republic for instance. Isn't it true that you withheld information from the committee? That you lied to Mrs. Simms and again to Mr. Clause? That you searched the private property of Jonas Singer and John Sparhawk, committing the same crimes for which you accuse the Crown?" Jefferson was silent in the face of the accusations; they were all true! He had done all those things in the name of a higher cause, but did that make them wrong? "And Mr. Hamilton," continued D'Estaing, "didn't you crassly blackmail Mr. Pembridge in an attempt to gain power over him and use him for your own purposes?"

Jefferson looked at Hamilton, who reddened and turned away.

"Well?" asked D'Estaing again.

"Yes, damn it!" shouted Hamilton, strangely more angry at what Jefferson might think of him now than of being exposed.

"Finally," said D'Estaing to Jefferson again, after a short silence, "I could mention your taking, shall we say, the better part of valor when, as governor of Virginia, you fled the capital before the advancing enemy..."

"That's a lie!" roared Jefferson, coming to his feet and frightening Tench enough to force him back a step. Immediately, he regretted his show of temper and hurriedly reseated himself.

"Tench, give the man a drink, he's distraught," said D'Estaing. "I know, you were exonerated of all charges by your peers, and personally, I know you were perfectly correct in what you did, but that hardly changes the fact of your demonstrated value of honor. And yet you were perfectly willing to compromise it in your recent investigations."

Tench held out the wine for Jefferson, but it was pushed away.

"What do you take me for?" asked the Virginian. "I'll take no poisoned wine from you."

"You're too excited," said D'Estaing. "Perhaps if we talked of something else..."

Jefferson needed no more invitation than that to speak up. "Why was Jonas Singer killed?"

"I'm sure someone as intelligent as you are, will have figured out..."

"Oh, I know what you've been up to. The contacts with Indian tribes all along the frontier, the payments to Spanish officials, the private mapping of the northwest and sitings for future trading posts, your Tory contacts and sympathies, and your connections with the Crown all point to some elaborate plan to establish your own empire in the west. But that still doesn't explain Singer's death."

D'Estaing leaned back, apparently satisfied. "I knew you were an intelligent man, Thomas. Singer was an influential, and wealthy Loyalist whom I recruited some years ago in my plans for the west. Unfortunately, my decision to wreck any treaty that would bring the war to a finish pricked his conscience. It was while he had been my guest for a few days at the house out on the Lancaster Road after I'd sent him the message to 'Come to the

Headquarters' that he threatened to expose the whole scheme to Congress. The morning before he left, I managed to give him a dose of *veratrum atra*; a dose I guessed would carry him to the halls of Congress at least. Why not kill two birds with a single stone after all? I'd rid myself of a threat and possibly scandalize Congress enough to jeopardize any treaty. It would've worked beautifully except for the unpredictable nature of the human metabolism. Singer fell dead in the halls of Congress, but in a relatively quiet backroom instead of the more public hall. Desmond here, had been delegated to keep a watchful eye on Singer to make sure he expired before being able to speak to anyone. When he saw him collapse in the committee room, he took it upon himself to make doubly sure he was dead by shooting him a couple of times." He shrugged his shoulders. "It wasn't necessary; but then it did ensure that murder had been done and that Singer hadn't simply succumbed to an innocent heart attack or unidentified ailment. Either way, murder was done, and the hope has been that scandal would ensue. Unfortunately however, by shooting Singer in the back, Desmond had given you more information than was necessary for your investigations. But then, how was he to know that Thomson would place you in charge of the affair? Anyone else, I'm sure, would have gotten nowhere."

"One thing," said Jefferson, his curiosity aroused despite the desperate situation. "How could Tench reload his pistol so quickly? And why were the balls of a frontier make?"

"I'm the owner of the Trans-Mountain Fur Co.," explained Tench, "but before I became a success, I spent many years on the frontier myself. The balls were merely those I've had in my possession for many years, and I've learned to be perfectly proficient with the loading of firearms on the run. A needed skill if one is to survive for long in a wilderness filled with bloodthirsty savages."

"And Pembridge? How does he fit into all of this?"

"Ah, if you don't mind the literary allusion, his was the most satisfying part in my little play," said D'Estaing. "Until he decided to part from the lines I had written him."

D'Estaing sighed.

"That has been the most trying aspect of this whole scheme; far from mere fictitious creations, real people can sometimes be unpredictable and so, can never be fully trusted. It happened with Singer and, I was certain, it would have happened to Pembridge as well if nothing was done. So I decided to preempt his inclinations to independent action...to continue the allusion...by eliminating him from the play. I visited him in his rooms, offered a bit of wine to lubricate our discussion and unknown to him, laced his share with a bit of *veratrum atra*."

"More than a share, I would say," interrupted Hamilton.

"Well, perhaps it *was* a bit more than was healthy for him." D'Estaing smiled at his own jest. "As you may have already guessed Mr. Hamilton, Pembridge had been more than just useful as a source of information on the progress of Thomas' investigations; as a secret member of Samuel Adams' cabal, he was able to keep me abreast of what the political opposition to the Peace Treaty was doing and thinking and in turn, offered me an unparalleled opportunity to subtly influence their deliberations. How much more valuable do you think he became after I learned that he had been forced to cooperate with you and your powerful backers?"

Hamilton squirmed a bit in his chair. Jefferson had said nothing, continuing to keep his attention focused on D'Estaing, but Hamilton knew that the revelation of his more or less secret associations had probably hurt his future relations with the Virginian.

"From that point, I was able to use Pembridge to influence all sides of the investigation," D'Estaing continued. "Although I have to admit, not as much as I would have liked to. The most glaring evidence of his usefulness to me was the opportunity he gave to have you followed Mr. Hamilton. That ability gave me the chance to make an attempt on your lives...which failed, of course."

"The runaway carriage," said Jefferson.

"Exactly. Unfortunately, events moved too quickly after that for a second attempt; you soon departed for the frontier and my agents lost contact with Mr. Hamilton when he abandoned his accustomed lodgings." The big man shrugged again. "It was just as well, however, since Pembridge began to show definite signs of a loss of nerve. Always high-strung and with an overly developed sense of honor, he began making noises about giving the whole business up, of not being able to live with his conscience because of his sense of betraying his friends and colleagues, etc. It was at that point that I decided to eliminate him as a risk to my plans. But having used *veratrum atra* once, and knowing that Thomas here had already determined that it was the true cause of Singer's death, I realized that attention would have to be diverted from the possible discovery of its use. Thus, after Pembridge had expired from ingesting the poison, I crushed his larynx myself and hung his body from the ceiling of his room."

"You cold blooded madman!" cried Hamilton, unable to control himself.

"I must say though," said D'Estaing, ignoring the outburst, "how very impressed I am at your resourcefulness, Thomas. Such ingenious methods as your use of the theodolite would never have occurred to me. In fact, with the success of your investigations and the loss of the opportunities at manipulation presented by Pembridge, I've been forced into a last resort of sorts with the local newspapers. Even now, they are being informed of the news of Singer's death and the attempt by Congress to cover up the affair. I'm afraid our politicians will not emerge unsullied and if I know our firebrand editors, the British envoy arriving with the treaty will take proper and understandable umbrage at the situation."

"Never mind that," said Jefferson, horrified, "what I want to know is, why is a man of your obvious talents bothering to indulge himself in sordid murder and betrayal for such an empty goal as personal power?"

"Personal power? Is that what you think this is all about? Do you think that I'd go to all this trouble, the personal risk, merely to establish myself as some cheap dictator of the west? A Ceasar over an empire of savages and log huts? Don't insult me, Mr. Jefferson!" To the Virginian's relief, D'Estaing had finally dropped his air of familiarity; a familiarity he had no right to.

"Then what..?"

"Utopia, sir." He saw the look of consternation on the two patriots' faces. "Have you ever heard of The College of the Six Days' Work?"

"Solomon's House?" said Hamilton, confused.

"A euphemism for the Creation, used by Sir Francis Bacon as the name of his imagined temple of wisdom in his philosophical work *The New Atlantis*," said Jefferson.

"Exactly," said D'Estaing. "Bacon was not only one of the most brilliant men of his day, he was also one of its most far-seeing. He envisioned a new land, a new country where the fruits of the mind would be its greatest accomplishments. In this utopian society, ideas would be its goods in trade and its Temple of Solomon the mine from which the product of men's minds would be tapped. Solomon's House would be used to 'exhibit therein a model...of a college instituted for...the producing of great and marvelous works, for the benefit of men.' The libraries of the New Atlantis would be filled with all the knowledge of mankind in the service of the future. There would be gardens and zoos where plants and animals of every kind would be kept for study and every one of man's senses would be listed and analyzed. Every citizen would be employed according to their own talents and wishes with the ultimate goal being 'the knowledge of causes and secret motions of things; and the enlarging of the bounds of human empire, to the effecting of all things possible.' It was all just the reason the Rosicrucians claim Bacon sent them to America to establish their society here; he saw America as his New Atlantis. Think of it, an empire of pure reason!"

"You miss the point of Bacon's book," said Jefferson when D'Estaing had finished. "It was meant only as an ideal for men to strive for, not as an actual, attainable goal. You, yourself once explained Hume's contention that perfect knowledge could never be grasped as long as men's minds are clouded by bias and personal experiences..."

"But you're wrong, Mr. Jefferson; I was merely playing at devil's advocate that time. The goal is more than just attainable. Haven't I very nearly done it?"

"You're getting ahead of yourself, D'Estaing. Even if your plot succeeds in delivering to you your western empire, it's still only a wilderness with savage Indians on all sides, and three nations vying for control of the continent..."

"I've gotten the Indians on my side already and as for Spain and Britain, why I've paid off the appropriate people in New Spain and the British will be glad to have a buffer zone between themselves, the new United States, and the Spanish..."

"But such an alliance will never hold," said Hamilton with customary cynicism. "The British and the Spanish have never been stopped by such petty inducements before; why there's a whole continent to be had! Of what importance to them are your paltry sums?"

"Those paltry sums have been placed in the hands that can do the most good for my plans. My New Atlantis will be perfectly safe; the political realities you cite, will play directly into my favor. And what's more, in my travels through Europe, I've recruited some of the greatest living minds to take part in the experiment."

Jefferson shook his head slowly. "Such ideas are outmoded. Republican governments will now become the wave of the future. Such an autocracy, even one by the most enlightened minds alive, would still be an autocracy."

"Why, Mr. Jefferson, are you suggesting the common people can rule themselves?"

"Of course..."

It was D'Estaing's turn to shake his head. "What of your own plan to create an educational system in your state of Virginia that would have been designed to weed out the less gifted members of society and develop an elite group of intellectually superior people who would be destined to rule the state? Where's your egalitarianism there?" Jefferson could not reply, he was right. "And what of the very republican government you preach about now? Is it not true that the members of Congress are of the opinion that the common man cannot be trusted to make the correct political decisions?" Jefferson remained silent, everything D'Estaing was saying was true and putting him in more and more of an awkward, intellectual position.

Hamilton sat quiet too, well aware of the discussions he'd already had with certain people on the matter of any new government's need for an electoral college that could, if necessary, supercede any political decision taken by the people. The distrust of the elite for the common man ran deep in the new country.

"So you see, what is so outrageous and cynical about the structure of a New Atlantis?"

Jefferson shook his head. "You're deliberately trying to confuse us. I've long since discarded any thought of an elite society, as have many of my fellow patriots. There shall never be a dictatorship of class ever again either political, social, or religious. A nation of free men will decide their own fate, and the consequences be damned; at least they'll have chosen their own fate and not one chosen for them by an unfeeling plutocracy that would see tens of thousands more people die in a war that need not be fought simply to establish a so-called 'utopia!' What legitimacy could such red-handed rulers have?"

At this, D'Estaing realized that further talk would be useless. His guests refused to be seduced by his smooth accusations and subtle hypocrisies.

He rose and gestured with his near-empty wine glass.

"So, gentlemen," he said, "I think you will have some wine now."

The two prisoners exchanged nervous looks as Tench, a pistol in one hand and a glass in the other, walked over to Jefferson and held out the wine. The Virginian took it, fingering the glass as he watched Tench return to the table and take up the second glass. In a moment, Hamilton was handed his own refreshment, the peculiar odor of *veratrum atra* identifying it as anything but the innocent vintage it appeared to be.

Tench stood back, and as two pistols were leveled in their direction, a tense, uncertain moment developed in which the two friends, independent of one another, began to weigh in their minds all the possibilities of their desperate situation. Only Jefferson's continued fingering of his glass and Hamilton's rock steady posture but constantly shifting eyes betrayed their thoughts.

D'Estaing, impatient and unfooled, spoke again. "Come gentlemen; there's no escape this time. I assure you, both Desmond and I are crack shots. We will not miss. The only decision you have is whether to exit this mortal plane with the dignity afforded by the *veratrum atra* or the crudity of a lead ball. I..."

There was an almost inaudible but definite creak from where Hamilton sat in his chair. The sound had not escaped D'Estaing's notice as he settled his attention on the New Yorker, but before Hamilton could do anything he might have planned, there was a knock at the front door. It was as if a blast of cold air had suffused the room. Everyone froze and for the first time, D'Estaing not only appeared annoyed but uncertain. "See who that is, Desmond. If it's any other but one of our own men, send him away."

With a last threatening gesture of his pistol, Tench left the room, its occupants still frozen in a grotesque tableau. Hamilton's eyes lay riveted on those of D'Estaing, his every thought perfectly legible to the traitor while Jefferson watched them both, mentally weighing every opportunity that either man could present to him.

They heard another knock followed almost immediately by Tench opening the door and his sudden gasp of surprise. Then a new voice filtered down the corridor to the parlor that sent chills of hope along Jefferson's spine and caused D'Estaing's head to involuntarily snap away from his guests to the entrance of the corridor. Immediately, he was struck by Hamilton's hurtling form, whose momentum was propelled by long minutes of tension filled preparation for just such a desperate lunge.

Unfortunately, the weight difference of the two men was too much for the lighter Hamilton to completely topple D'Estaing. Instead, the frontiersman seemed mostly to stumble back, his free hand dropping his glass and groping the mantelpiece over the hearth for support as the New Yorker fell to the floor. The immediate result of Hamilton's attack however, was the involuntary discharge of D'Estaing's pistol which, filling the room with its hollow boom and acrid stench, sent its ball flying toward Jefferson.

The Virginian had only half risen in response to Hamilton's quick action when he was thrown from his feet by the force of the wild ball that ripped into his shoulder and buried itself into the wall behind him. Stunned more by the jolting, indoor discharge of the pistol, it took him a second or two to realize that the shot had not drawn any blood, but only tore a clean gash in his best coat!

In the meantime, Hamilton was not having the best of it in his struggle with D'Estaing. Both men had lost their wigs in their initial contact, but the traitor had somehow retained his feet while Hamilton had slipped to the floor. Now D'Estaing had him by the front of his coat and was dragging him to his feet, shaking him like a stray dog. But Hamilton was not completely helpless as he brought up a knee to D'Estaing's groin, bending his opponent double and forcing a grunt of pain from his lips. The hold on his coat momentarily weakened, Hamilton broke free with a sweep of his arms, then clenching his hands together, brought them down hard across the back of D'Estaing's neck forcing him to one knee. Even Jefferson could see that the double blows had the big frontiersman reeling, and felt cold admiration for Hamilton's martial prowess. But that did not stop him from picking up the traitor's heavy pistol.

Suddenly, with a roar of anger, D'Estaing was on his feet again, the sheer animal nature of his savage upbringing was like a physical thing that forced the surprised Hamilton back a few steps. That momentary hesitation was enough for D'Estaing as he rushed forward and grasped the New Yorker in a mad bear hug whose force even Jefferson seemed to feel and that elicited a cry of pain and anger from Hamilton as he struggled desperately to escape the hold. In the confines of the deadly embrace, Hamilton struck back in the only way he could. He kicked wildly with his feet, and at one point, smashed his head down over D'Estaing's face, breaking his nose and covering the two men with his blood; but he refused to release his victim, and instead, increased the pressure. All this happened in a matter of seconds, ending with the gradually weakening struggles of the New Yorker. It was at that moment Jefferson struck. Holding the pistol by the barrel, he swung its heavy hilt at D'Estaing's skull with all his might. Staring in amazement as the traitor merely loosed Hamilton, who crumpled groaning to the floor, the Virginian swung again. Incredibly, D'Estaing somehow retained his senses long enough to try to break his fall as he toppled slowly to the floor like some great tree falling in the forest.

Jefferson dropped the pistol and went to help his friend to his feet and settling him down on the nearest chair. "Are you all right?" he asked.

"I think I might have a rib or two cracked, but I'll be all right. You saved my life," he gasped.

"Then we're even," said Jefferson lightly. Then he remembered the familiar voice from the front door...and Tench! Picking up a poker from where it had fallen during the struggle, he moved toward the corridor; but before he had taken five steps, a familiar, stocky shape stepped into the parlor, a broad smile on his face and Tench's pistol in his hand.

"Samuel Adams!" said Jefferson, relieved. "Then it *was* you."

"Of course," said the old patriot easily. "I hope you didn't have too much trouble in here."

"Some," said Jefferson, his fingers exploring the tear in the shoulder of his coat. "Alexander here might've suffered some broken ribs."

"Was that the ruffian who did it?" asked Adams, moving over to where D'Estaing lay on the floor. "It seems our young Mr. Hamilton was lucky to escape with only so minor a set of injuries." Despite the nonchalance, there was obvious admiration in Adams' voice for the New Yorker.

"I wouldn't say that!" said Hamilton, still holding his side and gratefully accepting some wine from Jefferson. He sniffed it anyway.

"Don't worry," said the Virginian. "It's all right."

Hamilton downed the drink in a single gulp and thought he felt better right away. "Well, Adams," he said at last, "you warned me I hadn't seen the last of you, and you've kept your word. Thank God!"

"Yes, how did you manage to turn up here at so propitious a time?" Jefferson wanted to know.

Adams chuckled and said, "I have a personal rule that I've always found it safe to live by: namely, never believe more than half of what anyone tells you. Well, after the little talk Mr. Hamilton and I had after Pembridge's unfortunate death, I decided to keep a personal surveillance of him. Unfortunately, Mr. Hamilton managed to lose me soon after when he changed address, not an easy thing to do I must tell you. In any case, I remembered that Mr. Hamilton had once disappeared from the city at exactly the same time and, more significantly, for the same *length* of time as you, Thomas. Finding that just a bit too coincidental, I consulted a map and figured out all the places you could have gone to and returned from in that space of time and decided the only worthwhile direction must have been out Lancaster way. And so, I took a bit of a ride out there; not something I care much to do with my delicate backside you know.

Anyway, asking about, I discovered that two recent visitors answered remarkably to your descriptions and one even referred to himself as 'Mr. Pass;' a name Pembridge once told me, Thomas, that you used with Mrs. Simms. Once I knew of your association with Mr. Hamilton, it was a simple matter to follow you when you returned to the city from the frontier. You led me here. But really, Thomas, you shouldn't make it so easy to be followed..."

"But how did you know what was going on in here?" asked Hamilton.

Adams smiled. "I looked in at the windows."

"Is there nothing you won't stoop to?" demanded Hamilton in mock indignation.

"And you still interfered, despite your wanting the treaty destroyed?" asked Jefferson.

"Sir! What do you take me for? Some blackguard? It's one thing to want to block a treaty, but quite another when the lives of two fellow patriots are in jeopardy," said Adams, offended. "Besides, I've seen the preliminary treaty, and I can assure you both, that you'll be very pleased with its contents."

"What!" cried both Jefferson and Hamilton at once; the New Yorker, wincing in pain as his surprise almost brought him to his feet before he was so forcefully reminded of his injuries.

"You mean the diplomatic ship has docked?" said Jefferson worriedly as Hamilton lay back gasping. "That we're too late?" He looked over at the unconscious D'Estaing. "That even in defeat, D'Estaing has managed to succeed in delaying us long enough..." He stopped. "What did you say? You've *seen* the treaty?" He shook his head, as if to clear it. "Did I hear correctly; you say you've seen the treaty? But how?"

Adams smiled again, emitting a groan from Hamilton. "Oh come now, Thomas; you know I can't tell you how! Suffice it to say, that I have my ways. In any case, I *have* seen it, and I think that I can say with all familial pride that my dear cousin John has done quite admirably for himself in getting the British to cede to the United States the entire Ohio country; every British possession in fact, north of New Spain and south of the Great Lakes. An empire sirs!"

It was too much for Jefferson to take standing up. He collapsed into a wing back, taking a pull himself from the bottle from which he had served Hamilton. An empire! "No, not an empire," he said at last. "An opportunity to allow our new nation to grow with the addition of new states, new governments, in every way equal to the original thirteen. A nation where every member is an equal and no one merely a colony."

"As you will," said Adams. "As long as our nation is in possession of the western lands, I'm satisfied."

Hamilton had gathered enough strength at last to say, "I still doubt whether you'd have been so helpful to us if you hadn't seen the treaty first." Adams scowled and Jefferson was too overwhelmed by the vistas opening up for the new nation to take Hamilton to task for his ungrateful remarks, even if they were well founded. "But right now, I think it would be appropriate if someone tied up D'Estaing and Tench...I assume Tench has been taken care of?"

Adams rubbed a fist. "When he turned at the report of a pistol, I struck him down. A single blow proved sufficient. By the way, will either of you tell me what's going on here?"

CHAPTER TWENTY-TWO

Jefferson stood on the deck of the *Ceres* watching the gray New England coastline shrinking along the horizon. He smiled to himself. It was hard to believe that he had finally gotten that nomination for minister plenipotentiary; no more ribbing from his friends! The only thing was, with the treaty situation on firm ground, there was really very little for him to do in regard to his original mission of negotiating with Britain. Instead, his new assignment would be to conclude treaties of commerce between the United States and other sovereign powers. He smiled again (he was doing that more often now), and savored the idea of his new nation being sovereign and free. A country ruled not by kings or potentates, but by ordinary men who would set their own destinies among the nations of the world.

He leaned against the rail and watched some seagulls dipping by the masts. But it had been a near thing. D'Estaing had almost succeeded in his plan to seize the west and emasculate the new nation with the continuation of a ruinous war. He had richly deserved his fate. After Congressional authorities arrived at Tench's house, it was decided to keep the whole thing a secret from the public. Jefferson objected, seeing in the action, the very points raised by D'Estaing about the elitism of elected officials in their regard for the common man. It bothered him more than he cared to admit how close the villain had been to the truth. The irony of the decision even escaped Hamilton, who thought it best to hush everything up. Suddenly, it seemed, their developing friendship had been set back to the grudging admiration they had had for each other before the whole Singer affair started.

Luckily, one headache had been removed in the death of Desmond Tench; it seemed Adams' blow had knocked him down, causing him to strike his head so violently against the corner of a marble topped table, that it killed him, sparing his colleagues in Congress from prosecuting one of their own. As a result, Tench's reputation was secure, he gave his life in the effort to save the new nation from D'Estaing's threat. In the meantime, information gleaned from Tench's house servant enabled Congressional authorities to round up other members of the conspiracy including those delegated to inform the newspapers of the scandal before they had a chance to carry out their orders.

D'Estaing himself, had not been so lucky as Tench. Tried in secret, with the British charge d'affairs present for the proceedings, he was found guilty of conspiracy and murder and sentenced to death. Jefferson had been present at the hanging and the destruction of all the court records. The affair would remain a secret, but it would hardly stop the further plots and conspiracies that he knew continually boiled all along the restless frontier. But he resolved to leave those worries to other men for now; today he was his nation's ambassador to Europe, perhaps its future representative to Versailles, and he intended to give his new responsibilities his fullest attention.

"Father! Father!" cried a voice from along the deck.

Well, maybe not his *fullest* attention...

His twelve year old daughter, Martha, or Patsy to members of the family, ran along the deck, her hair and petticoats flying.

"What is it Patsy?" he said.

She came to a halt with a rush of air, holding her little hand demurely to her chest and making a big show of catching her breath. "I...I saw a shark! Come and see!" She took his hand and began tugging toward the bow of the ship. Jefferson doubted very much that she had seen a shark; a dolphin at the most, but characteristically quizzed her in a fashion that allowed her to use her own deductive reasoning to arrive at a more logical conclusion.

"How did you know it was a shark?" he asked.

"Because it was too big to be anything else!"

Together, father and daughter went to investigate this curious phenomenon.

EPILOGUE
May 1784

John Adams was impatient and in a hurry to leave. There was another financial crisis brewing in Holland among the Dutch bankers with whom he had arranged loans for the impoverished United States. But of course, once again, the unpredictable Franklin was nowhere to be found. At the moment, Adams was pacing in the sitting room of his colleague's home in Passy, fuming at the delay and trying to imagine how wonderful it would be when the most agreeable Jefferson (whom he enjoyed working with when the two of them were on the committee to draw up a Declaration of Independence), arrived from home to replace the ailing and aged Franklin. There was a sound behind him and he turned to see his colleague being rolled into the room by a servant on some sort of wheeled chaise. His foot was bandaged again and sticking straight out from an extended board attached to the chair.

"Please excuse my tardiness," said the old gentleman. "My gout's been acting up again." Hc was pushed over to the window and deserted there by the servant who exited the room, closing its doors behind him.

"The latest news from home," began Adams, "is that Thomas Jefferson will be coming out to replace you."

Franklin breathed a sigh of relief, much to the surprise of Adams. "It's about time; I've enjoyed my visit here in France, but I'm getting on in years and there's nothing like the familiar surroundings of youth to ease one's declining years. I think things here aren't too shabby at the moment, and young Jefferson should be able to jump right in. I'll introduce him to all the proper people of course."

"What about Vergennes? Will Jefferson be able to handle him? Does he know that the French aren't as altruistic as the people back home think? Jefferson must be his own man here, he can't allow himself to be manipulated by the French."

"I'm sure there won't be any problem in that regard, John. After our having signed a treaty with the British, the French will be anxious to stay on good terms with us. In fact, if we play our cards right, we should be able to get the best out of both of them."

"That strategy doesn't seem to be helping us in the Ohio country. Even though the British have ceded us the territory by treaty, they continue to man forts all along the frontier with no sign of any inclination to move them."

"That *is* a sticking point," admitted Franklin, adjusting his pince nez. "But at least our main objectives have been gratified in that all British troops are gone from the thirteen states. New York and South Carolina are now free of them."

"But those troops on the frontier still bother me..."

"You've been letting the news from your cousin upset you too much..."

"It's not completely unfounded as you must know." Although no official news had reached them on the Singer affair, both men had their ways of keeping abreast of happenings across the ocean.

Franklin shrugged. "I'm not at all sure what happened, but the crisis, whatever it was, has passed. And in any case, at the moment our real problems are not on the frontier, they're in the thirteen states. The Articles of Confederation are too weak to hold the nation together for long. Sooner or later, we must form a stronger central government. Even now, mutiny threatens with the Continental Army and the Congress lacks any power to make the corrections that will prove necessary to defuse many of these crises."

Adams knew all that was true. "Nevertheless, I think that with the war behind us, and with the new loans I've procured, the nation has a good head start." He turned to face Franklin, determined to ignore the things he never liked about the man and to remember only the good that he had done. He extended a hand to the surprised Philadelphian. "I'd like to wish you good luck, Dr. Franklin," he said stiffly. "You know very well, that I never approved of some of your behavior while you were here, but I'll admit you've served your country with distinction and honor."

Franklin suppressed a chuckle, knowing how much it took for the prudish New Englander to say those words and took the proffered hand. "Compliments accepted, sir. And may I say, while it hasn't been a complete pleasure working with you, it has been a consolation never to doubt that whatever you did, you did for the best interest of our new nation."

The two men shook hands and a few moments later, Franklin heard Adams' coach as it moved up the driveway to the road. "Denis!" he called. "Fetch my carriage, isn't it almost time for Madame Brillon's bath?"

www.ingramcontent.com/pod-product-compliance
Lightning Source LLC
Chambersburg PA
CBHW020600260626
47157CB00003B/795